JUSTICE FOR HOPE

BADGE OF HONOR, BOOK 12

SUSAN STOKER

CHAPTER ONE

*C*alder Stonewall stared at the woman and little boy who were huddled against the wall of the adjacent building. He'd actually walked right past them when he'd gotten to the scene. He hadn't even looked twice, all his attention on the dead body lying on the ground halfway down the alley.

But now he couldn't take his eyes off of the pair. For the first time in his life, Calder was more concerned about something other than preserving and taking in a scene. All he could think about was getting to Hope and her son, Billy, before they disappeared into thin air.

He'd spent the last couple months doing everything possible to find them. He'd found out about them from Blythe, who was engaged to his firefighter friend, Squirrel. Blythe had spoken so much about the other woman that she'd lit a fire under *his* butt to find her.

Hope Drayden was homeless—at least, she had been the last time Blythe had seen her.

Calder would bet any amount of money the pair in front of him was Hope and her son. If they were, then it made sense why he hadn't been able to find them. He'd been looking on the wrong side of the city. The shelters Blythe had assumed Hope would most likely show up at had been dead ends. He hadn't branched out to looking in this area because the only nearby place for the homeless was a men's shelter.

"I'm going to go question the woman," the SAPD officer said to Calder, bringing his attention back to his surroundings. "If necessary, I'll take her to the station and question her further if her statement sounds hinky."

"No," Calder protested immediately. "I'll talk to her. I need you to stay here and make sure no one gets near the DB. Don't touch him and don't put a sheet over him until the CSIs get here."

"I know the protocol," the officer mumbled.

Calder knew the man wasn't happy to be put on dead-body guard duty, but after hearing Blythe talk about how Hope was essentially on the run from her abusive ex—who just happened to be a police officer—he had a hunch she'd feel more comfortable talking to him rather than the cop assigned to the scene.

Calder wasn't wearing a uniform; instead, he had on a pair of black jeans, a striped shirt, and he'd thrown on a dark blazer as he'd walked out of the house. Even though it was late, Calder always liked to look professional. His badge was also clipped onto his belt, just in case someone questioned who he was.

Without another thought for the ticked-off officer, Calder walked slowly toward who he knew had to be Hope and Billy. She had her son's face tucked into her side, obviously shielding him from the sight of the body. Her polyester dress was light blue, with a white square in front, made to look like an apron tied around her waist. It had red piping around the collar and the sleeves. It wasn't especially attractive, although it somehow seemed flattering on her.

She was slender—too slender. She was shivering in the night air. It wasn't exactly cold, it was Texas after all, but between the shock of what she'd seen and the knee-length dress, she was probably chilled.

Her red hair was coming out of the ponytail she'd put it in at some point that day. Wisps of hair hung around her face, and the dark circles under her eyes stood out clearly in the street light at the end of the alley. As he got closer, he could see her eyes were a dark green that made him think of the pine trees that surrounded his house.

"Hope Drayden?" Calder asked as he approached. "Are you okay?"

She looked startled for a second, then tightened her arms around Billy and asked, "How do you know my name?"

Calder swore under his breath. Dammit. There he

went, saying the exact wrong thing. He'd been trying to put her at ease, not spook her.

He stopped several feet away, not wanting to crowd her, and said, "I've been looking for you."

When she flinched and actually took a step away from him toward the street, Calder knew he'd screwed up again. He spoke fast to try to do damage control.

"Your friend Blythe has been worried about you. She got into an altercation the last time she came downtown to search for you, and her fiancé managed to get her out safely. But he doesn't want her coming down here again, for obvious reasons, so I've been keeping my eye out for you. It's not safe. There are gangs, ruffians, and homeless people who wouldn't hesitate to rob you...and more." Calder took a breath, wanting to impress upon Hope how dangerous the streets were, while not coming out and saying in front of her son that she could be raped.

"I know *exactly* how dangerous it is down here," Hope said quietly, with a hint of steel in her voice.

Calder noticed an ambulance pull up next to the curb, as well as a couple more cop cars. It was getting more and more crowded, and he wanted to get Hope and Billy farther away from the DB so they didn't have to watch the detectives and crime scene techs do their thing.

He shrugged out of his sports coat and held it out to her. "Right. Of course you do. My apologies. You look cold. Take my jacket."

She shook her head. "I'm fine."

"You're not fine," he said, and winced at how it sounded. "I just mean, you're cold. Please, take my jacket.

Pressing her lips together, Hope took it. Probably to shut him up more than anything else, but he couldn't help but feel pleased when she wrapped it around her shoulders. She didn't put her arms through the sleeves, but hopefully it still provided her a little bit of warmth.

"Come on," he said quietly, holding out his hand, indicating the sidewalk outside of the alley. "While the boys take care of that, I need to talk to you."

"That?" Hope asked.

"Uh…"

"*That* is Willie Waters. He was seventy-two years old and a Vietnam veteran. He was awarded a Silver Star after the war. He had four children, eight grand-kids, and two great-grandkids. He was married forty-one years to the love of his life and after she died of a heart attack, he had no will to go on. He eventually lost his house and ended up here on the streets. He some-times watched after Billy while I looked for work, and he was one of the kindest, most gentle people I've ever known. I don't know why someone shot him, but if they'd simply asked him for whatever they wanted, he would've given it to them. He didn't give a crap about material possessions and frequently gave away things that would've made his life much better."

Calder lowered his head and stared at the filthy

ground. He very rarely thought about the bodies he worked with on a daily basis as people. It hurt too much to think about their loved ones left behind. When he'd first started as an ME, he'd gone out of his way to befriend and comfort the families of the deceased, but after a while, it took too much of a toll on him.

Not only that, but he'd said the wrong thing to her...*again*. It really didn't surprise him, but for the first time in a really long time, he wanted to give a woman a good impression instead of sticking his foot in his mouth. Wanted her to look at him with something other than disdain.

At forty years old, Calder had pretty much written off ever finding a woman to share his life with. He was too old. Too set in his ways. Too...odd.

From a young age, he'd always managed to say the wrong thing to girls. He never meant anything bad, but it frequently seemed to come out that way.

Like the time he told a date that her clothes were baggy...he'd meant to compliment her on losing weight, but of course, the girl took offense and that was the end of that date.

Then there was the time in college he'd told a woman he was attracted to that he'd been following her when she walked home from class...he'd meant that, since it was dark and he was worried about her, he wanted to make sure she got back to her dorm all right. She decided he was a weird stalker and threatened to get a restraining order against him.

The examples could go on and on. Calder got along with his friends' wives and girlfriends okay, because they knew him. Knew how he was. Also, he didn't seem to say as many odd things to them...maybe because he wasn't attracted to any of those women.

"You're right," he told the ground. "I was out of line. I apologize. Can you tell me what happened?" Calder forced himself to look at her again.

Her brows drew down in confusion but she quickly recovered. "I was walking home after my shift. Billy and I passed the alley and he saw something. I was going to walk by, but he insisted that someone was back there and was hurt and needed help. We went into the alley and found Willie. I could tell he was already...gone. We hurried out and went to the little convenience store on the corner to call the police."

Calder nodded and looked behind him. He could see the crime scene techs taking pictures and putting down the little yellow cards with numbers on them, cataloging evidence. He turned back to Hope and Billy and immediately crouched down until he was eye-to-eye with the little boy.

"Good job, Billy," Calder said softly. "You did the right thing."

The little boy shifted his head so he could see Calder, but didn't speak.

"You could've ignored what you thought you saw, kept going. But you didn't. You got your mom to stop. That's amazing. What did you see that made you realize someone needed help?"

He waited patiently for the little boy to answer his question, but it was Hope who replied for him.

"He doesn't talk."

Calder stayed on the ground but looked up. "What?"

"Billy doesn't talk. Ever since…there was an incident a bit ago. He hasn't said a word since then. I took him to the free clinic, but they said there was nothing wrong with his vocal cords. They wanted to do more intensive testing, but I refused." She ran a hand over her son's red hair and said, "When he feels comfortable enough to talk again, he will. I'm not going to make him." The last was said with a bit of force, as if daring him to do anything that would further emotionally scar her son.

Looking back at Billy, Calder saw the little boy hadn't taken his eyes from him. "Well, I'm sure glad you saw whatever it was that you did so we could come and find your friend Willie."

After a second, Billy lifted his hand and pointed.

Calder turned his head to see what the little boy was pointing at and saw a paper bag lying next to the wall, with an unopened bottle of water nearby. Calder's eyes swept from the entrance of the alley, to Willie's unmoving body, to the paper bag once more.

His mind immediately whirled with possibilities. There was a store around the corner. Willie could've bought himself a bottle of water then walked this way. Someone could've seen him and thought he had alcohol. The water bottle would look the same as alcohol inside the brown bag. If he was held up, and if what

Hope said was true, he probably gave up the water easily. But whoever held him up had shot him anyway, maybe out of frustration that the bag contained water instead of booze, before fleeing the area.

It was possible the bag and the water had nothing to do with Willie's murder, but Calder had learned over the years that generally the simpler scenarios were usually more likely to be closer to the truth than convoluted and complicated ones.

He whistled at one of the crime scene guys and indicated the bag and bottle with his head. He knew the team would've seen it sooner or later, but figured he might as well bring their attention to it now.

Calder turned back to the little boy. "Good job, Billy. I'm impressed. Not everyone would've noticed something as small as that. That could end up being just what we need to figure out what happened, and to hopefully find the people, or persons, who hurt your friend."

Billy didn't say anything, but his lips twitched in a small smile.

"In fact," Calder said, "I think you've more than earned this." He reached down and unclipped his medical examiner's badge from his belt and held it out. It was made of silver metal and was in the shape of a star. He had some fake badges back in the trunk of his car that he usually gave to children when he gave talks about his job, or in situations like this, but he wanted to do something special for this little boy. He wanted to

SUSAN STOKER

do something to remove the look of pain and distrust from Billy's face.

Billy looked from Calder to the star sitting in the palm of his hand.

"Mister, look—" Hope began, but Calder interrupted her.

"Go on, Billy. Take it. I have another. You earned this tonight. It's not a police badge, because I'm not a police officer. I'm more of a scientist, really. But I think the cops felt bad that us medical examiners didn't have a nice fancy badge like they did, so they designed this for us to wear. See?" He didn't move closer but held the badge up so Billy could see it easier.

It wasn't exactly true that he wasn't an officer. He'd gone through the police academy to make him a better ME. He had training and experience with pathology, toxicology, as well as having his paramedic certification. He'd taken classes on human behavior and psychology to help him understand the why's of a crime scene better, and over the years, he'd learned a lot from simply listening to and being around police officers.

His job required him to investigate all unnatural or unexpected deaths in the county, or cases where a doctor couldn't certify a cause of death. He was called in on accidents, suicides, homicides, and undetermined deaths to figure out the cause and manner of how people died.

Most people thought his job was morbid and weird,

but Calder loved it. Loved solving the puzzle of how a person died. Enjoyed giving families some answers.

Unfortunately, it was those why's that were harder to determine, and those were what kept him up at night.

Billy bit his lip and looked up at his mother uncertainly.

Hope sighed and tried one more time to reject the gift. "It really is too much...uh...I didn't catch your name."

"Shoot. Sorry. I'm Calder. Calder Stonewall. One of five medical examiners in Bexar County. Friend of Blythe's. Totally harmless, run-of-the-mill, forty-year-old guy who only wants to make sure the woman I've been searching for is safe, and to show her son that not everyone who carries a badge is a bad guy."

She stared at him for a long moment before looking back down at Billy. "It's okay, son."

Billy reacted so quickly, Calder hardly even saw him moving. He snatched the badge from his hand and was looking down at it with curiosity, turning it over to see that it didn't have a pin on the back, but rather a clip so it could be attached to a belt or a waistband and worn that way.

"What do you say?" Hope asked her son.

Billy looked up at Calder and nodded at him.

Smiling, Calder said, "You're welcome." Moving slowly, so he didn't startle mother or son, he stood, making sure to keep his distance.

"Can we go?" Hope asked. "It's late and I have to work early in the morning."

Calder nodded immediately. "I'll need your contact information in case we have any more questions."

She bit her lip and looked behind herself nervously. "Oh, well…"

"I swear that while I often say things that are odd, I'm a good guy. I just don't seem to have the gene that allows me not to mess up casual conversations. I don't mean anything by it. The state of Texas trusts me… don't you think you can too?"

Calder winced as soon as the words were out of his mouth. Jesus, he was an idiot. He reached into his pocket even as he was shaking his head. He pulled out a business card and a folded piece of paper he'd been carrying around for months, just in case.

"That's my business card," he said, holding it out for her. "It has my office number and my cell written on the back. Call me. Anytime—for anything. I mean it. The other is a note from Blythe. I've been carrying it around for when I found you."

"How'd she know you would?" Hope asked quietly, as she took both the card and the note from him.

"She didn't. But she was hoping," Calder told her. "Look, I really do need to get your contact info for the report. I'll get my butt chewed out if I don't. But I swear, after my investigation is over, I won't include it in my official report. I know, Hope, why you're reluctant to share it—but he's not going to hurt you or your son again. I swear it."

12

Calder wanted to come right out and tell her that if her ex tried to get anywhere near her, he'd call on every resource he had—Cruz with the FBI, Dax with the Texas Rangers, Quint with the SAPD, Hayden in the sheriff's department, former sniper and highway patrolman TJ, and even Conor in the game warden's office—if it meant keeping her safe.

They may have just met tonight, but he felt as if he knew her...because of everything he'd learned about her from speaking with people on the streets who were acquainted with Hope. He'd do what he could to make sure her asshole ex, a cop from Washington state, didn't get anywhere near her ever again.

"We're staying at the Sun Motel on Presa Street." Her words were soft and uncertain, but Calder heard them.

He wasn't *happy* about hearing them though. The Sun Motel was notorious for drug and prostitution raids. Not only that, but he'd been called there on several occasions. It was cheap and rundown. But...it was close to the diner listed on the name tag she was wearing, and it was a roof over their heads. He couldn't, and wouldn't, judge her for where she lived, even if it was what she expected him to do.

"I know the place," was all he said. Then he took a deep breath. "Can I tell Blythe that I found you?"

Hope slowly nodded.

"Her number is in the note, so you can call her, but I want you to know that you can always call *me* as well."

She nodded, but Calder knew she wouldn't. Why

SUSAN STOKER

would she? He was a stranger to her. One who reminded her too much of what she was running from. *Who* she was running from.

"Great. Then you're free to go."

Hope nodded and took off his jacket and held it out to him. "Thanks for this."

Taking it back reluctantly, wanting to tell her to keep it, Calder shrugged into it, liking the slight scent of her shampoo he could smell on the material, even after she'd only been wearing it a short time. It was faint, almost covered by the smell of fried food, but it was there.

"I see you work at the Alamo Diner," Calder said inanely.

She simply stared at him.

"Right...ah...okay then. I guess I'll see you around." Calder stumbled over the words.

She turned to leave, towing Billy behind her as she went.

Calder waited until they were about thirty feet ahead of him, then he quietly began following. There was no way he was going to let a woman with a kid walk on the streets at this time of night and not make sure they got to where they were going safely.

The Sun Motel wasn't far, only about five blocks. Calder stopped at the far end of the building and watched as the duo entered room ten, right in the middle of the complex. He would've preferred that she was next to the office, but it was probably noisier

14

there. At least she wasn't on the end, where the light was crappy.

Calder stood there and watched the area for five minutes before forcing himself to turn and go back to the crime scene. He hated to leave them there. *Hated* it. But he had no claim on Hope Drayden or her son. He'd also left the scene he was supposed to be investigating for the first time in his career. Nothing ever got between him and a case…until now. Until Hope.

CHAPTER TWO

*H*ope dropped the curtain in her motel room and took a deep breath. She was utterly exhausted. She'd worked breakfast to close today, which meant she'd been on her feet literally all day and night. She'd taken the dinner shift for another waitress who had called in at the last minute, when her boss didn't have anyone else to do it. Tomorrow, she was working her usual breakfast-to-dinner shift, which meant another ten hours. But that was ten hours of wages and tips. She couldn't afford to be tired.

But she wanted to make sure the medical examiner guy had left. She'd known he was following her. She'd gotten really good over the last year at spotting people who had gotten too close to her, or who'd followed her for more than a few blocks. Intellectually, she knew he'd probably followed her for her own safety, but after her experiences with her ex, not to mention the other creeps she'd come into contact with on the streets, she couldn't be sure.

Calder. His name was as unusual as the man himself. Yes, he'd said some things that weren't exactly appropriate, but he'd seemed adorably flustered and contrite after he'd said them, so she couldn't be mad at him.

Hope mentally slapped her forehead. What was she thinking? She couldn't seriously be attracted to him. He was good-looking, there was no doubt about that. He had short dark hair and a close-cut beard and mustache. She'd never dated a man with facial hair, but that didn't mean she was turned off by Calder's. His cheekbones were well defined and his eyes were an unusual copper-brown color. He was slender, had intriguingly large hands, and most importantly, he'd been amazing with Billy. He hadn't talked down to him and didn't even seem fazed when she'd told him that her son didn't talk.

But Calder was also a glorified cop. He might not wear the uniform like her ex, but she had no doubt he was the same kind of man. Possessive, used to being in control, and exacting when it came to who his wife talked to, what she did in her spare time, and how she kept house.

Looking around the room, Hope sighed. She was a neat freak. She hadn't always been that way, but her ex had hammered home, with his fists if he had to, that the house should be immaculate at all times. But more than that, being homeless had taught her to take care of her possessions. Even the motel room they were currently living in was neat as a pin. She'd cleaned it when they'd first moved in because it had smelled a little funky and she wanted to make sure Billy had as clean an environment to live in as possible.

The housekeepers at the rundown motel weren't exactly the friendliest or the most thorough, so most weeks she just borrowed various spray bottles and disinfectants from them and cleaned her own room. They were happy to let her…it was one less room *they* had to worry about.

Billy yanked on Hope's dress and she smiled as he posed with the medical examiner badge clipped to the waistband of his jeans. The pants were too short—her son was growing like a weed—but Hope couldn't afford to buy him new clothes just yet. He looked as proud as could be of the badge, regardless of the clothes he was wearing.

"Looks good, kiddo. Did you get your schoolwork done tonight?"

He nodded.

Hope knew he had. Joseph would've made sure of it.

Joseph Roberts was the owner of the diner. He was in his mid-sixties and as gruff as all get out. He'd scared the crap out of Hope when she'd first met him, but he'd turned out to be one of the nicest men she'd ever met. Without his help, she wouldn't have been able to get back on her feet. Not that she was all the way back, but she was getting there.

She hadn't had any waitressing experience, was a

single mother, and was desperate to find some sort of job to get her and her son off the streets. Joseph had hired her on the spot, walked her down to the motel, paid for her first two weeks, and he even let Billy hang out in his office while she was working.

It wasn't ideal. Billy should be in school, but Hope had no real address and didn't want to bring him to the attention of child services. Besides, there was the matter of him not speaking. Hope knew it was because of the recent trauma of being kidnapped. Billy had been held captive by a crazy man, who'd wanted information about a woman he was stalking.

Blythe had been the one to bargain with the sadistic man, and Hope owed her more than she could ever repay. She'd been frantic when Billy had been abducted. A familiar volunteer at one of the shelters had been watching him while Hope was interviewing for a job, and one moment he was there, and the next he was gone. Blythe had done what was necessary in order to get the location of where the man had stashed Billy.

That had been the impetus Hope had needed to leave the area. She'd gone to the other side of the city where the gangs weren't as prevalent. She was still in the city, but on the outskirts. The only issue was that there were fewer places to get food and shelter for someone homeless like her. Luckily, Joseph had turned out to be their guardian angel within two days of her being in the area. The older man loved sitting in the back office of the large diner and helping Billy with his schoolwork while Hope worked her shift. She knew she'd have to get her son in a proper school sooner rather than later, but for now, she was taking baby steps.

"Go on and get ready for bed, baby," Hope told her son. "Put that badge somewhere safe so it doesn't get lost."

He nodded and headed to the small bathroom.

Hope sat on the edge of the lumpy mattress on one of the double beds and sighed. She was sad about Willie. He was a good man, one of the few she'd met on the streets, and she hated that he'd been killed. She was relieved she and Billy were relatively safe at night now, at least safer than sleeping in a park or a shelter, but she hated that the good men and women she'd met on the streets were still dealing with the uncertainty and dangers each day brought.

Taking a deep breath, Hope tried to stay positive. She had a roof over her head. She had a job, even if it didn't pay a whole heck of a lot. She had her son with her and they were safe.

She'd been gone for a year and a half now, her ex had no idea where they were, and hopefully it would stay that way.

When she heard the water in the bathtub running, giving her some much needed "alone" time, Hope pulled both the letter and business card out of her pocket and stared at them. Blythe had been one of her true friends on the street. She missed her, and was happy she was apparently safe and doing well.

She slowly unfolded the note and read what her friend had to say.

Hope,

If you're reading this, it means that Calder found you—thank God! I've been so worried about you and Billy. I hope you're okay. First, you can totally trust Calder. I know he's sort of a cop, but he's nothing like your douchebag ex. Nothing. If you need anything, all you have to do is let him know and he'll make sure you get it.

Second, I have a place for you and Billy to live.

Hear me out before you say no.

I don't know if you remember me talking about Sophie, who works in the lab next to the hospital downtown? Anyway, she has a house out here in the suburbs that she doesn't use. She let me live in it, rent-free. I'm not kidding. It's a long story, and one I'll explain when I see you in person. But I don't need it anymore because I'm getting married and I'm pregnant (again, I'll tell you all about it later), so the house is empty.

You and Billy can live there. Get back on your feet. Calder and his friends will even help you hide from your ex. They're good men, Hope. I promise.

Anyway, please please please call me! I need to know you're all right. That Billy's all right. I've been worried sick about you both.

When I was living on the streets, I refused to accept help from Sawyer (my fiancé) because I thought he pitied me. But the truth is, I should've accepted his assistance before I had no choice. He changed my life. Let me help you, Hope. For Billy's sake.

Love, Blythe

Hope took a deep breath and read the letter again. Blythe had left her phone number in a PS at the end of the letter, but Hope wasn't sure she was ready to talk to her friend yet. She was happy for her, thrilled that she'd found a man who saw the good person Hope knew Blythe to be. She'd brought her son back when he'd been snatched; that was something she didn't think she'd ever be able to repay.

The reason why no one could find her was because she wasn't hanging out at the shelters anymore, she was either working at the diner or in the motel room. She kept a low profile and did nothing to bring attention to herself.

She'd started a new life for her and Billy...and irrationally, it scared her to death to think about talking to anyone from her old life as a homeless mother. As if talking to them would somehow jinx her. Though she missed having friends. Once upon a time, when Billy was little and before she'd begun dating Earle, she had a lot of friends. They'd get together for moms' days out, for wine, or just to hang out and chill. But her ex hadn't liked her doing anything outside his home. Said it was dangerous. Said he was protecting her. Said Billy needed her to stay home with him. He'd alienated her from her friends before she realized what was happening. By the time she'd figured out what he'd done, it was too late. She was too worried about doing whatever Earle wanted her to do so he wouldn't hit her.

Looking up when she heard something off to her right, Hope saw Billy standing in the doorway of the bathroom. He had on his pajamas and his hair was wet.

Standing, Hope folded the letter and put it on the dresser, then hurried toward her son. She took the towel from his hands and put it over his head, tousling his hair with it to get as much water out as possible. "Have a good bath, honey?"

Billy nodded his head.

"You ready for more *Tom Sawyer* tonight?"

He nodded again.

Joseph had given the book to Billy one day and they'd made it their nighttime tradition to read it together. Hope wasn't sure how far they'd get tonight, as Billy looked dead on his feet, just as she was.

She missed the days in Washington when she got to stay home with him. Missed being able to make him three nutritious meals a day. Missed simply being able to sit on the couch and watch him play.

But she didn't miss the stress that came with making those meals, wondering if Earle would approve. Didn't miss cleaning the house from top to bottom, only to have to do it again when Earle came home and decided she'd been sitting around on her ass all day doing nothing, and she needed to clean up the "shithole" they lived in.

"Go on and get in bed, Billy. Grab the book. I'll be there in a minute."

Billy smiled at her and ran toward the nightstand where she put the book each night before she went to sleep.

Hope stepped into the bathroom and looked in the cracked mirror at herself. She looked like hell. She had dark circles under her eyes. Her hair was coming out of the ponytail she'd put it in that morning. And Hope thought the lines around her eyes were getting more prominent with every day that passed.

Taking a deep breath, she pushed the negative thoughts away. She was alive. Her son was alive. She had a job and a place to live. Both she and Billy were healthy. Things were fine. They could always be worse, so she needed to look on the bright side.

Hope stripped off the uniform she was wearing and hung it over the shower curtain. She'd come back in and wash it in the sink after Billy fell asleep. She took off her beige cotton bra and her undies as well. She reached under the sink and shook out the extra-large T-shirt Joseph had given her that she used to sleep in. After brushing her teeth, she filled the sink with hot water and quickly washed her underclothes. She hung them in the shower to dry. She knew from experience they'd be fine to wear in the morning. Hope didn't bother looking at her reflection again before she headed out of the bathroom to her son.

An hour later, Hope lay in her double bed with her head on the crappy feather pillow and stared at the other bed and her son. She'd made mistakes in her life, that was true, but she'd always done what she thought was best for Billy. The moment she became a mother, he was the most important thing in her life. Everything she did now, she did for him. She would've given up way before now if he wasn't around.

"Love you, Billy," she whispered.

He didn't respond because he was already fast asleep, but she hoped he heard her anyway.

CHAPTER THREE

*H*ope sighed in irritation the next morning. She'd arrived at the diner at four-thirty, just like she did every morning. The restaurant officially opened at five, but there were a handful of regulars who Joseph let in early to pick up a coffee and muffin to go.

But five o'clock came and went and Tori, one of the other waitresses, hadn't shown up yet. She wasn't the best employee, but Joseph didn't have much choice to keep her, as there weren't a lot of waitresses willing to work the morning shift. So, Hope was serving more than her share of tables and was irritated as a result. She was tired because she hadn't slept well last night, thinking about Calder, and because she was sad about Willie.

The bell over the door rang and Hope said without looking, "Welcome to Alamo's. Someone will be with you in a moment."

"Take your time," a deep voice returned—and Hope turned to stare at Calder in shock.

"What are you doing here?" she asked, a little harsher than the situation warranted.

But he didn't take offense to her tone. "Having breakfast," he said with a smile.

Hope sighed. It looked like it wasn't going to be as easy to blow the man off as she'd thought. The night before, she'd come to some conclusions about him. With her background, she should've been afraid of him, but there was just something about Calder that made her believe he was one of the true "good guys" in the world. Though, that didn't mean she was ready to be buddy-buddy with him either.

Without a word, she turned her back on him and went to the drink station and grabbed a pot of freshly brewed coffee. She made the rounds in her section, refilling cups and making sure no one needed anything.

Out of the corner of her eye, she saw Audrey, another waitress, seat Calder in her own section. Hope tried to tamp down the slight jealousy that rose within her. She had no claim on the man and if Audrey wanted to serve him, she could go right ahead.

She tried to go on with her normal routine and pay no attention to Calder…but it was impossible.

Hope simply couldn't ignore the man. For some reason, her eyes were drawn to him time and time again. He smiled at Audrey, and even Hannah when she went over to his table to make sure he didn't need a refill. Calder didn't try to talk to Hope, but she was more than aware of his eyes on her. It should've been creepy, but just like last night, it felt more protective than anything else.

She was proved right when one of her customers put his hand on her ass and pulled her into his side as he said, "Hey, baby, how 'bout lettin' me fill *you* up sometime?"

Before she could respond, someone jostled her from behind, forcing the man to let go as she stumbled from the contact.

"I'm so sorry, are you okay? I didn't mean to run into you."

Hope turned and saw Calder standing there. He put his hand on her elbow and pulled her away from the handsy customer.

"I'm fine."

"Good. Wouldn't want anyone getting hurt," Calder said with a smile. He'd moved so he was standing between her and the table, and the badge on his belt was on display right in front of the man who'd touched her.

With a nod in her direction, and a wink, he ambled back to his table nearby. Hope didn't have any further issues with the overly aggressive man at her table—or anyone else, for that matter.

Calder was friendly and gracious to everyone, and Hope overheard Audrey gossiping with Hannah about the fact he'd even requested that she tell the cook how good his omelet had been.

Hope wasn't surprised when Billy poked his head out of the back office to let her know he was done eating his breakfast muffin. But she *was* shocked when, the second he saw Calder, he made a beeline for his booth.

Smiling big, he showed the medical examiner the badge he was wearing on his jeans.

Hope moved closer to the table, telling herself she was simply looking out for her son, not trying to get closer to Calder.

"Hey! That looks good, Buddy," Calder told her son. "Fist bump."

When Billy just stood there looking confused, Calder didn't get irritated. Didn't make fun of him. He simply explained what a fist bump was, then smiled at the little boy when he shyly bumped his small fist to Calder's larger one.

"That's it!" Calder said excitedly. "Good job. Hey, you hungry?"

Hope opened her mouth to tell Calder that Billy had already eaten, but her son bobbed his head up and down with such force that she blinked in surprise.

Calder patted the seat next to him in the booth and Billy climbed up without hesitation. It was a bit astonishing because, since Earle, Billy had been reticent around most men. Being kidnapped hadn't helped either.

But he didn't act the least bit shy around Calder.

Hope watched as Calder's dark head leaned closer to Billy's red-haired one as they examined the menu.

Calder patiently read off every single item, trying to figure out what Billy wanted to eat. Billy could read, but he was apparently enjoying Calder's attention and didn't insist he could do it himself, as he would've if she was sitting with him.

Audrey wandered back over to their table then and Hope's attention was diverted by one of her customers wanting to pay for his meal. By the time she looked over at her son again, Joseph had joined the duo in the booth. He was sitting across from Billy and Calder, and the men were watching Billy tuck into a stack of chocolate chip pancakes with whipped cream piled high on top.

Hope wanted to be upset at Calder for letting her son eat so much sugar this early in the day, but Billy was obviously still hungry. She refused to make a scene over food when they'd had so little of it in the past.

By the time she got a break, Billy was finished eating and Calder and Joseph were having a conversation, making sure to include her son.

Hope walked up to the table and told Calder a little harsher than she meant it to sound, "Looks like you've made yourself quite at home."

But again, Calder didn't seem to take offense to her tone. He merely said, "Yup. I'm sorry for not asking you if Billy could have something. He told me he'd never had chocolate chip pancakes and that's just not right."

Hope knew her son hadn't actually said he'd never had the pancakes, but he still must've communicated that somehow to Calder. She smiled at her son and tousled his hair. "Were they good?"

Billy nodded happily.

"I think your break is over, honey," Hope said. "How about you go wash your hands and face then head back to the office? Joseph will be there soon."

Showing how great a kid he was, Billy didn't pitch a fit, simply nodded and raised his fist to Calder.

"It was great having breakfast with ya, kid," Calder said as he bumped his fist to Billy's.

Then Billy scampered down from the booth and headed to the restroom.

Hope kept her eyes on him until he disappeared through the door, then turned to Calder.

He held up his hands. "Don't get mad," Calder said before she could say anything. "I figured he was hungry, because when I was his age, I was *always* hungry. My mom used to swear I had a hollow leg."

Hope realized that any irritation she'd had over Calder getting a second breakfast for her kid disappeared with his casual words. Billy *was* always hungry, and she hated that she didn't have enough food for him most of the time. Joseph was great, feeding both her and Billy when they were at the diner, but she hated to take advantage of the older man's generous nature.

"It's okay. But, Joseph, I'm afraid you're going to have your hands full after all that sugar he ate."

The older man smiled, his bushy beard hiding most of his face from view. "No problem. He's a good kid."

"Just deduct the cost of his second breakfast from my wages," Hope told him.

"No," Calder said. "I've got it."

Hope shook her head. "I can't ask you to—"

"You didn't ask, although I wish you would. *I'm* the one who offered to get him something, so *I'm* paying."

Hope put her hands on her hips and glared at Calder.

"That glare isn't going to change my mind, Hope," he said softly. "So save it for someone it might work on."

Hope pressed her lips together, then said, "Thank you." She had a lot of things to do still, and standing there arguing with Calder definitely wasn't on that list. It wasn't that she was upset he wanted to pay for the food, exactly, it was just still extremely hard to accept help. Not to mention she was still trying to figure out what Calder's deal was. Why was he so eager to help her all of a sudden? While she wasn't scared of the man, he did make her uneasy, and that put her on edge.

It wasn't too much later when Calder left. He nodded at Hope but didn't try to talk to her. Glancing at the clock on the wall, Hope saw that he'd been there for two hours. She shook her head in exasperation but didn't have too much time to think about it, as the diner got their usual mid-morning rush not too long after that.

The next morning, Hope wasn't too surprised to see Calder appear around the same time he had the day before. Although this time, he sat in a booth in *her* section. He'd obviously had time to check out which tables the waitresses served the day before.

Tori had managed to show up to work today, and she immediately commented on the hot guy who had walked in. She asked Hope to switch tables with her so she could wait on him, but Joseph overheard and read her the riot act.

Hope was secretly glad, but she did her best to keep her mouth shut. Tori was notorious for flirting with every good-looking man who came through the doors, even though she had a boyfriend of her own. Caleb worked in the diner as well, as a line cook. It took a lot of guts to flirt with customers the way Tori did with her boyfriend around, but Caleb either didn't notice or didn't care. Not to mention, he wasn't exactly model material, at least in Hope's eyes.

"Hey," Hope said as she came up to Calder's booth.

"Hi."

"I suppose you're gonna tell me it's a coincidence that you're here for breakfast?"

Hope was stunned to see Calder blush, but he kept his gaze on hers as he said, "Nope. I'm here because you are."

"Calder, I don't—"

He held up a hand to forestall her words. "I know. You don't need any help and you think I'm a creeper. But I made a promise to Blythe that I'd look out for you."

"I don't need looking after," Hope protested, feeling

let down for some reason that he was there because of Blythe.

"I know you don't. You've proven that time and time again," Calder said, surprising her. "But…I need to eat every morning. And this place has one of the best omelets I've ever had. Not to mention, I get to hang out with Billy."

Hope opened her mouth to protest, but Calder had already turned his attention from her to someone behind her. She turned to see Billy. He crawled into the seat on the other side of the booth from Calder and held out his fist.

Calder bumped it and asked, "You got your badge on today?"

Billy nodded and came up on his knees on the bench to show it off.

"Good job." Then Calder looked at her again. "Is it okay for him to eat something?"

Hope sighed, then nodded, pleased that he'd asked permission. "Yeah, but not anything full of sugar like yesterday, okay?"

"Got it."

Hope heard her name being called from nearby and said, "I'll be back to get your order."

"Take your time. We're good here," Calder told her.

By the time Hope got back to the booth, Calder was deep in conversation about his friends and their women. Billy was paying rapt attention, but Hope figured Calder could talk about the trash and her son would still be interested. It was a little disconcerting, but nice.

"Did you guys decide?"

Calder ordered a fully loaded omelet and told Hope that Billy wanted an omelet as well.

"He doesn't like eggs," Hope informed him.

"He'll like this."

Hope resisted the urge to roll her eyes. She'd tried to get Billy to eat eggs for ages, but he'd always turned up his nose at them. But she wasn't going to waste time trying to explain that to Calder. She recognized the same stubborn look on his face that her son sometimes got. He'd just have to figure it out on his own.

Fifteen minutes later, Hope placed the plates on the table and smirked at the way her son's nose wrinkled at seeing the omelet in front of him. "Here ya go!" she said in a cheerful voice.

"Thanks," Calder said. "Can you get me a refill of coffee and a large glass of orange juice?"

She wanted to stand there and watch Calder fail at getting Billy to eat eggs, but instead turned and went back to the drink station to fetch the coffee and OJ.

When she got there, Tori was there bitching about one of their regular customers. "Instead of a tip, *again*, all I got was another stupid lottery ticket. I swear to God, someone needs to tell him he's being rude and disrespectful."

"Right?" Audrey agreed. "I mean, it's highly unlikely any of us are gonna make it big off a two-dollar scratcher."

"If he tipped us with money instead of those worthless lottery tickets, I might be able to afford to get that new lipstick I've had my eye on," Hannah threw in.

"I think it's kinda sweet," Hope chimed in as she filled a glass with juice. "He told me one day that he gives the scratch-offs because if one pays out, it'll be more than he could ever afford to give as a tip."

"Whatever," Tori said with a roll of her eyes. "I'd much prefer the cash."

"Me too," Hannah piped in.

"Ditto," Audrey said.

Hope liked the older man. Eli Hyde was around eighty years old, and he always ordered the same thing for breakfast...coffee, plain toast, a bowl of fruit, and a cinnamon roll. He'd never been married and lived in a condo nearby. He always had a smile on his face and was the highlight of Hope's mornings. Well...he had been until Calder started showing up. She'd been pretending to be annoyed with the guy, but that was because deep down, she was attracted to him...and that freaked her out.

Bringing the drinks back to the table where the man she couldn't get off her mind sat with her son, she was prepared to order Billy something else—but was shocked to see that her son had eaten half the omelet and was shoveling another piece in his mouth even as she approached the table.

"What the heck?" she said under her breath. Then turning to Calder, she asked, "How did you get him to eat that?"

Calder smiled at her, then winked at Billy. "Cheese."

"What?"

"Cheese. Lots of it. Everything tastes better with cheese. And salsa. Your son loves spicy stuff, and the salsa pretty much blocks out the taste of the eggs. Right, Buddy?"

His last words were said to Billy, and the little boy nodded happily and forked another piece of the omelet into his mouth.

Hope was irked. She'd done everything she could think of to get Billy to eat eggs, but hadn't thought about salsa. Then Calder comes in, after knowing him for two days, and gets him to eat them? Annoying.

"You're annoying," she said quietly, turning so she was facing Calder.

"I know," he replied, still smiling. "But you like me anyway."

Hope opened her mouth to refute his statement... but couldn't. Calder was right, she *did* like him. He was...easy to be around. He didn't demand she tell him her life story. Didn't lecture her on how she was living. And he seemed to enjoy being with Billy. All pluses in her book.

"Maybe. But there's always tomorrow," she quipped.

Calder threw his head back and laughed at her response, and Hope just stood there staring at him. She couldn't remember the last time she'd been so easygoing with another person, especially a man. And to see Calder laugh, truly be amused, and to know that she'd done that, made her feel all tingly inside.

Billy reached across the table and tapped Calder's hand. When he looked at the little boy, he wrinkled his brows and shrugged his shoulders.

Hope was going to interpret his nonverbal question for Calder, but she should've known the man didn't need her help.

"I'm laughing because not only is your mom beautiful, she's funny too," he told Billy.

His compliment hit Hope hard. It had been a really long time since she'd had anyone say something nice about her. She didn't believe she was beautiful for a second, but it was nice to hear anyway.

Deciding she couldn't deal with the compliment, she ignored it and instead told Billy, "Finish up here. You've got math to work through with Joseph this morning."

Her son scowled at her and glared down at his plate.

"You don't like math?" Calder asked Billy.

He shook his head vehemently.

"Hmmm, math is fun. I use it every day in my job."

Billy's head came up at that.

"I do. Seriously. You want me to help you this morning?"

Billy's eyes got wide and he nodded vigorously.

Hope blinked. Calder couldn't really be offering to help her son with his schoolwork, could he?

"Hope? Would that be all right? I can't stay all morning but," he looked at his watch, "I can stay for another forty minutes or so."

"I...uh...are you serious?"

"About you and Billy? Absolutely."

Hope got the message loud and clear. She just wasn't sure what to do about it. Wasn't sure she was ready for another relationship. Especially with someone so closely related to law enforcement. And she had to protect Billy.

But then Billy climbed out of the booth and stood next to her. He looked up at her and put his hands together and pouted, begging her to say yes.

She rolled her eyes and said, "Okay, but when he needs to go, you need to be a big boy and let him leave. Don't harass him to stay longer, all right?"

Billy nodded happily, then ran off toward the office and his worksheets Hope had made up for him.

Once he was out of earshot, Hope turned to Calder and said, "The only reason I'm letting you do this is because I haven't seen him take to another man like he has to you. He doesn't like most men, they scare him, and I can't blame him after the experiences he's had. But if you do anything to hurt him, I'll kill you. I'm not kidding either."

Calder didn't even blink at the threat. "I'm not going to hurt him...or you, Hope," he said softly, looking her straight in the eyes. "I admire you. You've been through a hell of a lot, and the only thing I want to do is get to know you, and your son, and give you a helping hand."

"The only thing, huh?"

He smirked. "Okay, you got me. That's not the only thing, but it'll do for a start."

Hope took a deep breath. Once upon a time, she'd been good at flirting, but that seemed like ages ago. Speaking quickly, because she knew she had to get back to work and because Billy would be back any second, she said, "He struggles with math. He's really good at writing and reading, but math confuses him. I know I need to get him in school, but until I get more on my feet, I don't trust that the system won't try to take him away from me. Besides that, he doesn't do well with strangers. Go easy on him, okay?"

Calder reached out and took Hope's hand in his. "I'm not going to judge you, or him, Hope. He does need to be in school, but believe it or not, I understand why he isn't. I can tell he's a smart kid. He'll bounce back from this."

"I hope so."

"I know so."

And then Billy returned, clutching a few papers in one hand and a pencil in the other. He pushed past his mom and climbed into the booth next to Calder.

Her son didn't spare her a single glance. Since the kidnapping, he'd constantly wanted to be near her, wanted to be able to see her, but somehow Calder's attention meant more to him at the moment than she did. Hope didn't know whether to be thankful or hurt.

"Hope," Tori called out. "Order's up!"

"Go," Calder ordered gently. "We got this."

"If you need me, just let me know," Hope said.

"Of course."

He said it in a tone that comforted Hope. Of course, Calder would call her over if her son needed her. But she had a feeling she wouldn't be needed anytime soon. Billy was staring up at Calder with adoration.

Wishing she could sit on the other side of the booth and watch the two together, Hope took a deep breath and got back to work.

That morning was the first in a long line of mornings. Calder came in, had breakfast with Billy, then the two of them worked on whatever schoolwork Hope had prepared for her son the night before.

She had a feeling if her son was talking, all she'd hear about was Calder this and Calder that…which she would be okay with.

As it was, she was fielding questions from Audrey, Tori, and Donna. They wanted to know what the deal was with the hot guy who kept coming in every morning and sitting in her section. Tori tried to complain to Joseph that Hope was spending too much time chatting with a customer and neglecting her duties, but Joseph merely said, "If you were as concerned about getting your ass to work on time every day as you are with what Hope's doing, I'd be a much happier boss. Leave her alone, Victoria."

Hope had wanted to laugh, but she also wanted to stay on Tori's good side. She'd learned the hard way from her time in the shelters that making enemies made her life harder. So she simply shrugged and made a mental note to ensure none of her customers had to wait for her because she'd been talking to Calder and Billy.

A week and a half after Calder started having breakfast at the diner, Hope was walking back to the motel with Billy skipping happily in front of her and Joseph at her side. This was the fourth time he'd insisted on walking them home after her shift. It wasn't dark outside, but he wouldn't take no for an answer.

"What's the deal, Joseph?" Hope asked quietly.

"Not right to let you walk home alone," Joseph said.

"Since when? I've been doing it every day since I started working at the diner."

"Since Calder mentioned it. I'm sorry, hon, I should've done this way before now."

The warm feeling in her belly spread at hearing Calder was looking after her, even though he wasn't physically there. "Joseph, I'm fine. This part of town isn't as bad as where I used to walk the streets at all hours of the day and night."

The older man scowled. "Don't remind me of that shit," he growled.

"I don't see you accompanying Tori home. Or Donna or any of the others," Hope protested, not letting it drop.

"That's because Tori has Caleb with her. And Donna drives, as do Hannah and Audrey. They also don't have a seven-year-old to keep an eye on."

Hope wanted to protest more. She wasn't sure how much protection a sixty-five-year-old man would be if someone wanted to start trouble, but she appreciated his concern anyway. "Then, thank you."

"Don't thank *me*, thank Calder," Joseph said gruffly. "He's the one who pointed out that you shouldn't be walking the streets by yourself."

"I know, but it's more than just walking me home," Hope persisted. "It's everything. Letting Billy stay at the diner all day is going way above and beyond. And giving me the job in the first place. And letting me work all the overtime you do. It's…just thank you. I'm going to pay you back."

"Don't want your money, girl."

"I know. I didn't mean monetarily. But there'll come a time when you need something, and I'll hopefully be in a position to provide it. To help *you* out for once."

"I'm not doin' anything for payback," Joseph said without looking at her. "My Madelyn was always happiest when she was helpin' others. She said that success to her was based on serving others, not at the expense of others."

"That's beautiful," Hope breathed.

"*She* was beautiful," Joseph countered. "I'm a grumpy ass, I know it. But every day, I try to live like my Madelyn would've wanted me to."

"She would be so proud of you," Hope said, putting a hand on the older man's arm.

Joseph shrugged. "Maybe. Maybe not. But you remind me a lot of her."

"I do?"

"Yup. You don't care what someone looks like, or what they smell like for that matter. You treat everyone who walks through the door of that diner as if they're a treasured, welcomed guest. I've seen you pay for a meal for someone who can't afford it, even when you yourself don't have any extra money. You don't complain if someone leaves you a shit tip. Hell, you even defend that crazy old coot, Eli, when he leaves fucking lottery tickets instead of money."

"Hey, Hannah once won twenty bucks on one of those. That's way more tip than she would've gotten from him otherwise."

"Yeah, except she's served him twenty times or more, so that comes out to only a buck for every time."

Hope shrugged. "One of these days, someone will win big on one of those scratch-offs, then you'll be saying that Eli was a genius."

Joseph shrugged.

"Besides, Billy loves scratching them off. I use them to teach him about probability."

"You're a good mom," Joseph told her. "Me and Madelyn didn't have no kids, not for lack of trying; it just wasn't meant to be. But if I had a kid, I'd want her to be just like you."

They'd arrived at the motel and Hope wasn't sure what to say. Joseph had just given her the best compliment she could ever remember getting. Her own parents had washed their hands of her when she'd had Billy out of wedlock. They didn't want anything to do with her or their grandchild. She'd been upset but would never expose Billy to their censure.

"Thank you," Hope said quietly.

"You're welcome. Now…get some sleep. Morning comes early."

"Yes, sir," she said with a smile, then leaned up and kissed Joseph's bearded cheek. "Thanks for walking us home."

With a grunt, Joseph turned and headed back toward the diner.

Hope stood in the doorway of her motel room until she could no longer see Joseph, then closed it securely behind her. Nighttime at the Sun Motel was when things got dicey. Sometimes all was quiet, and other times the evening was filled with fighting and a visit from the police.

I'm gonna get us out of here, Hope vowed silently. She didn't know how, or when, but she was saving every penny she earned so she could get a safer place to live. Billy needed to be in school. She was doing her best, but she was well aware that her best wasn't good enough.

But as much for her son, she wanted to move out of the motel so *she* could feel more normal. She wanted to be the kind of woman Calder wouldn't be ashamed to be with.

No, not that. He wouldn't give one shit if the woman he was dating was penniless.

She wanted to be proud of herself. Wanted to be someone *she* wouldn't be ashamed of.

Taking a deep breath, Hope turned to face Billy. She had lessons to come up with for the next day, a son to keep entertained until it was bedtime, and rent to the motel manager was due. She needed to count out her tips and figure out how much extra she had this week, and see if she had enough to go down to the thrift shop a couple blocks over to find Billy some clothes that fit his growing body.

CHAPTER FOUR

*I*t had been a month since Calder had started eating at the Alamo Diner, and he already couldn't imagine a day that didn't start with seeing Hope and Billy. He hadn't realized how lonely he'd been until he had them in his life.

Driving downtown to the diner was a little out of his way, but he'd go double the distance if it meant seeing Hope.

The feeling that Hope might be someone special when he'd heard Blythe talk about her had been spot on. He admired the hell out of her. She'd somehow managed to climb out of the gutter, literally, get a job, support both her and Billy, and get on with her life.

A part of Calder had wanted to be the one to find and "rescue" her, but it turned out Hope Drayden hadn't needed rescuing at all. He longed to give her money so she could move out of the shithole motel she was living in, but he knew better than to even offer. He knew instinctively she needed to make her own way. It killed him, but he understood it.

He'd once tried to give her a hundred-dollar tip with his breakfast, but she'd stormed out of the diner after him and shoved the bill back at him. She'd said in no uncertain terms that if he left her more than the normal amount of tip again, she'd get Joseph to bar him from the diner.

That wasn't exactly possible, and Calder had a feeling Joseph wouldn't do anything of the sort, but because Hope had been extremely upset, he'd immediately agreed. So now he left a generous but not over-the-top twenty-percent tip...but that didn't mean he didn't order more food than he really wanted most of the time. More food meant a higher bill, which in turn meant a higher tip.

He really hoped both Hope and Billy saw him as a friend after all this time. They needed a friend more than anyone he'd ever met. Even Blythe'd had Tadd and Louise when she'd been homeless. Hope didn't seem to have anyone. Except Joseph. The gruff elderly man had taken them under his wing and treated them as if they were his own child and grandchild.

Calder hated not being able to make sure Hope and Billy got home safely every night, but after speaking with Joseph about his concerns, the man had volunteered to walk them home. It wasn't the ideal solution, Calder wasn't sure what Joseph would do if someone tried to harm them, but it was better than nothing.

More and more, he loved spending the two hours

each morning with Billy and chatting with Hope when time allowed. Billy was a smart kid. He might not speak, but he didn't miss anything going on around him. He'd asked, by writing the question on a piece of paper, if Calder had figured out what had happened to Willie, the old man who'd been shot in the alley. He'd put off the kid's question until Hope could join them, and then informed Billy the bag and water he'd seen had been the evidence they'd needed. They'd finger-printed the bottle and had tracked down the man who'd touched it.

After bringing in the petty thief, he'd admitted exactly what Calder had hypothesized had happened. He'd thought the older man had just bought a bottle of booze, and when he found out it was only water, had shot him in disgust. Both Draydens had been sad, but Calder praised Billy for finding the evidence needed to catch the guy who'd shot his friend.

Billy showed his intelligence in other ways as well. Calder had a feeling he was reading well above the level of other children his age; he was also observant and took in everything anyone said around him. He didn't hesitate to try to protect his mother either. One day, when Hannah was yelling at Hope, Billy slid out of the booth and went up to the other woman and pushed her thighs, making her step away from his mother. Hannah wasn't happy, but she backed away and went to gossip with the other waitresses.

Calder definitely didn't care much for the other waitresses Hope worked with. They were catty and didn't seem to care that he was clearly interested in Hope. When he rebuffed their advances, they refused to take the hint and continued to flirt with him whenever they could.

Every morning he sat in Hope's section, but he was well aware of the fact that the other women manipulated Hope as much as they could. They'd beg her to take tables outside her section and then, when she was busy, poach her regulars before she could get to them. Hope also frequently took more tables than were assigned to her when customers had waited too long to get served. And when the other waitresses didn't show up altogether, she never hesitated to take on extra shifts.

It wasn't lost on Calder that most of the regulars did their best to sit in Hope's section each morning. It was the drop-ins and newcomers who had to settle for Hannah, Tori, Donna, and Audrey.

All in all, Hope was an amazing person. Thoughtful, considerate, and just plain nice.

And Calder wanted her more than he'd ever wanted anything before in his life.

He should've been concerned about that revelation, but he wasn't. At forty years old, he'd just about given up on getting married and having a family of his own. But from the first time he'd heard about Hope, he'd been intrigued. Meeting her had simply increased his interest.

That morning, Calder was moving on to plan B. Hope and Billy had been living in a solitary bubble.

She'd done an amazing job getting herself back on her feet, but it was time to expand her circle of friends. He knew she hadn't called Blythe yet, but he felt as if he understood why. Blythe knew the life Hope had lived. And Hope wanted to put as much distance as possible between that life and the new one she was forging.

He'd passed on as much information as he could to Blythe and reassured her over and over again that Hope was fine. Blythe still wanted her to move into Sophie's empty house, but Calder didn't want to suggest anything that would make Hope apt to cut him out of her and Billy's lives.

This morning, he'd invited his friends Daxton Chambers and TJ Rockwell to have breakfast with him. He knew he was taking a risk, as both men were police officers, but he'd asked them to come in their civilian clothes. Though, he'd also asked them to make sure to bring their badges. Dax was a Texas Ranger and TJ was a highway patrolman.

He was sitting in his usual booth when his friends entered the diner. Calder wasn't surprised when Tori and Donna both immediately went up to them and tried to seat them in their areas. His friends were good-looking. Calder might be a guy, but he was well aware that women were attracted to his friends. It had been amusing, and welcome, to the men when they'd been single. But now that everyone had women of their own, who they loved with all their hearts, the attention was merely annoying.

Calder hid his grin behind a hand when the men

blew off the desperate attempts of the waitresses to gain their attention and headed his way. Standing, he greeted his friends.

"Hey, Dax. TJ."

"Good to see you," TJ said as he shook Calder's hand.

"You've been busy lately," Dax observed as he too shook his friend's hand, then sat in the booth.

Calder grimaced. "Yeah. It seems as if there have been more deaths this year than last. I don't have official numbers, but I wouldn't be surprised if, at the end of the year, we've set some sort of record."

The other men shook their heads in commiseration.

"I hear the woman you're interested in works here," TJ commented once they'd gotten situated.

Calder knew TJ was teasing him, but he stiffened anyway. "Yeah. Got a problem with that?"

TJ's eyebrows shot up and his eyes got wide. He immediately shook his head. "No, man. I think it's awesome. I've known you a long time and I haven't ever seen you this…intense about a woman before."

Calder tried to relax. "Sorry. I didn't mean to jump down your throat. Yeah, Hope is special. And wait until you meet her son. He's somethin' else."

"Happy for you," Dax said quietly. "There's nothing in the world like knowing someone's waitin' for you at the end of a long shift. I don't know what I'd do without Mack. She can make me smile when I've had the absolute worst day in the world."

Calder opened his mouth to respond, but when he heard a commotion to his right, he turned.

Billy was running toward the booth with a huge smile on his face. But the second he saw that Calder wasn't alone, he skidded to a stop and stared at Dax and TJ.

"It's okay, Billy," Calder said, holding out his hand. "These are my friends, Daxton and TJ. They're nice."

Billy stared at his friends for a second, then, melting his heart even more, finally took a step forward and grabbed Calder's hand as if it were a lifeline and Billy was drowning in the ocean.

He pulled the little boy forward and formally introduced him to his friends. "Dax, I'd like you to meet Billy Drayden. Billy, this is Dax. And that is TJ. He used to be in the Army."

"Hey, Bud," Dax said.

"Good to meet ya," TJ told Billy.

It took a moment, but eventually, Billy nodded at the two men in greeting.

"Billy doesn't talk much," Calder informed his friends. "But he's super smart, aren't you?"

Billy smiled up at Calder and nodded happily.

Everyone chuckled.

"Hi."

Calder looked up from Billy's happy face into Hope's. She was standing by their table, looking unsure and shy. He smiled up at her and repeated the introductions. She didn't shake his friends' hands, but she did smile at them and nod her head. "I see you've met my son. If you need to talk, let me know and I'll send him back to the office."

"No, it's fine," Calder was quick to reassure her. "I wouldn't know what to do if I didn't get to have breakfast with him."

Billy blushed and bent his head to stare at the tabletop. Calder made a silent vow to praise the boy more often. He tousled his hair and looked back up at Hope. "Three coffees?"

"Of course," she said, seeming to shake herself out of whatever trance she'd been in. "Cream or sugar?" she asked Dax and TJ.

They both declined and said they took it black, and Hope said she'd be back with their drinks and to take their orders.

When she left, Dax grinned at Calder. "She's pretty."

"I know."

"You realize the second the girls figure out who she is to you, they're gonna want to meet her," TJ said.

"Yup."

"That's it? Just yup?" Dax asked.

"Yup," Calder repeated with a grin.

The others smiled back at him. "So, does that mean I can tell Mack tonight?"

Calder quickly shook his head. "I wouldn't go that far. We haven't even been on a date yet. Not sure she's ready for Mackenzie."

The others chuckled.

Billy pulled on his sleeve and pointed to the paper in front of him. On it, he'd written:

tonite

"Tonight what, Buddy?"

Billy painstakingly wrote on the paper again then turned it to face him.

date

"You think your mom would say yes if I asked her out?" Calder asked.

Billy nodded happily.

"What about you? You want to come too?"

Billy looked surprised for a second, then grinned and nodded.

"I'm not sure she'll agree, but I'll ask. And if she says no, you'll have to work on getting her to say yes the next time I ask, deal?"

Billy smiled even bigger as he nodded. His slightly crooked teeth making him look endearing as hell.

"Here you go," Hope said as she put three coffees down on the table and a glass of orange juice for Billy.

"Thanks."

"Thank you."

"'Preciate it."

Hope smiled at them all, then pulled out a pen and a

pad of paper. "Now, what can I get you for breakfast this morning?"

Calder took the time to drink in the sight of Hope as she took his friends' orders. She was wearing the same light blue polyester uniform she wore every day. Her hair was pulled back into a neat ponytail and she had no makeup on. Not that she needed it. Calder loved being able to see her freckles and the way she blushed when he complimented her. Her skin was naturally pale, and he wanted to run his fingers down her cheek to see if it was as smooth as it looked. Of course, he hadn't earned that right yet, but he had high hopes that one of these days he'd get the privilege of touching more than her cheek.

"Billy, do you want pancakes or your special omelet this morning?" Hope asked her son.

He pointed at Dax.

"Omelet?" Hope asked, obviously a pro at interpreting her son's nonverbal requests.

Billy nodded.

"Okay. Calder? What can I get for you?"

"I'm going to try the special this morning," he told her.

"Not the omelet?" she teased. "Cook's not going to know what to do."

Calder smirked. "I figured I'd try something new. Be brave. You won't let me down." His eyes bored into hers, willing her to read between the lines of what he was saying. To know that he'd never let her down either.

She licked her lips nervously but didn't take her eyes from his.

Billy interrupted the moment by pulling on her dress.

"Yes?" she asked.

Billy pointed across the restaurant at an old man sitting at a table by himself. Hope smiled. "Yes, you can go say hello to Eli. But he's almost done, so don't dawdle. Okay?"

With a nod, Billy hopped down from the booth's bench seat and scampered over to the elderly man who was getting ready to leave. The four adults watched as he patted the man's hand then gave him a hug.

"He's a good kid," Dax noted.

"Yup," Hope said without hesitation.

Wanting to get the awkwardness out of the way while Billy was otherwise occupied, Calder reached out and took Hope's hand in his, both for support and to keep her from bolting, as he said, "Hope, TJ is engaged to Milena Reinhardt."

She jerked, and Calder felt her tug at her hand, but he refused to let go. He'd known that learning TJ was with Milena would make her nervous and uneasy, but he wanted to make sure she knew that no one held any ill will toward her or her son.

"Easy," TJ said, leaning back in his seat, putting a few more inches between them. "I'm sorry that your son was involved in that fucked-up situation with that asshole, Jonathan Jones. Only a lowlife like him would see nothing wrong in using a child to force someone else to give him what he wanted. Is Billy doing okay?"

Calder answered for Hope. "As you can see, he's bright and happy, but he hasn't spoken since he was kidnapped."

"Shit," TJ muttered.

"The doctors say it's not anything physical. They think it's a mental thing," Hope said, and Calder felt her hand relaxing in his.

"Trauma," Dax stated. "I've seen it happen before. You just keep on loving him, Hope, and he'll be fine."

"I hope so," she whispered.

"I know so," Calder said as he brought her hand up to his mouth and kissed the back of it.

She stared at him with eyes so wide, he could see the whites all the way around her irises.

"One more thing..." Calder said, not taking his eyes from hers.

"Shit. What now?" she whispered.

Calder couldn't help but smile. She was funny, even if she wasn't trying to be. "Dax and TJ are cops. No—please don't pull away. Listen to me."

Hope stopped trying to yank her hand away, and he saw her eyes dart to the men on the other side of the booth before coming back to his. She took a step away from them, which brought her closer to Calder.

"They're good men," he told her. "The best. They'd no sooner hurt a woman or child than I would. You can trust them just as much as you trust me. They aren't him, honey."

He watched as Hope took a deep breath then nodded. He was impressed with the way she'd controlled her fear.

"Dax is a Texas Ranger and TJ works for the highway patrol. I trust them with my life."

"Texas Ranger?" Hope asked quietly. "Do you wear the cowboy hat and everything?"

Dax chuckled. "Yes, ma'am."

Hope licked her lips then pressed them together before saying, "Thank you both for what you do. I know it can't be easy."

Calder wanted to stand up and hug Hope so badly. She was being extremely brave, considering what he'd learned about her ex. He'd had Cruz do some discrete inquiries about the douchebag. He was a city cop in Seattle who had a few reprimands in his file, but nothing serious enough to get him fired.

It was no wonder she was nervous around law enforcement. After reading the report Cruz had given him on the number of times Hope had gone to the emergency room for broken bones and "accidents," he'd understood what had made Hope flee across the country with only her little boy and what she could carry on her back. Thinking about it made Calder want to fly to Washington and confront Earle Thyne in person—and teach him what it felt like to be on the receiving end of flying fists.

"You gonna stand there all day or what?" Hannah said under her breath as she walked by the table.

Calder saw Dax's and TJ's jaws tighten, but Hope

merely turned her head and said, "Of course not," before she turned back to the table.

"I need to get your orders turned in and get back to work, but I have to say...I know that just because one person isn't nice, doesn't automatically mean everyone who does a similar job is the same way. But my son has had a rough young life. First, he was scared to death of my ex. Earle had no problem yelling at him when he touched his police stuff. Then he was kidnapped and stuffed in a closet in an abandoned building. Don't scare him. He's just starting to become the little boy he was before I made the biggest mistake of my life by hooking up with my ex. I don't want him to turn back into the scared little boy who wouldn't dare leave my side to say hello to a lonely old man."

"He's safe with us," TJ said immediately. "I have a two-and-a-half-year-old son myself. If Jeremiah Jones had his way, he would've taken him across the border and raised him to be just like him, a perverted asshole who preys on children. I would sooner kick my own ass than do anything to scare your son."

"And I don't have kids yet, but you need to know that Calder is like our brother. We'd do anything for him. *Anything*. He's been there for us when we've needed him, and if he ever needs us, we'll be there in a heartbeat. Any friend of his is a friend of ours. Including you."

Hope cleared her throat twice before she croaked, "Thanks."

"And also," Dax added, "Calder has kept you under

wraps, but I can guarantee after we get home to our women, they're gonna want to know everything about breakfast…and about you and Billy. Don't be surprised if a group of women show up sooner rather than later for lunch, asking to sit in your section."

He smiled when he said it but Hope still looked surprised.

"Why?"

"Because…" Calder said, deciding enough was enough. His friends meant well, but they were freaking Hope out, and he hated that. "They just can't help themselves. They're happy, and they want everyone else to be happy too. Besides, once they hear how awesome Billy is, they won't be able to stay away."

Hope nodded but still looked confused. Finally, she gamely said, "Billy *is* pretty awesome."

Calder kissed the back of her hand again then gently shooed her away. "Go on. You've got work to do and the others are glaring at you."

She rolled her eyes. "Whatever. They're always glaring at me," Hope said matter-of-factly. "Let me know if you guys need anything else."

With that, she turned and headed for the drink station.

"I like her," Dax said.

"Me two," TJ echoed.

"Me three," Calder agreed.

All three chuckled.

* * *

Hope tried to get her heart rate down as she walked toward the drink station to grab a pot of coffee and make the rounds of her tables with refills.

Tori and Hannah were standing there laughing. When she approached, Tori said, "Look! old man Eli actually gave me a tip today!" She was holding up two one-dollar bills. "He's still a cheapskate, but at least I got some cash this time."

"Ooooh, you're soooooo rich," Hannah said, laughing.

Hope looked over and saw Eli leaving. She waved at him, and he winked in return then shuffled out the door.

"I thought I was going to have to seat him in *my* area today, but luckily I was full," Hannah said. "So you got him, Tori. Sucker."

Hope frowned. They were always so mean to poor Eli. She swore that the two waitresses didn't have a compassionate bone in their bodies.

"The only reason he gave me cash is because I saw him give the stupid scratch-off to the brat," Tori said.

"I've asked you not to talk about my son like that," Hope reprimanded. She hated when Tori called her son names. It wasn't normal that he was always hanging around the diner, but he was anything *but* a brat. He was well behaved and never got in the way.

Turning her back on the two women, Hope got to work making sure her customers were happy and didn't need anything. She thought about Eli. He was eccentric, that was for sure, but that didn't mean he wasn't a good person. Or that he didn't have feelings. There were times when she really, really needed cash, but she'd never take that out on Eli. She knew he loved giving the lottery tickets as tips.

He didn't have a ton of money, lived off social security, but he always went out of his way to be nice to Hope. The least she could do was humor him about the lottery tickets. It was obvious he saw them as harmless fun. Every time he came in, he'd ask the waitresses who'd last served him if the ticket he'd given them was a big winner, and every time, when it wasn't, he'd look extremely sad.

When Donna had won that twenty bucks, Hope swore the old man smiled for days after. He wasn't jealous that she got the money and not him, he was genuinely happy that he'd given her something that paid off.

Making a mental note to come up with another math lesson with the scratch-off ticket her son had gotten from Eli, Hope smiled at one of her regular customers as she refilled his coffee cup.

Glimpsing Billy returning to the men sitting in her section, Hope's thoughts turned to Calder and his friends. Meeting Dax and TJ had been daunting, more so when he'd told her they were cops, but she'd clearly come a long way since Earle. She couldn't say she was all that thrilled being around law enforcement, but she knew that not everyone was like her ex.

She'd stayed with him way longer than she should have. When she'd tried to leave him the first time, he'd tracked her down and literally dragged her and Billy back to his house, where he'd proceeded to beat the shit out of her and told her there was no way she was leaving him.

She'd pretended to be cowed and repentant, but secretly began plotting her escape. With no friends, and her family having washed their hands of her, she was on her own. She'd managed to get out with the basic necessities for her and Billy by pretending she was going to the grocery store. She'd ditched the car in the parking lot, because Earle had a tracker on it so he could yell at her if she went anywhere he didn't approve of, and they'd hopped on a bus. She and Billy had switched buses so many times, she couldn't even remember what cities they'd been in. She'd had the vague thought to head to Mexico, but she'd run out of money in San Antonio.

At thirty-two, Hope sometimes felt more like eighty-two. She was exhausted, and many nights she wanted to simply give up...but then she'd glance at Billy, and remember that whatever she did would forever affect her son. So, she kept on going. One day at a time, one dollar at a time.

Billy was getting better. She could feel it. He smiled more. His mouth actually moved when he was writing something out on paper, and she could tell he was getting more and more impatient with not being able to communicate what he wanted, when he wanted. She figured if she didn't push, he'd start speaking again on his own.

At least she hoped so.

By the time the cook rang the bell announcing that an order was up, Hope already felt a little better about Calder's friends. They were handsome men, that was for sure, and it was obvious how much they cared about their fiancées. And knowing that TJ had a son, and seeing the pride in his eyes, went a long way toward making her less nervous around them.

When she made her way back to their table, she saw Billy had four badges on the table in front of him. Two were in the shape of a star—his and Calder's medical examiner badges—and the other two were round, one with an outline of the state of Texas in the middle and the other with a star. He was examining each of them intently and running his finger over the words on each.

"Breakfast is ready," she said cheerily as she set the tray down on the table next to them. She began to pass out the plates and told Billy, "Give the badges back. It's time to eat."

He looked up at her impatiently and shook his head.

"Billy," Hope warned.

Her son shook his head again and pressed his lips together stubbornly.

She opened her mouth to reprimand him once more, but Calder spoke before she could.

"How're you gonna grow big and strong if you don't eat breakfast?" he asked. "Our badges will be there when you're done eating."

Billy looked up at Calder, then down at the badges again.

Hope could practically hear his mind working. They'd had to leave his toys behind time and time again. She only had room to carry the basic necessities. He'd been sad each time, but hadn't ever protested too hard. But he'd obviously been affected more than she'd thought.

Then slowly, one by one, he picked up each of the badges and put them on the seat between him and Calder, as if that could keep them safe. He lined them up, alternating between a round one and a star one. Then, finally satisfied, he looked up at Hope and waited for her to place his plate in front of him.

There were a lot of things she wanted to say to her son. She wanted to promise that he wouldn't have to give up anything he loved again. That he'd always be safe by her side. That they'd move into an apartment soon. That he'd get to go back to school soon. But she couldn't guarantee any of that. The only thing she could promise was that she'd always love him, and she'd put him first in her life. But at seven, he probably didn't care much about that.

Sighing, she tried to smile at the group. "Enjoy. Let me know if you need anything else."

She turned to leave when Calder said, "Wait."

She faced the table again.

Calder looked down at Billy and said, "You owe your mom an apology, Buddy."

Hope could only stare at him in shock as he continued speaking.

"You were rude to her, and she didn't deserve it. I

know you were happy playing with our badges, but that's no reason to glare at your mom. You should always respect her—*always.*"

Further breaking her heart, Billy looked confused.

Calder put his hand on Billy's shoulder and looked him straight in the eye as he spoke. "I know you haven't had the best examples of how a man should treat a woman, but I've been coming here for a month now. You ever hear me raise my voice to your mom? Or any of the other waitresses?"

Billy shook his head.

"When I was reading the newspaper that one day, and your mom brought our breakfast over, did I glare at her and tell her I wasn't done reading, and she should come back later?"

Billy again shook his head.

"Right. Because she was doing what I asked her to do. Bringing me breakfast. She was being nice, and if I refused to move my paper and glared at her, *that* wouldn't've been nice back."

Billy frowned and looked down at the badges next to him. He traced the star of Calder's badge for a second then sighed.

"There's nothing wrong with saying you're sorry," Dax said from across the table. "Heck, I'm always apologizing to Mackenzie. I don't mean to mess up, but I do sometimes. I forgot to call her once to let her know I would be home late, and she'd made us a fancy dinner, and by the time I got home she was crying and upset because she thought I'd been hurt and was scared for me. I told her I was sorry and she forgave me right away."

"I had to tell my son I was sorry just last night," TJ offered. "I was supposed to stop and pick up some applesauce on my way home from work, it's his favorite, and I forgot. I told him I was sorry and that we'd have to eat something else for dinner, but that I would make sure I picked it up today. He forgave me too, and we had a yummy dinner with some corn instead of applesauce last night."

When Billy looked back up at Calder, the man said softly, "There's nothing wrong with saying you're sorry...as long as you mean it. Don't say it if you're just trying to get out of trouble."

Billy nodded then looked up at his mom. Then he got up on his knees in the booth and held out his arms.

Hope wanted to cry. She immediately took her little boy in her arms and hugged him. "It's okay, Billy. I know you didn't mean it."

Billy pulled back and smiled at her, then sat back on his bottom and picked up his fork.

"Thank you," Hope mouthed to the men at the table.

They all nodded at her, but it was Calder whose smile made her weak in the knees.

Nodding back at them, she turned away to regain her composure, missing the way the man she was quickly falling for held out a fist to her son. When he gave Calder a fist bump, the man said, "Good job, Billy. I'm proud of you."

She also missed the way her son sat up straighter,

and how his entire countenance changed from trying to be invisible, to being proud of sitting next to Calder. Sitting with his friends.

Calder gave his friends a chin lift as they headed for their cars. He was standing near the door, waiting for Hope to have a second to be able to say goodbye. He wasn't sure this was the time or the place to ask her out, but he also wasn't sure when *was* the time or place. Hope worked her ass off and was at the diner more than she was at the shitty motel she and Billy were living in.

Joseph came out of the back room and Calder caught his eye. He'd talked to the owner of the diner earlier and had gotten his approval. Calder figured the older man was as close to a father as Hope had, and he wanted to do this right.

Joseph went over to Hope and took the pot of coffee out of her hand, then said something to her. She looked over at him, then back at Joseph.

Her blush was easy to see even from across the room. Calder smiled as she walked toward him.

"Hey. Joseph said you wanted to ask me something?" she said as she got close.

Calder nodded. "Yeah. I wanted to know if you'd go out with me."

She stared up at him in surprise. "Really?"

"Really."

"Oh...I would, but I work here every day until six-thirty. Sometimes later if one of the other waitresses doesn't get here on time. And I can't leave Billy alone."

"I talked to Joseph, and he said he'd let you off at four on Friday." Calder didn't tell her that Joseph had also said he'd pay her for the two hours she'd be missing at work. She could work that out with her boss. "And of course you can't leave Billy alone. I'd love it if he came with us."

At that, Hope stared at him in disbelief.

Nervous now, Calder kept talking. "I'm not on call, so we shouldn't get interrupted by me having to leave to go investigate a dead body or anything. That sometimes happens, I'll probably have to bail on you sooner or later and you'll get pissed, but I can't exactly tell the dead body it'll have to wait. But Friday I'm not working. So, I thought we could maybe go out to dinner and then go back to my house to watch a movie or something. If that's too weird, we can probably find something to watch in a theater if you wanted. I just want you to be comfortable. I can drop you both back at the motel anytime you want."

He forced himself to stop talking and stared at Hope, holding his breath, wanting her to say yes more than he'd wanted anything in his life.

"Yes."

"Yes?" It was his turn to question her response.

She smiled slightly. "Yeah. As long as dinner isn't anything fancy. We...uh, we don't have any dress-up clothes."

Calder wanted to jump up and down in glee, but he refrained. "Cool. And no, nothing fancy. Promise."

"Hope. Order up!" Audrey bellowed.

She turned to look behind her, then at him again. "I guess I need to go."

"Me too," Calder said, then he reached up and smoothed a piece of hair that had come out of her ponytail behind her ear.

"Thanks," she whispered.

"I'll see you tomorrow," Calder told her. He reached for her hand and turned it over. Ignoring the calluses, he kissed her palm, then closed her fingers into a fist as if she were holding his kiss in her hand. "Thanks for saying yes. I haven't been this excited since my junior prom."

"Yeah?" she asked.

"Yeah." Then Calder stupidly kept talking. "I was taking Jeni Hamilton, and she'd told all her friends that she was going to go all the way with me and I couldn't wait." The second the words were out of his mouth, Calder knew he'd said the wrong thing. Again. "I mean, I don't think that *you're* going to want to go all the way with me Friday. We haven't even kissed yet. I want to, but I'm not going to insist on..." His voice trailed off, and he muttered, "Shit."

He stayed tense until he heard Hope chuckling. Looking up, he saw she was smiling at him. "It's okay, Calder. I know what you meant. And I'm looking forward to it too. I haven't been on a date since who knows when. It feels nice."

"Yeah." It did feel nice. "I already told Billy I was going to ask you out, and that he was hopefully coming along, so you might let him off the hook and tell him you said yes. He seemed pretty excited."

"I bet he did. He likes you, Calder."

"And I like him back. He's an amazing kid, Hope. I know things haven't exactly gone your way lately, but you're an amazing mother."

"That's the nicest thing anyone's ever said to me," she said softly.

Calder vowed to do his best to tell her more things that would make her smile just like she was right that moment. "Go on," he urged. "Audrey looks like she's gonna blow a gasket if you don't get back to work."

Hope rolled her eyes. "Like she can talk. She took a twenty-minute break to smoke earlier this morning, and she doesn't even smoke! She just wanted to go gossip with Tori, who *was* smoking."

"See you in the morning, Hope," Calder said. Then, moving slowly, so she could protest if she wanted, he leaned down and kissed her cheek. "Be safe getting home." He smiled at her, ran his hand down her arm, and turned to leave.

He looked back once and saw Hope still standing at the door watching him. He waved and headed to his car, suddenly impatient for the next two days to go by quickly, so he could have Hope and Billy all to himself without any distractions for any of them.

CHAPTER FIVE

*H*ope ushered Billy inside their motel room and closed the door behind them. Calder was waiting for them in his Ford F250 in the parking lot. He'd picked them up at the diner right at four and driven them the couple blocks to the motel.

She had to get both her and Billy changed, then Calder was going to take them to dinner.

"Billy, go put on the jeans you were wearing the other day," she told her son.

He frowned at her.

"The ones you had on when you met Calder's friends," Hope specified. "I folded them and put them in the drawer after your bath."

He grabbed hold of his shirt and pulled it away from his belly and tilted his head at her.

Hope eyed the black T-shirt Billy was wearing. It only had a small stain on the front, so it would do. It wasn't fancy, but then again, it wasn't as if either of them *owned* anything fancy. "Yes, you can wear that one. After you change, go wash your hands and face."

Having gotten Billy situated, Hope pulled out the only pair of jeans she owned. She mostly wore her uniform and hadn't had a chance to put on anything else for quite a while. She tugged on the jeans, happy that they still fit. With Joseph insisting on them eating at the diner, she knew she was gaining weight. But when she looked in the mirror, Hope was happy to see that she now filled out the jeans in all the right places rather than having them hang on her butt and thighs.

She tore off her uniform and let it fall to a heap on the floor. She'd wash it when she got home later. Going to the closet, she looked at the three blouses that were hanging there. Making a split-second decision, she grabbed the emerald-green top. Earle had told her she looked ridiculous in anything green and had gone out of his way to belittle her whenever she dared defy him. But Hope had always thought she looked good in green. The color brought out her eyes and complimented her red hair.

When she'd seen the blouse in the thrift shop, she hadn't been able to resist getting it. Miraculously, it fit her perfectly and, more importantly, Hope felt pretty wearing it. The material was something silky and soft. Hope wished she had an appealing bra to wear under it, but her plain cotton one would have to do, as it was the only one she owned.

Hope pulled the elastic out of her hair and winced at the unruly mess. She attacked it with her brush and did her best to get the kinks out of it from having been restrained all day. She didn't have time for a shower, but when Billy came out of the bathroom, Hope used water to dampen her hair, and then she washed her face and arms. She had no perfume, makeup, or jewelry to put on, but she pinched her cheeks to give them some color and tried to relax.

Calder knew what she looked like. It wasn't as if he'd expect her to emerge from the motel room looking like a runway model. But she wanted to. For the first time since she'd left Earle, Hope wanted to look pretty. Wanted Calder to take one glance at her and be spellbound.

Sighing in exasperation, Hope turned from her reflection in the mirror. She was who she was, and she'd made a promise to herself when she'd left Washington to never fundamentally change for a man ever again.

"Ready to go?" she asked Billy, even as she eyed him up and down, making sure he looked presentable.

He nodded enthusiastically, putting his hands on his hips and smiling up at her.

Hope could see the medical examiner badge he'd proudly clipped to his belt, just peeking out from under his shirt. He hadn't taken the thing off since Calder had given it to him.

"Remember what we talked about, okay?" Hope warned her son.

Billy nodded again.

Before he'd fallen asleep last night, she'd gone over

how she expected him to behave when they went out with Calder and warned him not to be demanding. Told him not to scowl at people, and to smile. Since he wasn't speaking, she didn't have to worry about him back-talking, though he somehow managed to get his point across even without saying a word. But she didn't want him to take advantage of Calder's obvious fondness for him. Not that he would…Billy was a great kid and always managed to make her smile.

"All right, let's not keep Calder waiting any longer."

Billy ran to the door and opened it, knowing to wait for Hope as she made sure the door was securely locked behind them. Calder had climbed out of his truck when he'd seen them exit the room and met them at the passenger side of the pickup.

Billy climbed into the back and Calder helped him buckle the seat belt and shut the back door before turning to smile at her. "You look great," he said.

Hope couldn't tell if he was merely being polite or if he really did think she looked good, so she just said, "Thanks."

Then Calder blew her mind by leaning close and whispering, "I have a feeling it's a good thing your son will be our chaperone tonight. I'm not sure I'd be able to keep my hands off you otherwise."

Blushing, Hope smiled. Guess that answered her question about whether or not he really thought she looked okay. Deciding to say what she was thinking for once, Hope said, "I'm sure there will be a minute or two tonight when he's otherwise occupied."

She watched in fascination as Calder's pupils dilated.

"Damn," he said softly. Then he warned, "I'm going to kiss you."

"Right now?" she squeaked in surprise.

"Right now," he confirmed. He put one hand behind her head then leaned down and covered her mouth with his own.

Hope was too surprised to do more than breathe in sharply before the kiss was over. She grabbed hold of his biceps and looked up at him in shock.

Calder licked his lips and groaned. "Fuck, I want to do that again. But I can feel Billy's eyes boring into the back of my head. It'll have to wait."

"Mmmm," Hope said, having a hard time putting her thoughts into words at the moment. She could still feel the pressure of Calder's lips on hers. Smell whatever soap he'd used. She licked her own lips. Could taste the mint he'd probably eaten while waiting for her and Billy to get ready.

"You agreeing to go out with me means a lot, Hope. I'm trying to go slowly, let you and Billy get used to me."

"This is going slowly?" Hope asked in surprise. "We only met a month ago."

"If it was up to me, you'd be living in Sophie's old house right now. Billy would be in school and I'd be over for dinner every night. So yeah, this is me moving slowly."

Hope blinked. "Seriously?"

"Seriously."

She wasn't sure how to respond to that.

"I'm old enough to know what I want, and you're it. You and Billy. But I knew if I pushed too hard, you would've shut me down. Closed yourself off. So as much as I hated you living here in this place, I've not butted in. But now that we're dating, sweetheart...you should know that I'll probably start pushing. It's just how I am. I want you out of here. Living somewhere safe."

Hope's mouth opened then shut again. Then she asked, "We're dating? But we haven't even left on the first date yet."

"As far as I'm concerned, yes. I've been coming to see you every day at the diner for the last month."

"But that was so you could eat breakfast," Hope protested.

"Fuck, you're cute. Hope, I'm forty years old. I've been making my own breakfast since I was sixteen. I've been coming to the diner to see *you*. And Billy. It seems that if I don't get to see you at least once a day, I'm impatient, grumpy, and a pain in the ass to be around. So, yes. We're dating," Calder finished definitively.

They heard Billy pound on the window impatiently.

Calder smiled. "Sounds like someone is hungry. You ready to go?"

"Calder, we need to talk about this," Hope protested.

"Later. Right now, we need to feed your son." And

with that, Calder opened the door and held out a hand to help her inside.

Sighing, Hope let him help her and shook her head in exasperation when he insisted on leaning over and buckling her seat belt. She was perfectly able to latch it, but she'd be lying to herself if she said she didn't like it. No man had ever done that for her before. It felt…nice.

Calder walked around the truck and climbed into the driver's seat. After he'd buckled his own belt, he turned to her and Billy. "Anyone hungry?"

Billy raised his hand and waved it in the air enthusiastically.

"You like tacos?"

He nodded.

"Then tacos it is," Calder said with a smile and started up the truck.

* * *

Hope sat on Calder's couch in a food coma, not wanting to move an inch. Instead of bringing them to a restaurant, like she'd thought was the plan, he'd pulled up outside a beautiful two-story house in a very nice suburb of San Antonio.

He'd informed them it was his house, and instead of going to a restaurant where it would be crowded and loud, he thought having a nice, relaxing dinner at his place would be more comfortable for them.

At first, Hope was uneasy. She wasn't sure she was ready to be alone with Calder. Not because she didn't trust him, but because everything seemed to be happening so quickly between them. She'd moved extremely fast with Earle too, and look how that turned out.

But Calder had gone out of his way to be nonthreatening and entertaining. He'd given her a glass of wine when they'd arrived and told her to sit and relax while he got everything ready for dinner. He'd enlisted Billy's help, and Hope had nothing to do but sit and watch Calder with her son.

From the start, she could tell Calder was nothing like Earle. Her ex had always seemed impatient with Billy. But Calder was relaxed and genuinely seemed to be having a good time. Even when Billy dropped the bag of shredded lettuce on the floor and it spilled everywhere, Calder simply laughed and cleaned it up, ignoring the way Billy's eyes filled with tears and how he'd flinched away from Calder when he'd first dropped it.

Hope's hand had clenched around her wine glass at seeing the reminder of why she'd ultimately left Earle. When she'd noticed Billy acting scared to death around him, it had been the final straw. She'd put up with him hitting her, but once she realized Billy felt threatened, she was done.

But Calder was giggling and joking with Billy. He got him a small stool and showed him how to stir the ground beef cooking in the pan. Hope hadn't seen Billy smile so much in quite a while.

Billy had set the table while Calder stole a couple

brief kisses, making Hope feel even more giddy than she had earlier that night. The tacos were perfect. Dinner was perfect. Laid-back and comfortable. Calder went out of his way to include Billy in their conversation, asking lots of yes and no questions that her son could easily answer.

They were now sitting in his living room watching a movie on the television. Well, Billy was watching. Hope was fixated on Calder.

"Did you get enough to eat?" he asked.

Hope nodded.

Calder was sitting next to her on his extremely comfortable black leather couch. Billy was in a giant beanbag off to the side. Hope could see his legs sticking out of the thing, and that was about it. It was like a giant cocoon.

"Everything was delicious, thank you."

"It was my pleasure. Come here," he ordered, holding out his arm.

Hope took a deep breath and did what she wanted, rather than what her brain was telling her she should do, which was put some distance between them. She was falling for Calder, which scared her to death. But she snuggled into him, loving the weight of his arm across her shoulders.

Calder nuzzled her temple and Hope sighed. She ducked her head, laying it on his chest, and pulled her legs up until her knees were touching his thigh. "Tell me about yourself," she blurted, desperate for something to talk about to keep her mind off of wanting to rip all his clothes off right there on the couch. "Did you always want to be an ME?"

He chuckled, and Hope could feel his warm breath waft over her head. "Nope. I kinda fell into the job, but I honestly love it. It's a perfect blend of solving puzzles and getting my hands dirty, so to speak."

"Ewww, but I guess I understand."

He chuckled again, then shifted and put his feet up on the coffee table in front of them so he was slouched down a bit more on the couch. He pulled one of Hope's arms across his belly and rested his hand on her arm.

Hope tensed before relaxing into him a bit more. Calder was warm, and she loved the way his fingers gently caressed her arm as they talked.

"I majored in biochemistry in college. I wasn't sure what I wanted to do, but I had being a doctor in the back of my mind. Then I took a forensic pathology class and that was that. I knew that was it. I went to medical school, did an anatomic pathology residency, worked a fellowship in forensic pathology...and here I am."

Hope snorted. "You make it sound so easy."

Calder shrugged. Hope could feel his shoulders move under her, but she didn't pick up her head. "Honestly? The schooling wasn't that bad simply because I enjoyed it. Was interested in it. Every day, I'd learn new things. I even attended the police academy in Austin because I wanted to get the law enforcement experience, so I could use that to help me know what I was looking at when I got to crime scenes. Try to get into the mind of the person who might've murdered someone else. I know people think what I do is morbid, and I guess on one hand it is, but I find the human body fascinating. It boggles my mind how we can start out as a single cell inside a drop of sperm, and in nine months or so grow into a human. The body is so complex, and it's amazing how much abuse it can take before throwing in the towel."

"I envy you," Hope whispered. When he squeezed her, she kept going. "I got a general studies degree in college because I didn't know what I wanted to do. Even after I graduated, I had no clue. Nothing really spoke to me. Then I met Billy's father and thought he was the man I was going to spend the rest of my life with. I had a job at a middle school as an administrative assistant and when I got pregnant, I was so excited to let my boyfriend know. I thought he was going to be ecstatic. That he would propose, and I'd quit my job and get to be a stay-at-home mom. That's really what I wanted to do…" Her voice trailed off as she remembered what had actually happened.

"I take it he wasn't happy."

Hope snorted. "To say the least. He didn't want kids. Said I'd tricked him. I tried to explain that birth control wasn't always one hundred percent effective, but he accused me of purposely sabotaging it by not taking my pills properly."

She felt Calder kiss the top of her head then leave his lips against her. "That sucks."

"Yeah. I tried to go home, but my strict, very religious parents weren't thrilled I was knocked up and not married. They kicked me out and told me I'd made my bed so I had to lie in it."

"Assholes," Calder murmured.

"So, I had Billy and was struggling with the single-parent thing."

"Then you met Earle," Calder surmised.

"Then I met Earle," she confirmed. "Things moved really fast with us. I moved in with him within two months of us meeting. He swept me off my feet. Said all the right things. Told me I could quit my job and stay home with Billy. Told me everything I was desperate to hear. I finally thought my life was on the upswing."

"I'm not him," Calder said forcefully, straightening and putting his finger under Hope's chin so she had no choice but to look at him. "Things are moving fast with us too, but I will never, *ever*, do anything to hurt you or your son. I've never lied to you. I want you, Hope, but at your pace."

"I...I know."

"No, you don't. Not yet. But I'm making a promise to you here and now that I'm not him. I won't hit you. I won't hit Billy. I'll support you in whatever you want to do in your life. You want to become a doctor? I'll bend over backward to make that happen for you. You want to stay at home and raise your children, I'm on board with that too."

Hope stared at him, wanting to believe him, but she'd been let down too many times in her past to blindly do so.

He sighed and pressed his lips together in frustration before kissing her forehead and dropping his hand from her chin. "I get it," he said softly. "It's easy for me to say. I'll give you as much time as you need to believe me. To understand down to the marrow of your bones that I'm the man you were supposed to be with all along. I hate that you had to go through what you did in order to find me, but I'm here now. I want you to be the woman you were meant to be, and I'll do whatever it takes to help you get there."

Hope squeezed her eyes shut to keep the tears from falling. He was saying all the right things, but didn't Earle do that too? Hope knew Calder was nothing like her ex. He'd already proven it time and time again, but it was still really hard for her to trust her own judgment.

"What are your parents like?" she asked after an awkward silence, wanting to get their conversation back on safer ground.

"I guess they're your everyday normal couple. They live up in Dallas. Dad works too hard and Mom does what she can to get him to relax as much as possible."

"What does he do?"

"He's an accountant. So the first four months of the year, he's gone a lot. He works an insane amount of hours preparing taxes and helping his long-time customers. But after April, things calm down and he and my mom take their RV out and travel. They've been to all fifty states and are planning on spending six weeks in Alaska soon."

"They sound nice."

"They *are* nice," Calder agreed.

"Any brothers or sisters?"

"Nope. Just me. I've been blessed in that my parents have always supported me. They don't understand why I like examining dead bodies and dissecting them, but they're proud of me all the same."

"I don't care what Billy wants to do with his life. I want him to start talking again, but even if he doesn't, I'll always support him. I'll never turn my back on him like my parents did with me," Hope said firmly.

"Of course you won't," Calder said. "You're an incredible mother."

"Thanks. Most of the time I don't know what the hell I'm doing, but I'm trying."

"I think most parents think like you do."

Hope shrugged and looked over at Billy. His eyes were glued to the television screen as he watched dinosaurs trying to eat the characters on the screen. "Calder?"

"Yeah, honey?"

"I like this."

"Me too."

"If it was just me, I'd probably jump into something with both feet and say the hell with the consequences."

"But it's not just you," Calder said. "I understand, Hope. I do. And I'll say it as many times as you need to hear it, I'm perfectly willing to go at whatever pace you want. I like you. A lot. And I want you and Billy in my life however I can get you. I've been focused on my career for a long time because there wasn't anything else to be focused on. But I want a family. A big one. I figured it was probably too late for me to have that, but then you came into my life. If you let me in, I'll do everything I can to make sure you and Billy have everything you need and want."

Suddenly there was a loud grunt from next to them.

Hope jerked and turned to look at Billy. He was struggling to get out of the huge beanbag and trying to get their attention.

"I got him," Calder said, gently easing out from under Hope and standing to go help Billy. He reached down and grabbed his hands and helped him stand without difficulty. Hope knew she probably would've had to grunt and groan a little more to assist her little boy, who was quickly growing taller and bigger every day. Soon he'd not only be taller than her, but would weigh more too.

Billy nodded his thanks and ran down the hall toward the bathroom.

Chuckling, Calder sat down next to her on the couch once more. "Guess he had to pee."

Hope smiled. "Guess so."

Billy reappeared minutes later and came up to them on the couch. He held out a piece of paper and had a huge grin on his face.

"What's this?" Hope asked, taking it from him. "Oh! This must be the scratch-off ticket Eli gave to us the other day. You know, when Calder's friends were there.

I guess we left it in your pocket and forgot about it. You wanna do it now?"

Billy nodded his head enthusiastically.

Calder chuckled and reached into his pocket and pulled out a quarter. "There ya go, Bud."

Hope kneeled by her son's side at the coffee table and instructed him on what to scratch off. It was the One Million Dollar Big Money scratcher. It was somewhat complicated, so it took several minutes for Billy to use the coin to uncover everything he was supposed to.

Hope studied it for a long, silent moment, then turned to Calder. "I think we messed it up."

"How?"

"Because it says we just won a million dollars."

CHAPTER SIX

*C*alder stared at Hope. She wasn't kidding. "Can I see the ticket?"

She nodded and handed it to him without hesitation.

He looked it over once. Then again. Then he raised his eyes to hers. "Hope, even if you scratched off everything on the ticket, it would still be valid. The machines in the stores use the code at the bottom to determine if it's a winner. No matter *what* you scratched off, or didn't scratch off, the outcome would be the same. You didn't mess it up—you won a million dollars."

"Are you sure?" she whispered.

Calder nodded and held the ticket out for her, grinning. "I'm sure. You won, Hope!"

She didn't reach for the piece of paper, just stared at the thing as if it were a snake about to bite her. "That's impossible."

"Hope," Calder said again. "You just won a million dollars. Well, after taxes it'll be less, but it's a winner."

Billy made an excited noise in his throat and Calder looked at him. "You won, Billy! You and your mom won."

The little boy began jumping up and down in excitement. Calder had a feeling he didn't really understand what had happened, but it was adorable anyway.

"Calder," Hope said in shock. "What am I going to do?"

He grinned again. "You're gonna call the lottery board and tell them you have a million-dollar winning ticket and arrange to pick up your money."

When Hope didn't react, he stood and pulled her to her feet. He swung her around in a circle. "You can move into a safe apartment. You can quit your job and find something better out here in the suburbs where it's safer. You've done it, Hope! You've made it!"

He stumbled a little when Hope struggled in his arms. He stopped and put her on her feet, confused when she took a step back and stared up at him. "I'm not going to quit," she said firmly.

"What? Why not?"

"Because. I can't just up and quit on Joseph. He needs me. You've seen the other waitresses, they're not exactly reliable."

Calder understood what she was saying, but what he *couldn't* understand was the upset look on her face. "Hope, you just won a ton of money. This will help solve a lot of your problems."

"So my life was a problem?"

Calder frowned at her. "That's not what I said."

She turned away from him and picked up the ticket he'd put on the coffee table. "I'm not sure this is real," she said. "Maybe it's one of those trick tickets. Maybe Eli bought it as a joke."

"It looks real to me," Calder told her.

"Well, I'm not making any snap decisions."

Calder was getting irritated now. "So, you don't want to live somewhere safer?"

"I didn't say that," she fired back. "But you sounded a lot like my ex when you insisted I move out here."

That did it. Now Calder wasn't irritated anymore. He was mad. "I didn't insist you do anything, and I am *not* him," he enunciated slowly. "You said yourself that you wanted to get out of the city."

"I know. But...this is...I can't wrap my head around it."

Calder took a deep breath and tried to relax. She wasn't rejecting him. She was just freaked out that she'd won. He gentled his voice and took her shoulders in his hands and turned her to face him. "You don't have to do anything right this second, honey. In fact, I would recommend that you talk to someone about the money before you made any big changes in your life."

"Like who?"

"An accountant. An investor. A lawyer. Someone who can help figure out what to do with the money so you pay the least amount of taxes possible."

He saw the panic on her face again. "I don't know anyone like that. And I can't afford a lawyer, I—"

Calder kissed her quickly, stopping her words. "You might not know someone, but I do. My dad would jump at the chance to help you. And you *can* afford a lawyer now, hon. You just won a million dollars."

"I just... Oh, shit..."

He felt Hope begin to shake and lowered her to the couch. "Billy, run to the kitchen and pour your mom a cup of orange juice, okay?"

Billy had been hovering nearby, but at seeing his mom's pale face, he ran to do as Calder suggested.

Calder cradled Hope's face in his hands as he crouched down in front of her. "Breathe, Hope. This is a good thing. I know it's scary and you're in uncharted territory, but this is amazing."

"I can't believe it. I won't. Not until I know something official," she whispered. "I can't make plans in my head to move, to quit, to do anything until I know it's not a cruel joke."

"I understand," Calder said, enfolding her in his arms. "I'd feel the same way if I was in your shoes."

They stayed like that until Billy ran back into the room with a half-filled cup of OJ. Both man and boy watched as Hope sipped it. "Thanks, Billy. I appreciate it," she said with a small smile for her son.

Billy picked up the ticket and held it up. He put his hand on Hope's arm and raised his eyebrows.

"I don't know, honey. Calder thinks it's real, but I won't know until I talk to the lottery board."

Billy opened his mouth a couple times, then pressed his lips together in frustration. It was the first time Calder had seen the little boy even try to speak, and he hated seeing him so upset at not being able to say what he wanted.

He reached out and put a hand on Billy's shoulder. "Your mom doesn't want to get her hopes up in case it's not authentic. But nothing will change in your life until she gets the final word, okay?"

Billy shook his head violently back and forth and raced out of the room once more.

"What is he trying to say?" Calder asked Hope.

"I don't know. I hate when this happens. Most of the time I can read him pretty well, but I have no idea what he's thinking right now."

Billy ran back into the room holding a pen and an old take-out menu that had been on the counter in the kitchen. He fell to his knees next to the coffee table and started to painstakingly write something on the paper. When he was done, he held it up to his mom.

move?

"No, honey," Hope said.

Billy scowled, then leaned over the paper once again.

Calder looked at her and bit his lip, but they both turned back to Billy when he held up the paper again.

school?

"Not for a while," Hope told him.

Calder was surprised when Billy threw the pen and menu on the floor and stomped over to the beanbag. He threw himself into it and crossed his little arms over his chest.

Hope turned distraught eyes to him, and Calder was moving before he'd thought better of it. It probably wasn't his place to comfort the little boy, but he couldn't stand seeing him so upset. He walked over to the beanbag and got on his knees in front of it so he and Billy were eye-to-eye.

"Can we talk?"

Billy turned his head away. He looked mad, but Calder had also seen the tears in the little boy's eyes. "Do you want to go to school?"

Billy didn't respond, so Calder continued. "Because I know your mom wants you to. But she's worried about you. I know this might be hard for you to believe, but when you were taken, it was just as hard on your mom as it was on you."

Billy's eyes met Calder's.

"Everything she's done in her life has been for you. She loved you the second you were born. Every decision she makes in her life, she makes with you in mind. Moving to Texas, getting the job at the diner, living in that motel. She worries when you're out of her sight because she doesn't want something to happen to you again, like when that bad man took you. Do you understand?"

Billy nodded.

"Right, so she wants to believe that winning the money is real. That she'll have the money to move out of the motel to a bigger and safer place, but she doesn't want to get your hopes up, or hers. You understand that, right?"

Calder waited until the boy nodded before continuing.

"You're going to go back to school, Billy. But not until your mom knows it's somewhere safe. Where you can relax and trust the people around you, so you can start talking again. She's gonna find a safe place to live where you can both let down your guards and just be yourselves."

Billy bit his lip but didn't take his eyes from Calder when he pointed to the floor.

Calder looked down but didn't see anything there. "I don't understand, Buddy."

Billy pointed to himself, then to the floor once more.

Calder shook his head in confusion.

Then he watched as Billy mouthed a word and repeated his pantomime. It was the first time Calder had seen him do that. No sound escaped his lips, but he could clearly read the word he was mouthing.

"Here?"

Billy nodded.

"Here what?"

Billy pointed to himself, then to his mom, then back to the floor as he mouthed words again.

"You and your mom would be safe here?"

Billy's eyes lit up as he nodded once more.

"Oh, honey," Hope said as she came over to the beanbag. "I'm sorry. I'm so sorry. I've been doing everything wrong, haven't I?"

"No, you haven't," Calder said before Billy could respond. "Listen to me. Are you listening?" He waited until she nodded before continuing. "I can't imagine how things have been for you, but I know with everything in me that you've done everything exactly right. You're here, aren't you? You and Billy? That tells me that you're an incredible mother, and that when life gave you lemons, you didn't bother to make lemonade, you crushed those things and made an entire lemon meringue pie."

Her lips twitched, but he kept talking. "The money's nice, but you would've made it without it. And if the money turns out to be nonexistent, you'll *still* make it." Calder turned to Billy. "You have to trust your mom. I know you want to go to school, and you want to move out here, but until you're eighteen, you have to go with the decisions your mom makes. That can be frustrating, I realize that, but always remember, deep in your heart, that your mom loves you and only wants the best for you. Can you do that?"

Billy reluctantly nodded.

"Now, I want you to know that you are *always* welcome here at my house. This will always be a safe place for you. I like your mom. A lot. And I want to date her, and I'd love nothing more if you guys moved into my house for good and for always, but…that's not my decision to make. And it's not yours. You know whose it is?"

Billy pointed at his mom.

"Exactly. And we have to trust her to make the best decision for not only herself, but for you too, Bud."

"Calder," Hope protested.

He turned to her. "I'm done. No, wait, I'm not. There's a school a couple blocks from here. I moved to this neighborhood in part because of the awesome school system. I didn't have kids but I hoped to have them someday, and when I did, I wanted them to get the best education possible. There's a nice apartment complex not too far from here as well. Once we find out about the scratch-off ticket's authenticity, I could help you see if there are any vacancies."

Calder watched as Billy leaned over and tugged on his mom's blouse sleeve, and once he had Hope's attention, he clasped his hands together under his chin and gave her the most pathetic puppy dog eyes he'd ever seen.

He tried not to laugh, but he did grin at the pleading look on Billy's face.

Hope chuckled and rolled her eyes. "You really want to go to school again?"

He nodded.

"Even though you aren't talking and the kids'll probably make fun of you?"

Billy nodded again.

"You'll probably be behind academically. Joseph has been working with you, but it's still gonna be a lot of work to catch up."

Billy kept nodding.

Hope looked from her son to Calder, then back to Billy again. "*If* the ticket is real, and *if* the money comes in…I'll look into the apartments near here."

With a loud whoop, Billy threw his arms into the air and tried to jump to his feet. The beanbag, of course, prevented that. So Calder picked him up and as soon as he was on his feet, Billy ran around the room like a crazy man, his arms waving wildly over his head, looking like one of those air-dancer things businesses used to advertise outside their stores.

"Did you hear that?" Hope whispered. "He made a sound."

"I did," Calder told her with a smile. "He also was mouthing words earlier…he's gonna talk again soon. I know it."

"I think so too." Hope got to her feet with a smile, and Calder followed suit.

"I meant what I said," Calder said. "You and Billy are always welcome here. You'll be safe with me."

"Thank you. I…appreciate it, but I'm not ready for that yet."

"I know. Which is why I suggested the apartments. If I can't have you in my house, at least you'll be close by."

"You really do like me, don't you?" Hope asked.

Calder couldn't help it, he laughed. Threw his head back and guffawed like she'd said the funniest thing imaginable. When he got himself under control, she was glaring at him.

Grabbing her around the waist and pulling her into his embrace, he picked her up off her feet and fell sideways onto the beanbag. She screeched, and then laughed when she realized what he'd done.

"Yeah, sweetheart. I like you a heck of a lot."

Calder let out an *umph* when Billy threw himself on top of them on the beanbag. Putting an arm around the little boy, he ignored the badge Billy was wearing as it dug into his side and did his best to block out how good Hope's body felt against his own.

"Now you've done it, Billy," he teased. "Since we're all in this thing, who's gonna help us out?"

The giggles that erupted out of the little boy's mouth were music to his ears.

Three hours later, Calder stood in the doorway of Hope's motel room. He didn't want to leave them there. It wasn't too late and all was quiet in the parking lot, but he knew that could change in a heartbeat. He'd tried to convince Hope to stay the night at his place, but she insisted that since she had to work the next morning, she needed to get back to the motel.

"Will you let me call my dad and tell him about the ticket and get his advice?" Calder asked Hope.

She slowly nodded. "I'm still not convinced it's real, but if so, I have no idea what to do with the money, so

I'll need help." She reached into her pocket and took out the ticket in question. "Will you keep it for me?"

Calder blinked. "Seriously?"

"Yeah. Why?"

It hit him then. Deep down, Hope trusted him. There's no way she'd hand over a million-dollar winning scratch-off ticket if she didn't. He could call in and claim it himself and there would be no way for her to prove it was hers.

Calder reached out and wrapped his hand around hers still holding the ticket. He flattened it on his chest, the ticket between her palm and his shirt, and leaned down to kiss her.

This time, he took it slow and tried to show her with his kiss how much she meant to him. He felt her lean into him, and he took a step forward, taking her weight against his own. The kiss was deep, but not nearly long enough. He pulled back, well aware that Billy was probably watching them from inside the motel room. "I'll keep it safe for you, sweetheart. You'll call tomorrow, right?"

She sighed. "Yeah."

"Good. Do it first thing. I'll also talk to my dad tomorrow morning before breakfast."

"Calder! That's too early."

"Nah, he'll be up. He's always been an early riser. Guess that's where I got it from."

"Thank you," she whispered.

"You don't have to thank me," he told her. "I'd do

anything if it made you feel safer and more comfortable."

Then he brushed the back of his hand against her cheek and tucked the ticket into his back pocket. "Goodnight, Billy," he called out. "See you tomorrow, Hope."

"Tomorrow," she echoed.

Calder backed away and said, "Shut and lock the door."

Hope rolled her eyes. "Bossy."

"When it comes to your safety, yup," he returned.

He kept eye contact with Hope until the door was shut and he heard the lock snap into place.

Calder took a deep breath and looked up at the sky. The night had been full of ups and downs, but he also felt as if he was one step closer to his goal of making Hope care about him as much as he cared about her.

CHAPTER SEVEN

*H*ope hadn't planned on telling anyone at work about the winning ticket...at least not until she'd had it verified by the lottery people that it was authentic. And even though she'd made Billy promise to not say a word, she'd forgotten that he was only seven and that secrets were literally an impossibility for him.

Within ten minutes of Eli walking through the door of the diner, Billy had spilled the beans. He'd written the words "we won" on a napkin and that was that. Hannah, Audrey, Tori, Donna, Joseph, and even the cooks and busboys were all talking about it.

By the time Calder arrived for breakfast, Hope was ready to scream.

"I suppose now that you're rich and your boyfriend is here, you're gonna want to take a break and have us serve your tables, huh?" Tori sneered.

"Yeah, little Miss Moneybags doesn't need to do any actual work anymore," Donna threw in.

Hannah and Audrey just turned up their noses at her.

"Problems?" Calder asked as he sat in his usual spot.

Hope sighed. "They found out."

"I guessed as much. Billy?"

Hope nodded. "How'd you know?"

"Hunch. How are you doin'?"

That was one of the things Hope liked most about Calder. He always worried about her. Always wanted to know how she was doing. She'd never had someone so focused on her before. And Earle didn't count because he was focused on her for all the wrong reasons...namely, to ferret out whatever she'd messed up so he could punish her for it.

"I'm okay."

"How about you try again, and be honest with me?" Calder asked dryly.

"Fine. It sucks. Everyone's treating me differently, and I hate it. The customers are giving me the side-eye. The other waitresses hate my guts and the cooks aren't much better. You know, if someone else had won, I'd be happy for them. I wouldn't flat-out ask them for money. I wouldn't try to guilt them into giving me some. I wouldn't ask for a loan. It's crazy."

"Fuck. You've been asked for money?" Calder asked.

Hope sighed. "Yes."

"By who?"

"Everyone. Okay, that's a lie. Eli didn't ask me for

any, although out of anyone, he'd be the one I'd probably give some to."

"And Joseph?" Calder asked.

Hope smiled. "Of course not. He has a hard-enough time asking for help with little things, there's no way he'd ever even hint that he wants some of my winnings. Besides Eli, he's the only one who's acting halfway normal."

"When are you going to call the lottery board?"

"I was going to put it off until this afternoon, but now I'm thinking I need to call as soon as they open."

"Good idea. What did Eli say when Billy told him about the ticket being a winner?"

"He's been beaming all morning. He said he just knew one of these days one of the tickets would pay out big."

"He wasn't wrong."

Hope smiled at Calder. "How are *you* this morning?"

"Good. I missed you last night."

Hope knew she was blushing but tried to control it. "We weren't apart all that long."

"Doesn't matter. Still missed you. The house seemed empty after you and Billy left."

Hope opened her mouth to respond but was interrupted by Tori.

"If you're done chatting, table four needs more coffee."

Hope looked over and, sure enough, the mugs sitting in front of the couple at the table were empty.

"On my way," Hope told Tori. "You want your usual this morning?" she asked Calder.

"Of course. But I'll wait for Billy."

"Okay. He should be out in a few. Joseph was working on some math with him this morning. He wanted to show him exactly how much a million dollars was."

"I'll be here when he's done," Calder said.

Hope turned from him, extremely aware that his eyes were on her as she made the rounds to all her tables, refilling coffee and making sure no one needed anything else.

When she went back to the drink station to put down a pot of coffee and start a new one brewing, Tori and Hannah cornered her.

"You know that was supposed to be mine," Tori said.

"What was supposed to be yours?" Hope asked, playing dumb.

"That lottery ticket. He was sitting in *my* area the other morning."

"If I remember correctly, you were happy that you actually got a cash tip instead of the, and I quote, 'stupid scratch-off.'"

Hannah's lip curled and she leaned into Hope. "Listen, bitch, you need to split that million bucks between us all. We've all served that old coot, and we've all gotten lottery tickets, except none of *ours* was ever worth more than twenty bucks. It's only fair."

Hope probably *would've* offered to split the money

SUSAN STOKER

—if the women she worked with were halfway nice to her. But they weren't. They were terrible waitresses, gladly leaving her to work their shifts when they didn't bother to show up, not caring if they were late in the mornings, taking extra-long breaks, and not bussing their tables, leaving that to the overworked and under-paid busboys.

No, she had no intention of giving these horrible women a dime of her winnings. If that made her a shitty person, so be it.

"Why should I give you guys any of it? You hate Eli. You do everything you can to have him sit in my section whenever possible. Hannah, you were even glad when Eli wasn't in *your* section the other morning."

"You might be the boss's favorite, but that doesn't mean shit when—"

"Time to get back to work, ladies." Joseph's words interrupted whatever Hannah was going to say.

"You'll regret not sharing that money!" Hannah hissed before she and Tori slunk away to the other end of the counter, where they immediately started gossiping with Donna and Audrey, no doubt telling them what a bitch Hope was and how she wasn't going to share her winnings.

"They aren't going to lighten up on you," Joseph said.

Hope turned to the man who'd literally changed her life and sighed. "I know."

Joseph opened his arms and pulled Hope into his

embrace. She was startled for a moment because he wasn't an outwardly affectionate man. He hugged Billy all the time, but Hope couldn't remember a time he'd even touched her other than to shake her hand.

But without hesitation, she snuggled into his embrace. He smelled like onions and grease from the grill. It was somehow comforting.

"It's time for you to move on, Hope," he said quietly.

Hope shook her head.

Joseph pulled back. "You don't want to? Hell, girl, I know you've been savin' every penny you've earned here to move, why are you hesitating now?"

"I don't want to leave you. You're more like a father to me than my own ever was."

"That's sweet and all, but it's not like I'm gonna disappear. And you're not gonna move to Timbuktu. There're even these new-fangled things called telephones."

Hope gave him a small smile. "I'm scared."

"Of course you are. I don't blame you. But that never stopped you before."

"What?"

"When you walked in here that first time, I could tell you were scared out of your skull. You thought I was gonna kick you out. You stunk like garbage and had a haunted look in your eyes that I can't get out of my head, even today. Draggin' your son along when you asked for a job took a lot of guts, but I don't blame you. I wouldn't have left my son alone when I went lookin' for a job either. But none of that stopped you from asking if I was hiring. You were also scared to ask me if you could bring Billy in with you to work because he didn't have any other place to go, but you asked anyway."

"That's different."

"It's *not* different," Joseph argued. "The odds of one of those scratch-offs being a million-dollar winner is astronomical. Some rich college kid could've won it, but he didn't. *You* did. Use that money to get out of here. Get an apartment. Get your son into a good school. Live your life, Hope. As you've always meant to live it."

"I don't want to leave you in a lurch," Hope said softly.

Joseph shook his head in exasperation. "You've always been such a softie," he said. "Fine. You keep workin' here until I find a replacement. But I'm cuttin' your hours. Morning 'til noon only."

"But that's only seven hours!" Hope protested. "I need the hours, I need—"

"You don't need the hours anymore," Joseph said, shaking her gently. "You need to look for an apartment. A car. A school for Billy. There's other things you need to do, and I'm givin' you the time to do them."

Hope took a deep breath. Joseph was right, but it was really hard to change her mindset. She'd always worked as much as possible so she could save every penny. But now she didn't need to do that.

"That money you won ain't gonna last forever," Joseph told her. "After taxes, it'll be a lot less than a million, but it's a great foundation for starting over. You can find a job that you love and get yourself and that son of yours back on your feet. Not only that, but you need to get out of this neighborhood. You know as well as I do how fast information gets around. By tonight, everyone's gonna know that one of the waitresses at the Alamo Diner won a million bucks. If you thought the people *here* askin' you for money was bad, just wait until you try to walk down the street. Every single person you've ever even looked at will be comin' up to you with their hand outstretched. Be smart with that money, Hope. Get out of here while you can."

"Thank you," Hope said quietly.

"For what?"

"For being there for me and Billy. For looking out for us. For not judging. For giving me a chance."

"You're welcome. Now...looks like you have an order up, your son has made his way over to your man, and your regulars are busting at the seams to find out if the rumors are true and you really are a millionaire."

Hope rolled her eyes but quickly leaned forward and hugged Joseph once more. Then, without another word, she made her way to the food pick-up area and got the two plates waiting for her.

Around three o'clock that afternoon, Joseph told her to go home. Hope had called the lottery board and they'd confirmed that she really was the winner of a million dollars. They'd made arrangements for her to meet with them, and bring the ticket, and they'd give her an oversized check.

She felt numb. Yesterday, the fact that she'd won was still like a dream. Something that may or may not be true. But now that it had been confirmed, she was overwhelmed. There were so many things that she needed to do and think about, but she didn't have the foggiest idea where to start.

Joseph was right. So was Calder. She wanted to move out of the city. She actually hated it there, but it had been her home for a while now. It was scary to think about going anywhere else. But it was time. Through Eli's generosity and a bit of luck, she had the means to do it. Billy could go to school, she could get a job that she loved, and maybe, just maybe, continue her relationship with Calder.

She'd found out as she and Billy walked home that Joseph had been right, she'd gotten a lot more attention than she'd ever had before, as if everyone had already heard about the ticket. For the first time in a long time, she felt nervous about walking on the streets. She'd blended in with all the other people, first the homeless, and then those headed to and from work, for so long, she'd forgotten what it felt like to be an outsider.

And right now, she felt as if she had a giant bullseye on her back. And she hated it.

When Hope got back to the motel room, she called Calder. He picked up after only one ring.

"Hello?"

"Hi, it's me."

"Hope. Is everything okay?"

She chuckled. "Of course. Joseph sent me home

early. Billy and I are at the motel. I just thought…
Shoot."

"What, sweetheart?"

"I just wanted to talk to you."

Calder's voice lowered. "I'm glad. I've been thinking about you since I left the diner this morning."

"I called the lottery board."

"And?"

"And the ticket's authentic. I won."

"I'm so happy for you, Hope."

"Thanks." And the thing of it was, Hope knew he *was* genuinely happy for her. He'd been interested in her *before* she'd won. She knew without a doubt that Calder didn't want even one penny of her winnings. "The thing is…does the offer to talk to your dad about accounting and stuff still stand?"

"Of course it does. Why would you think other-wise?" Calder asked.

"I don't know…I just…I don't want to take advan-tage of you."

"Hope, I wish you'd ask *more* of me. I think at this point it's safe to say I'd do just about anything for you and Billy."

Hope had been standing next to one of the double beds in the motel room, and upon hearing that, she plunked herself down on the edge of the mattress. "You're too nice to me."

Calder snorted. "No, Hope. You've had too many people *not* be nice to you to realize that you deserve for *everyone* to be nice to you."

"That was...convoluted," she said, wrinkling her nose.

"I already called my dad this morning and he's more than happy to help you...especially after I told him that you're my girlfriend."

"You told him that?" Hope asked, shocked.

"Yup."

"I don't...was that smart?"

"Hope," Calder said gently. "If you don't want to see me, if you don't think of me like that, I need you to tell me. I'll still help you with the ticket and I'll still be there for Billy, but if you don't have any feelings for me, please tell me now, so I don't continue to fall harder for you and get my heart broken in the process."

Hope swallowed hard. "I can't believe you just said that," she whispered.

"Why? Because guys aren't supposed to admit it when they like a woman? Because we're supposed to be all manly and macho and shit? Screw that. I like you, Hope. I can easily see myself falling in love with you and being with you for the rest of our lives. But if you don't feel the same way, I need to know. It'll suck, I can't deny it, but I'd never force you into a relationship you don't want. That wouldn't be fair to either of us."

"No!" Hope blurted. "Of course I want you! I just can't believe that you'd purposely choose to be with me."

"Why *wouldn't* I want you? You're smart, loyal, beautiful, brave, and dedicated to your son."

Hope waited for him to say more, and when he

didn't, asked, "Are you waiting for me to actually answer that? Because I can think up a hundred or so reasons why."

"No, you don't have to answer it. But do tell me this…are you okay with being my girlfriend? With being in an exclusive relationship with me?"

"Yes," Hope blurted. "God, yes."

"Thank God," Calder breathed. Then he said, "I'll bring you my dad's number tomorrow morning and I'll let him know to expect your call. When are you supposed to meet with the lottery board?"

Relieved he'd moved on to safer subjects, still having a hard time wrapping her mind around the fact she and Calder were now apparently boyfriend and girlfriend, she said, "I'm not sure. I told them I'd call back and let them know. I'm not sure how I'm going to get there."

"Just let me know when it is, and I'll take you."

Hope bit her lip and didn't say anything.

"Hope?"

"I'm here. I just…"

"You are not taking advantage of me," Calder said firmly, reading her mind.

"But you have to work, and—"

"I'm not chained to my desk. I'm on call, yes, but that doesn't mean I can't help you out."

"Oh. Okay."

"There's something else I want you to consider."

"What?"

"Now that we're dating…would you consider

113

trusting me to claim the money on your behalf? I swear I'd never try to take it from you or anything. We'd deposit it into your account. But if *you* claimed the prize, it would make it really easy for Earle to track you down."

Hope bit her lip and thought about his offer. She'd already thought about Earle being able to find her based on the publicity that could happen when she came forward to claim the money. On the one hand, she wanted to be tough, and not let him scare her for one more minute, but she had to think about Billy's safety as well.

As if he could tell she was struggling with the decision, Calder said, "Why don't you start by calling them tomorrow and finding out when the first day they can do their thing is, and set it up."

"Why the rush?" Hope asked, twisting the phone cord around her hand.

"Hope, it's a million dollars. You're living in a crack-house motel. I want that money in your possession so you can get the hell out of there. Yes, selfishly, I want you nearer to me, but more than that, I want to be able to get a good night's sleep because I know you're safe. So I won't panic every time my pager goes off and I see a downtown address. So you can get Billy enrolled in school and start to really live your life, instead of simply making it through one day at a time."

"Yeah…okay, you're right."

"I know I am," Calder said without an ounce of humor.

Suddenly everything hit Hope all at once. She flopped back on the bed and whispered, "I won a million dollars."

"Yeah, sweetheart. You did."

"I can afford to move into an apartment."

"Yup."

"And get Billy clothes that fit."

"Uh huh."

"Go to the store and buy a cart full of vegetables and not have to worry about where I'm gonna put them or how fast I have to eat them before they go bad."

"Well, you might still have to worry about that last part, but otherwise, yes."

A tear fell out of her eye, dripping into the hair at her temple. Then another.

"Hope?"

"Yeah?"

"Are you crying?"

"Maybe."

"Shit, you need to stop," Calder said sternly.

Hope was so surprised, she sat up and asked, "Why?"

"Because I can't stand it. Because I'm not there to hold you. Because when you cry, it tears me up inside."

"They're happy tears," Hope protested, feeling warm inside at his words.

"Doesn't matter," he said without pause.

Hope wiped her eyes and grinned. "Okay. I'm okay now. Just overwhelmed for a second there."

"I'm gonna be at your side throughout this, Hope. I'm gonna help you pick out an apartment. Buy a reliable car. Go shopping for the first time. Even go to Billy's school to get him registered if you want. Whatever you need, whenever you need it, I'm there."

"I...Calder, you don't have to do that."

"I know. I want to."

Hope took a deep breath and jumped. "I want that too."

"Good. Hope?"

"Yeah, Calder?"

"Thanks for calling today. I was thinking about you all day and wondering what was going on with you."

"I was thinking about you too," Hope admitted.

"You know what else you can get now that you're rich?" Calder asked.

"What?"

"A cell phone. So you can call and text me all day, every day."

Hope smiled. "Yeah?"

"Yeah."

"Sounds good. But I'm not getting Billy one. Not until he's at least twelve. Maybe thirteen."

Calder chuckled. "Smart. Kids are way too connected to their electronics these days."

"But I might bend and get him a game console," Hope admitted. "It's going to be hard not to spoil him with a ton of toys and stuff. He's never had a lot of that sort of thing, and I feel like an awful parent as a result."

"Don't. He's a sensitive and caring kid. That's what's important."

"I guess."

"It is. You've done an amazing job with him. You're a wonderful mother."

"Thanks."

"What are your plans for the rest of the afternoon since you have unexpected free time?" Calder asked.

"I hadn't really thought about it. I don't want to go outside because someone will ask me for money, and that sucks. Maybe I'll see if I can find something on TV to watch with Billy. Do you...do you want to join us?" Hope asked the last part quickly before she lost her nerve.

"Oh, hon. I wish I could. I'm about to head into autopsy."

"I'm sorry. Did I interrupt you?"

"Absolutely not. I wouldn't have answered if I was busy."

"Okay."

"Would you mind if I sent something over though?"

"Sent something over?" Hope asked, confused.

"Supper. I know you usually eat at the diner, and I assume you didn't grab anything to go?"

"No. I didn't even think about it. But I've got some mac and cheese here, Calder. I can make that on my hot plate."

"Please? I don't like the thought of people asking you for money. If they don't get it, things could turn ugly...then I'd have to hurt someone if they touched one hair on your or Billy's heads. So since I can't come over and hang out with you guys, I want to do the next best thing."

Hope decided to ignore the part about Calder going after someone who might hurt them. It felt...good. Not like when Earle said it, since he was simply being possessive and crazy, but more protective and comforting. "Okay, but as soon as I get paid, I'm going to take *you* out. And pay."

"Deal."

Hope rolled her eyes. She had a feeling there was no way Calder would ever let her pay for something. She'd barely gotten him to stop giving her exorbitant tips.

"What time?" Calder asked.

Hope looked at the clock on the nightstand. "Maybe in a couple hours?"

"Perfect."

"And if you get done early, you're more than welcome to join us," she said.

"I wish," Calder said with a sigh. "When I go into autopsy, it usually takes hours. Even when it seems like an open-and-shut case, I always check every organ, every possibility, before I confirm the cause of death."

"That's smart."

"I don't want anyone coming back and questioning my methods and findings. And the last thing I'd want to do to a loved one's family is to force an exhumation because I was sloppy or because I rushed through an autopsy. And I'd do the same for an unidentified DB as

I would for the mayor of the city. If it was me, I'd want the medical examiner to do the same thing."

"You're amazing," Hope whispered. "Most people aren't like you."

"No, hon. I think most people *are* like me. You've just had the misfortune to meet more of the other kind in your life. But that stops now. You've got a ready-made family now. Between me and my cop friends and their wives and girlfriends, and the firefighter family, we're going to show you and Billy a whole new life."

She didn't really know what he was talking about, but agreed anyway.

"I'll set up the delivery to be there in two hours," Calder told her. "But don't open the door until you check to be sure it's the Battalion delivery guy."

"Who?"

"Sorry, Battalion is the name of the restaurant. It's an Italian place downtown that operates out of an old firehouse. Blythe's fiancé loves it, as do the other fire-fighters. Anything you and Billy won't eat Italian-food wise?"

"Oh, um...neither of us is that picky. It's hard to be when you're starving." There was silence on the other end of the line, and Hope closed her eyes and mentally slapped herself on the forehead. "Sorry, I mean, no, anything is fine."

"That shit is done," Calder said firmly. "Neither of you will *ever* have to eat something you don't like again."

"Okay, Calder," Hope said quietly, thinking it better to simply agree at this point than rile him further.

"I'll order a variety of dishes to make sure there's something you do enjoy."

"You don't have to do that. Spaghetti or lasagna will be perfect."

"Two hours, Hope. Don't open the door to anyone who isn't from the Battalion."

"I wasn't planning on it. Calder?"

"Yeah?"

"I've never felt about someone the way I feel about you."

When Calder didn't respond right away, Hope thought she'd gone too far.

"Good. Because as I said earlier, I have a feeling you're it for me, Hope. I've spent my life feeling like I'm on the outside looking in. Seeing all sorts of happy families and couples. Wanting that for myself. And for the first time, I feel as if I've found it. Sweet dreams tonight, sweetheart. I'll see you in the morning at the diner. Be safe."

"I will." There was so much more Hope wanted to say, but before she could get her thoughts in order, Calder had said goodbye and hung up.

Billy came over and pulled on her sleeve as if to ask what was up.

Shaking her head and smiling at her son, Hope informed him that they were going to have a lazy afternoon of TV and then dinner that Calder was sending over for them.

Billy jumped up and down in excitement and immediately went over to the crappy motel TV and clicked it on.

Later that night, after Billy was asleep in the bed next to her, Hope looked at the remains of the food Calder had ordered for them. He'd sent way too much, of course, but she put the leftovers in the small fridge she'd bought at Goodwill and shook her head.

He'd had the restaurant send over small portions of beef and pork meatballs, Italian salad, spinach manicotti, fettuccine, lasagna, chicken parmesan, green beans, potatoes, and cheesecake for dessert.

She and Billy had tried every single dish and loved every bite. Billy ate way more than a normal seven-year-old would eat, but Hope didn't scold him. She knew it would take a while for him to understand that he didn't have to stuff himself at every meal. In the past, they didn't know when they'd get to eat again, but now that she'd won the lottery, that wasn't an issue anymore.

Hope wanted to call Calder to see how the autopsy had gone...not the details, but to ask if he'd figured out how the poor person had died. She wanted to ask what he'd had for dinner. Wanted to thank him for sending over the food for them. Basically, she simply wanted to hear his voice. She had no idea how she'd managed to fall for him so quickly, but she had.

For the first time in ages, she was looking forward to her future. Wanted the night to hurry up and pass so she could start a new day. To see Calder.

CHAPTER EIGHT

$\mathcal{H}$ope was having a good morning. She'd gotten to see and talk to Calder when he'd stopped in for his usual breakfast. Billy had not only squeaked in happiness when he'd seen him, but he'd run straight to him and given him a big hug. Eli was back, and Audrey didn't even complain when he'd given her a lottery scratch-off as a tip—although she seemed a little annoyed when she didn't win anything from it.

Tori and Donna were being bitchier than usual, but Hannah wasn't there that morning, so that was a plus, even if it meant Hope had to do more work than usual.

There had been only two people who'd approached her and Billy on their walk to the diner that morning, asking for money. One slunk away when she'd told him she didn't have any. The other, however, a homeless man, had followed her for two blocks, saying things about Hope being too big for her britches, now that she'd won, and telling her that she should give to those less fortunate, otherwise people might "get offended" and possibly hurt her. That guy had scared her, but she'd done her best to ignore him and walk faster to the diner.

She'd thought long and hard the night before about whether or not to take Calder up on his offer to claim the money for her. She'd finally decided that if she was ever going to move on from her abusive relationship, she needed to stop being afraid to really live her life.

So, she'd called the lottery board and made arrangements to come to their office in a few days to take care of the formalities of winning. She'd ask if there was a way to either keep herself anonymous or at least keep her picture out of the press releases. Calder still had her winning ticket, which Hope was perfectly okay with. The last thing she wanted was to leave it in the motel room for one of the maids to find, or for someone to steal it from her on her way to or from the diner.

Calder was going to pick her and Billy up later that day to take them to his house for dinner, and Hope promised herself she'd tell him about the scary homeless guy—she didn't tell him that morning, not wanting to kill the happy mood everyone seemed to be in. And she'd also make sure he was okay to continue holding on to the ticket until they went to claim the money.

All in all, she was in a relatively good mood, even though she still had quite a few things on her mind—so she wasn't mentally prepared for the barrage of reporters who entered the diner right before lunch.

They pushed into the small building and immediately started asking, loudly, who was the waitress who had won a million dollars.

Tori, being oh so helpful, pushed her forward and pointed at her. "She is. Hope Drayden."

Hope's head spun with the questions that were immediately fired at her. She stared, frozen, at the cameras with wide eyes and couldn't think of one thing to say.

"What will be the first thing you buy with the money?"

"What did you say when you scratched off the ticket?"

"Are you going to share with the man who gave you the ticket as a tip?"

"Tell us about yourself, Hope!"

"What does your family think?"

It was the last question that made Hope finally shake herself out of her stupor. She spun away from the cameras and fled to the office, where Joseph and Billy were doing schoolwork.

Joseph looked up when she entered and asked, "What in the world is going on out there?"

"Cameras," Hope panted. "They're here because of the lottery. They got me on film, Joseph." The last was whispered, even though she was completely panicked.

"Shit," Joseph muttered. "Stay here. I'll deal with them."

Nodding, Hope wrung her hands together and stared at the door Joseph left through. She felt Billy come up next to her and put his arms around her waist. She put an arm around his shoulders and stood there in shock.

The entire reason she'd fled to San Antonio without a penny to her name was because of her ex. She'd wanted to get as far away from him as possible…to hide from him. He'd told her if she ever left, he would never rest until he'd tracked her down and dragged her back home. That since he was a cop, he had the resources to find her no matter where she went. And if she was on the news…it would make it easier for him to find her. To find *them*.

It was one thing to have her name in some lottery database, it was another thing altogether to have her picture plastered on local news shows that could be picked up across the country.

Being brave enough to live her life would be harder than she'd thought.

Hope began to shake, and she didn't even realize until she was sitting that Billy had led her over to the chair Joseph had been using next to the desk.

He made soothing noises in the back of his throat and petted her hair. Hope should've been thrilled Billy was making any noise at all, but now she couldn't think of anything other than her ex finding her and carrying through with the threats he'd made.

Ten long minutes later, Joseph came back through the office door. "They're gone."

Hope closed her eyes and sighed in relief. "Will they be back?"

"Probably. But you don't have to worry. If they come back, I'll just chase them off again."

"What am I going to do?" Hope fretted, more to herself than Joseph.

"You're going to hold your head up and not be scared anymore," her friend and mentor said firmly. "You aren't the same woman who lived with that scumbag. If he dares show up here, you've got friends who will stand by your side and support you."

"You don't know him," Hope whispered. "He's sneaky. If he wants me back, he'll find a way to make that happen."

"I've called Calder," Joseph said, ignoring her words. "He's on his way to pick you and Billy up."

"What?"

"You're taking the rest of the day off. Tomorrow too. You can come back the day after next if you want."

"If I want?" Hope asked. She felt like she was echoing everything he said, but nothing was making sense.

"Yup. Let's let things die down, then you can figure out what to do next."

Hope felt bad. She was disturbing Joseph's livelihood. "I'm so sorry."

"Don't be," Joseph said with a smile. "I guarantee when people hear that a customer gave a waitress a million-dollar tip, they'll be lined up around the block to eat here. I'm gonna make bank."

Hope couldn't help but smile. She knew Joseph was trying to make her feel better, but he was also probably right. "I can come in tomorrow and work."

"Nope. Those other girls can take care of it for once. You get your head together then you can come back. But you know you can't work here forever, right?" Joseph asked.

Hope sighed again. "Yeah." As much as she loved Joseph, she didn't exactly love being a waitress. The older man had given her a chance to get her life back on track, but now that she didn't *need* to work there, it was inevitable that she'd quit when she got an apartment in the suburbs. "I'm gonna miss you, Joseph."

He waved his hand. "Whatever. Like I said before, you'll have a car and a phone. You can visit and call me whenever you want."

Hope smiled. "You got it."

"Wait in here until Calder arrives."

"But my tables—"

"Audrey, Donna, and Tori can take them. Lord knows you've had to cover for them often enough."

Hope winced. The other girls wouldn't like that, but whatever. They were already pissed at her for not giving them any of her winnings. Besides, she *had* covered for them in the past. Countless times. She handed her order pad to Joseph and took off the apron around her waist. "I'll cash out before I go."

Joseph nodded. "I'd get on that if I was you. Calder was none too happy when I told him what was going on. I bet he'll be here before you know it." Then the

127

older man turned and left the office again, gently shutting the door behind him.

Hope wasn't thrilled with what was happening either, not in the least. But as a result, she was going to get to see Calder and spend more time with him. She couldn't be mad about that.

She counted out her tips and was watching Billy get his things together when the door to the office opened once more.

Before she could blink, she was in Calder's arms.

"Are you all right?" he asked, pulling back, putting his hands on her shoulders and inspecting her from head to toe as if the reporters had been holding weapons rather than cameras.

"I'm fine."

Calder chipped away at the shield around her heart a little more when he crouched on the floor next to Billy and asked him the same thing.

When Billy nodded, Calder gave him a huge bear hug too, then grabbed hold of his hand as he stood. "Right. Then we're outta here."

Hope didn't even protest when Calder put his arm around her waist and led her out the office door to the front of the diner.

"Where are *you* goin'? Tori asked as they passed her.

"Joseph gave me the rest of the day off. Tomorrow too," Hope said.

"What the fuck?" Tori huffed. "This place is gonna be crazy because of you, and you're fuckin' leavin'?"

"Yeah, she's leaving," Calder answered for her.

"She's been busting her hump for months while you and your friends do the absolute minimum possible. All the regulars want to sit in *her* area because they know they'll get served in a timely manner and won't have to put up with attitude while they're eating. Here's a tip—you'll catch more flies with honey than vinegar."

Hope could only stare at Calder as he chastised the other waitress. It had been a long time, if ever, since anyone had stood up for her like Calder was. She squeezed his waist with her arm, trying to let him know how much she appreciated it.

"I've *got* a man," Tori hissed. "I don't need to flirt and simper to make men interested in me either. Caleb likes what I've got just fine. This job is stupid, and Hope treats it as if it's the end-all, be-all of jobs. That stuck-up, stingy bitch wouldn't know what to do with a man's cock if her life depended on it!"

Halfway through Tori's rant, Hope had reached out and covered Billy's ears with her hands, not wanting her son to hear the filth spewing from the other woman's mouth. He'd heard his share of swearing since they'd been on the streets, but Hope tried to keep his exposure to a minimum.

"Get your shit and get out," a deep voice growled from behind them.

Hope turned to see Joseph standing there listening. His face was red and his fists were clenched at his sides.

Calder didn't say a word, merely stepped to the side, pulling Hope and Billy with him.

"Joseph, I didn't mean—"

"Oh, I think you meant every word," Joseph sneered, interrupting her. "You're lazy and a bitch to boot. You're done."

"Fine!" Tori spit out, then turned to look at Donna and Audrey. "Come on, we don't need to put up with this bullshit."

But the other two women wouldn't meet her eyes.

"Audrey? Donna?"

"I need this job," Donna mumbled.

"Me too," Audrey echoed.

"Fucking bitches," Tori said under her breath, then whipped her apron off and threw it on the floor in disgust. She turned on her heel and left the diner without another word.

It was so quiet in the diner for a moment, Hope would've sworn she could hear a pin drop...but then someone started chuckling. Then one of the customers started clapping. Soon, everyone in the diner was cheering and laughing.

Hope noticed Donna and Audrey slinking off to the drink station before she felt herself being turned. She looked up at Calder and saw that he was definitely not amused by what had just happened. "Are you okay?" he asked.

She nodded. "Are *you* okay?"

He looked pissed for a second longer, then she saw the anger fade away. He shook his head in exasperation. "Only you would ask me if *I* was okay after a scene like that."

Hope raised a hand and put it on his cheek. "No one's ever defended me like that before."

"Well, get used to it," Calder responded. "That's what boyfriends do when their girlfriends are unfairly and unjustly attacked. You ready to go?"

Hope blinked at him. She felt warm all over. She liked being his girlfriend. Just as she liked him being her boyfriend. Standing up on her tiptoes, she kissed him. It was a light, chaste kiss, but she still felt lightning move from her lips down to her toes.

His arm tightened around her waist, and she hoped that meant he felt it too.

Calder pulled back and looked into her eyes, and Hope felt as if he were looking straight into her soul. That he could read every heartbreak, every doubt, every dream she'd ever had about finding a man who would love her for who she was. He licked his lips, and his gaze darted down to hers before coming back to her eyes. His brown gaze was intense, yet soothing at the same time.

Then he blew her mind even more. After kissing her lightly on the forehead, he knelt down next to her son and asked him if he might be interested in a hamburger from Whataburger. When Billy nodded, Calder picked him up as if he weighed no more than an infant, when Hope knew that wasn't the case. Her son was a rapidly growing boy, and she'd long since given up trying to carry him.

Then Calder reached for her hand. He nodded at Joseph and they walked out of the diner toward his pickup. There were a few reporters standing around who called out questions, but Calder ignored them and got her and Billy inside his truck safe and sound before climbing in himself and driving off.

He took them to the motel, where he stood in the doorway while Hope packed an overnight bag of clothes for her and Billy. They hadn't really talked about it, but there was nowhere Hope wanted to be more than with Calder.

She was feeling off-kilter after everything that had happened that morning, and if for some reason Earle felt the need to hop on a plane and come to San Antonio, she felt much safer at Calder's house than in the crappy motel.

When Calder pulled into his garage, after going through the drive-thru at Whataburger, Hope marveled again at how beautiful his house was. It was huge...but then again, she'd been living in a motel room for the last few months, so anything above three hundred square feet seemed big to her.

Calder handed the bag of food to Billy and said, "Go on in, Buddy. Me and your mom will be there in a second."

Nodding, Billy ran off for the door to the house and disappeared through it.

"I'm sure you have to get back to work. I don't know what Joseph was thinking calling you. You're busy and—"

Calder interrupted by pressing his lips against hers and backing her up against the side of his truck.

Hope inhaled sharply at the move, but immediately melted into Calder as his arms came around her. One hand went to her head and he shoved his fingers into her hair, cupping the side of her face, and the other dug into her waist as he held her against him.

His head tilted and moved even as he held her still.

Hope groaned and raised her hands to press against his chest. But she didn't push him away, she dug her nails into his shirt and held on as Calder rocked her world.

How long they stood there making out, Hope couldn't have said. When Calder took his lips from hers, she was breathing hard, and when she shifted, she felt her damp panties rub against her core. More than that, she felt Calder's arousal hot and hard against her belly. But instead of thrusting himself against her lewdly or moving his hands to touch her intimately, he leaned his forehead against hers and simply stood there.

She felt his warm breath against her cheeks, and she didn't make any attempt to pull back or move. It felt as if they were talking without words. She'd never felt closer to another human being than she did to Calder at that moment.

"Thank you for coming over," he said after a couple minutes had passed.

"Thank *you* for showing up at the diner when Joseph called," she countered.

"I'll do my best to always be there for you," Calder said in what sounded like a vow. "There will be times I won't be able to, but you have my promise that if possible, I'll always drop whatever I'm doing to get to your side when you or Billy need me."

"Calder," Hope whispered, feeling overwhelmed. She'd been alone for so long, his words struck her hard. "Don't say that if you don't mean it," she said softly.

"I mean every word, Hope. I've never met a woman like you. I'd just about given up on ever finding a woman who could take me as I am. Every day I'm surrounded by death, by choice, but all I have to do is think about you and it's as if the sun has come up. When Blythe started talking about you and Billy, I thought she was exaggerating your goodness. That there was no way a woman who'd been on the streets, as you had, could be as nice as Blythe said you were. But the reality is a thousand times better than her stories."

"I'm not always nice," Hope said.

Calder chuckled. "Sure you're not."

"I'm not," Hope insisted.

Calder still had a hand tangled in her hair and they were still plastered to each other, but she felt as if she needed to make sure he understood.

"Tell me one time, recently, when you weren't nice."

Hope bit her lip and tried to think. It was difficult with Calder being so close. Her nipples were hard under her uniform and his body against hers was making it almost impossible to want anything other than for him to kiss her again.

"Um...one time at a shelter, I told another woman a

shelter nearby was giving out free socks when I knew they weren't."

"Why?"

"Why'd I tell her that?"

Calder nodded.

"Because I knew they were running out of spaces for the night and I wanted to make sure me and Billy got a bed there. She got out of line, and I was right, we got the last available bed."

"You did that for Billy. Doesn't count when you're protecting your son. What else?"

Hope pressed her lips together. "Calder, I don't—"

"Seriously, what else?" Calder asked.

"I don't know!" Hope whined.

"You can't think of anything that doesn't involve you trying to provide for your son, or you trying to protect yourself and him, can you?"

"I'm sure I can...but I can't think when you're all..." She shifted, and her nipples brushed against Calder's chest. Hope inhaled sharply, which only pressed her closer to him.

"I like nice," Calder said softly, then kissed her forehead. "As I said, my life is full of not-so-nice things," he kissed her temple, "and knowing you're here in my house," he tilted his head and kissed her cheek, "feels like a reward for all the shitty things I've seen while working as an ME."

Hope tilted her head back, not ashamed in the least for wanting Calder's lips on hers again. And he didn't disappoint. As soon as he finished his sentence, he was kissing her again. And once again, Hope was lost in sensation. Everything tingled, and she tried to press herself closer to Calder's hard-as-nails body. He was hard to her soft, and she loved it.

When he pulled back once more, Hope couldn't stop the small whimper that left her mouth. She wanted Calder. More than she'd ever wanted anyone before. More than Billy's father. Way more than her ex. She knew without a doubt that Calder was nothing like either of those men. There was no way he'd care more about his own satisfaction than hers. That wasn't the kind of man he was. He was honorable and giving. But when he pulled away from her for the second time and dropped his hands, she wished he was a little more selfish.

"Not here," he told her with a grimace.

"I want you," she blurted, then blushed.

"I want you too," he said immediately. "But not in the middle of my garage against my truck when your son is waiting for us to get inside so we can eat hamburgers together."

Hope closed her eyes in frustration. He was right, she knew he was, but it sucked. She kept her eyes shut as she said, "I know. But it's been a really long time since I've wanted someone the way I want you." Then, feeling brave, she opened her eyes and looked up at him. "I haven't ever really liked sex. I haven't understood what the fuss was all about. But...I think I'm figuring it out."

"Fuck, sweetheart," Calder said, as he pulled her

against him once more. He buried his face in her hair and held her tightly to him. She could feel his erection, just as he could probably feel her hard nipples against his chest. But this hug wasn't about sex. It was about connecting as man and woman.

Calder didn't say anything else, but eventually, he pulled back and intertwined his fingers with hers. He pulled her toward the door to the house and held it open for her. They walked into his home together, and Hope had a feeling her life would never be the same again.

CHAPTER NINE

Having Hope and Billy in his house made Calder feel less jumpy. Less paranoid. He hadn't been sleeping well recently, and he knew it was because he was worried about Hope staying in the rundown motel. He had nightmares about being woken up by his pager and heading to a scene, only to find it was Hope's dead body in an alley he had to investigate.

He couldn't have been happier that Hope had won the money. It solved so many of her problems. Money wasn't exactly the key to happiness, but in her case, it sure went a long way toward making her life easier.

Calder couldn't give a shit about the money, though, beyond the fact that it meant she'd be moving sooner rather than later. He would've done anything possible to get her to see reason and accept help from Blythe, Sophie, or himself, but this was even better. She didn't have to feel beholden to anyone and he didn't have to feel guilty for manipulating her into moving.

The night he'd brought Hope and Billy to his house had been both bliss and torture. He'd taken the rest of the day off after picking her up at the diner, and he'd also called out the rest of the week. The other medical examiners would have no issue taking his shifts, knowing he'd make it up to them in the future.

Billy had eaten his hamburger and fries with a smile on his face. Then Calder had called his father and put him on speaker, introducing him to Hope and letting them talk about the money she'd won. Wanting her to feel comfortable, he took Billy out to his yard and started to teach him how to throw a football.

Later, when Billy was engrossed in a movie, Hope stood at his side as they cooked dinner together. She told him everything his dad had said about taxes and investments and had thanked him for putting her in touch with him.

Calder had wanted to take advantage of the fact that Billy was otherwise occupied, but instead of hoisting her up on the counter and spreading her legs like he wanted, he'd satisfied himself with brushing up against her and touching her every chance he got.

She knew exactly what he was doing, however, and started returning the favor. When he was bending over looking for something in the fridge, she brushed against his backside as she went past. In retaliation, he moved behind her when she was chopping vegetables for a salad and put his arms around her, telling her she was doing it wrong. Keeping her in his arms, he took the knife from her hand and proceeded to show her the "correct" way to chop. Although, remembering back now, Calder had a feeling she'd won that round too with the way she'd pushed her ass back against his hard dick.

They'd teased, laughed, and generally enjoyed each other's company as they ate, then settled down to watch another movie.

Billy fell asleep in the beanbag, and as much as Calder wanted to carry Hope up to his bedroom and have her sleep there, in the end, he showed her to a guest room instead. Calder wanted to leave Billy in the beanbag, but Hope said he'd freak if he woke up in the middle of the night and couldn't see her. They'd been sleeping next to each other for months, and Calder didn't want to do anything to scare either of them.

He still remembered the way Hope had looked at him before she'd closed her door the night before. Her green eyes seemed frustrated yet relieved that he hadn't pushed for more. Calder vowed right then and there to make sure she knew he wanted her more than anything else in his life, but that he was willing to wait as long as she needed to feel comfortable with their relationship. He had a feeling she hadn't had that before. That she'd been rushed into relationships in the past, both with Billy's father and her douchebag ex.

They spent the next day much as they had the one before. Relaxing, laughing, and getting to know each other better. Every minute Calder spent with Hope and her son made the thought of bringing her back to that awful motel all the more terrifying and depressing. He didn't know what he'd do if something happened to them. Both meant that much to him.

Now they were on their way to the lottery board office so Hope could officially claim the million-dollar prize. She was nervous and excited at the same time. She'd barely eaten anything for breakfast, but Billy had eaten enough for both of them.

Calder had wanted to go into the office with Hope, but she asked if he would stay in the waiting room with Billy, and he couldn't say no to her. He handed the scratch-off ticket to her and kissed her lightly before sending her off with a soft, "You've got this, sweetheart."

Thirty minutes later, Hope had reappeared. Her cheeks were flushed and her eyes were sparkling. She came straight to him and Calder took her in his arms in a congratulatory hug. "I take it things went well?"

She nodded against his chest. "Yeah. I can't believe it."

Calder pulled back. "Believe it, hon."

"They gave me a check," she whispered.

"A normal-sized one?"

She chuckled. "Yeah. I'm supposed to take pictures next with a big ceremonial one."

Calder felt the smile fading from his face. "Pictures?"

She nodded. "I tried to tell them I wasn't comfortable with that, but they kept pushing. Said it would make a great rags-to-riches story. They want Billy in them too."

"Right this way, Ms. Drayden," a man wearing a three-piece suit said from the doorway of the waiting area.

"What do *you* want to do?" Calder asked, ignoring the man.

"Refuse the pictures."

"Hope?" the man from the doorway asked a little impatiently. "We really do need to get going."

Calder turned his head and looked at him. "Give us a minute."

"We don't have a minute," the man fired back. "We're on a schedule. The photographers are here now and we have a deadline to get the photos to the press. If we don't—"

"They're just going to have to wait. This isn't exactly the story of the century. Give. Us. A. Minute." He followed up his words with a hard stare until the man dropped his gaze and mumbled something before backing out of the room, leaving them alone.

"So you want to refuse to let them take pictures?" Calder asked again with no trace of the irritation he'd just displayed to the man in the doorway.

"You're doing it again," Hope said.

"What?"

"Standing up for me. Protecting me."

Calder couldn't tell how she felt about it. "I'm not going to apologize," he told her. "You've been on your own for too long now. I told you before, and I'll tell you again and again and again until you truly believe it. I'm on your side, and no one messes with you when I'm around to prevent it."

"I don't want any pictures," Hope said after licking her lips. "I'm afraid enough as it is that Earle will have seen those news clips that aired the other night, when those reporters were at the diner. I can't prevent the lottery board from writing a press release, I agreed to that when I accepted the money. I want to move on from Earle's abuse, but pictures are a bit too much for me at this point."

"Then you won't take them," Calder said definitively.

"But—"

"No buts," he said, interrupting her. "If you don't want to do it, you don't have to."

"I don't think it'll be that easy. You saw that guy. He was pretty insistent."

"Hope, they can't force you to have the pictures taken. They've given you the check, you can simply walk out."

She didn't respond for a long moment, then she smiled. "I can, can't I?"

"Yup."

"Then let's do that...but..."

"But what?"

"Maybe we can make up some reason so as not to hurt their feelings."

Calder chuckled. Only Hope would be worried about hurting the feelings of complete strangers who likely only cared about making money for the lottery. "Okay, hon."

"Thanks, Calder."

"No need to thank me."

"See, you say that, but it's so not true it's almost ridiculous."

"Come on," Calder said, kissing her quickly before taking her hand in his. He was happy to see that she was becoming more and more used to him touching and kissing her as time went on. It was a good thing, as he wasn't about to stop anytime soon. "We need to celebrate. Then we need to stop at the bank and deposit that check. Then we're going apartment shopping. Do you want to look at cars today or save that for another day?"

"We're looking at apartments today?"

"Is there a reason why we shouldn't?"

"Um…no, but it just seems fast."

Calder stopped in front of the door and cupped the side of her face. "Do you really want to spend another night at that motel when you've got the means to get out of there?"

She made a face. "No."

"Then we're going apartment shopping," Calder said decisively. He looked down at Billy. "What about you, Bud? Want to find a new place to live?"

The little boy made an excited sound in the back of this throat and nodded enthusiastically.

"We'll find a nice place where you can have your own room, what do you think about that?"

The happiness in Billy's eyes dimmed a bit, but he still gamely nodded.

Calder crouched down, keeping his fingers linked with Hope's. "Your mom is gonna be in the room right next to you. You can even keep your door open so if she needs you in the middle of the night, you can hear her when she calls out. That work?"

Billy smiled and nodded again. Calder stood and felt Hope's fingers squeeze his. He'd hoped mentioning his mother needing *him* would make Billy feel better. Calder knew it would take time for both mother and son to be comfortable sleeping away from each other, but it'd happen. When Billy figured out that their new apartment was safe and no one would be bursting in to hurt either of them, he'd relax.

"Come on, you guys," Calder said, smiling at two of the people who meant the most to him in the world. "Let's get outta here."

* * *

Hope stared in bemusement at the impromptu party happening around her. After telling the lottery board guy in no uncertain terms that she wasn't going to be taking pictures, Calder did just what he said they were going to do. He took them out to eat, then she deposited the biggest check she'd ever seen, money-wise, into her account at the bank, then they'd headed to the apartments around the corner from Calder's house to check them out.

They were all beautiful, and more than Hope had ever dreamed she'd be able to afford, but for some reason, none felt right. There was a three-bedroom apartment, which was way too big for just her and Billy. Calder refused to let her even look at the one-bedroom place. Then they toured two separate two-bedroom apartments. They were set up a little differently, and both were very nice, but something was holding her back.

Calder didn't pressure her to make a decision right that second, whispering in her ear that she and Billy could stay with him as long as they wanted. She liked that idea, but at the same time felt guilty. Calder had done so much for them already that agreeing to stay at his house felt...weird. Like she was taking advantage of him somehow.

But she liked him. A lot. Wanted to be with him but was afraid at the same time. She was scared that she'd seem like a tease if she initiated anything, then chickened out and changed her mind about sleeping with him.

They'd ended up back at his place, and somehow one call from one of his law-enforcement friends turned into another, which turned into a full-blown party at his house.

Hope had been introduced to so many people, her head swam. Luckily, she had a very good memory, so she could recall everyone's names.

First had been Dax and Mackenzie. Hope remembered Dax from when he'd eaten at the diner, but

Mackenzie had been a surprise. Two seconds after they'd been introduced, Mackenzie had hugged her and said she was so happy to meet Hope and that they were going to be the best of friends. She'd then proceeded to babble on without taking a breath for what seemed like several minutes about how much she liked Calder, and how she and the other women had worried that he'd never find someone to spend his life with, and how they couldn't believe he actually enjoyed looking at dead bodies all day.

When she finally wound down, Hope could do nothing but stare at her, speechless.

Calder had laughed and put his arm around her shoulders and said, "You'll get used to her."

Then there was Cruz and Mickie. Cruz apparently worked for the FBI, and he and his girlfriend had met when he was working undercover. Mickie was curvy with short black hair, and she had brought along a tube of uncooked cookie dough and a tub of ice cream, winning Billy's affection by declaring that "it was illegal to have a party and not have cookie dough and ice cream."

Corrie and Quint weren't hard to remember, as Corrie was carrying a white cane with a red tip. She was a little more laid-back than the other two women, but no less friendly. She had blonde hair and blue eyes, which stared into the room blankly but were still somehow very expressive. She was taller than Hope by a few inches and looked like she could be a model on a runway. She'd smiled and held out her hand in Hope's general direction. "Hi, I'm Corrie. As you can see, I'm blind, but don't let that make you feel uncomfortable."

Her disability *did* make Hope uncomfortable at first, as she hadn't had any experience being around someone who was blind, but after listening to Corrie talk to the others, she realized that there was nothing to feel awkward about. The other woman was funny, and open, and immediately did what she could to make her feel at ease.

Wes, a man she guessed to be a couple years older than everyone else, was next to arrive. He had black hair peppered with gray, but was as muscular, or more so, than the other men in the room. He was with a woman named Laine, who Mackenzie hurried over to meet. She introduced Laine as her best friend and said that if Hope needed assistance finding a place to live, Laine could help since she was a realtor. Laine had merely laughed at her friend's enthusiasm and pushed her back into the living room before shaking Hope's hand, saying how nice it was to meet her after hearing about her from the others.

Hope was still pondering that when the doorbell rang again. This time it was a woman with red hair much like her own, except hers was extremely curly. Hope would've killed to have her curls when she was younger.

"Hi, I'm Hayden," the woman said, introducing herself. "It's really good to meet you. I've talked to Calder a bit about your situation, and just for full disclosure, so it doesn't blindside you later...I'm a sheriff's deputy."

Hope blinked in surprise. She never would've guessed the beautiful woman was in law enforcement. She wasn't exactly comfortable with all the cops in the house, but since no one was wearing a uniform, it made things a little better. "You're a cop?" she asked in surprise before she could stifle the question.

Hayden and the man next to her laughed, making Hope blush even more.

"Calder told us that cops aren't your favorite people," he said, "but I promise, Hay is harmless... unless someone threatens someone she loves, isn't that right?"

Hayden nodded and explained. "I met Boone when his ex tried to falsely accuse him of abusing her. She was cray-cray but, blah blah blah, she learned not to mess with me or my man."

Hope could only stare at the extremely confident woman in surprise.

Boone definitely made her a little nervous. He was big, muscular like her ex, and even the cowboy hat couldn't put her at ease. But knowing someone had tried to frame him for domestic abuse, coupled with the loving way he looked at the woman at his side, went a long way toward softening her feelings about him.

"Wes is already here," Calder told Boone. "I heard him telling Dax that he wanted to talk to you about the possibility of bringing over one of his heifers to breed with your bull."

Boone nodded. "I'll just go and find him then."

When they were gone, Calder leaned down and asked, "You doing okay? I know it's a lot of people, but as is typical, when they heard you and Billy were here, they all wanted to meet you as soon as possible."

"I'm okay," Hope told him. "A little overwhelmed, but okay."

"Billy seems to be doing well," Calder said, turning to look into the living area. Billy was sitting on the couch next to Corrie, holding a small book in his hand as the woman explained how braille worked.

"Yeah. I'm a little surprised. He struggles in big groups sometimes."

Calder shrugged. "Our friends are good with kids. And Billy knows you're right here if he needs you."

"*Our* friends?" Hope grinned.

"Yeah, sweetheart. Ours."

The doorbell rang again before Hope could say anything else.

Next to arrive was Conor, a game warden for the state of Texas, and his wife, Erin. Calder had already told her about how Erin had been kidnapped so a crazy guy could hunt her in the forest. Hope didn't want to believe it, but after what had happened to Billy, she couldn't deny there were a ton of mentally abusive and deranged people in the world.

TJ arrived next with Milena, and while Hope was relieved to see another man she already knew from the diner, Milena made her nervous. She had a little boy perched on her hip who had his fist wrapped around a lock of her blonde hair, and that should've helped her relax. Still, knowing what happened to Billy was tied into what had happened to this woman, left Hope uneasy.

But she shouldn't have been. As soon as Milena saw her, she reached out and gave her a one-armed hug. The embrace was shorter than Mackenzie's, but no less heartfelt. "I'm so sorry about what that jerkface did to your son," Milena said.

"I'm sorry about what happened to you and *your* son. JT, right?" Hope said politely, having gotten the whole story from Calder about Milena's kidnapping by a pedophile.

Milena smiled and opened her mouth to say something else—when all of a sudden, Blythe was there. She'd arrived with a man who had to be her fiancé, Sawyer. He was tall and wore a pair of glasses better than anyone Hope had ever seen.

But Hope froze when she met Blythe's gaze. She hadn't seen the other woman since she'd been homeless on the streets—well, since they'd *both* been homeless on the streets—and she wasn't sure what to say.

Blythe didn't give her a chance to say anything. She burst into tears right on Calder's doorstep.

Moving without thought, Hope reached out and wrapped her arms around the other woman and held on tight. She felt tears spring into her own eyes, guilt filling her for not getting in touch with Blythe sooner.

"I'm sorry I haven't called," Hope said.

"No, don't be. I'm just so happy you're all right," Blythe said. "I was so worried about you guys."

Then Hope heard a noise next to her and looked down to see Billy. He'd heard the commotion at the door and had wandered over. She was worried about how he'd feel seeing Blythe again, as she was the one who'd found him in the abandoned building and gotten him out of there. Hope didn't want Billy to have any flashbacks.

But it seemed her worries were for nothing as Billy latched onto Blythe and buried his head in her stomach, holding on tight.

"Hi, Billy," Blythe choked out, overcome with emotion.

Hope felt Calder come up behind her. His arms snaked around her waist and crossed over her stomach, holding her tightly. It felt good, comforting and soothing. She ran a hand over Billy's head.

She hadn't been entirely thrilled with everyone coming to the house to check her out—because she knew that's what they were doing—but seeing Billy overcome with happiness at the sight of Blythe made it all worth it.

Now everyone was sitting around in the living room, laughing and talking as if they'd known each other all their lives. And more than that, they were including both her and Billy as if they'd know *them* their entire lives. No one seemed to care that Billy wasn't actually speaking. For the most part, they figured out what he wanted to communicate, and when they didn't, they were so nice and laid-back about it, Billy didn't get upset once.

Mackenzie was the leader of every conversation, but no one seemed to mind in the least. And Hope had to admit that the other woman had a way of making everyone relax and have a good time.

Calder had ended up ordering pizza to feed everyone. Hope had drunk three glasses of wine and was feeling mellow and relaxed...and more content than she'd been in a long time.

She and Calder had claimed the beanbag and were snuggled together from ankles to chest. He was behind her with his head propped up on a hand, his other one draped over her hip. Hope was mostly on her side in front of Calder, one hand holding her glass of wine, and the other was intertwined with Calder's at her hip. It felt intimate and comfortable.

"Just to get it said," Mackenzie announced, "I'm so happy, and jealous, that you won a million bucks!"

Hope stiffened in Calder's arms, but he didn't tense at all.

"I think it's the coolest story," Erin enthused.

"Right? You got the ticket as a *tip*. That's so cool," Milena piped in.

The comments flew around the room, ranging from agreement that it was extremely lucky to what Hope should buy with her newfound wealth.

It was Blythe who shut everyone up with her simple statement of, "Guys, Hope was homeless. She's not going to go out and buy designer shoes and bags. She's gonna use coupons, and shop at Walmart, and put every penny away just in case. Just like I'm doing. One million or one thousand dollars, it doesn't matter. It's all about making sure what happened in the past doesn't happen again."

The room was so quiet, Hope didn't think anyone was even breathing, much less willing to speak.

Then JT, Milena and TJ's son, broke the silence by saying, "Cookie!"

Everyone chuckled, and TJ got up to get his son another cookie as he'd demanded. Hope didn't like the way everyone was now looking slightly awkward, as if they weren't sure what to say next.

"You're right," Hope told Blythe. "Having the money seems like a miracle. For so long, I had nothing, and finding a quarter on the street felt like I'd hit the jackpot. But money can't buy friends, and it's been forever since I've been able to sit in a room with a group of people and feel completely at ease. It's been even longer since I've felt safe. And that's something money can't buy either. But I have a feeling relaxing and watching TV would be what we'd be doing tonight even if I *hadn't* won the money. Calder is the best thing to happen to me and Billy, and through him, we're all here now."

"I like her," Cruz said suddenly, and everyone laughed.

When they all started talking at once, agreeing with her, making the awkward silence a thing of the past,

Calder leaned forward and spoke in her ear. His warm breath gave her goosebumps and made her shiver. "Damn straight, I'm the best thing that's happened to you."

Hope grinned.

"And you're the light in my otherwise lonely life. You've done what no one has been able to do before… made me see that there's more to life than work. Made me look forward to something other than getting a call to break up my monotonous days. Thank you, sweetheart."

If they'd been alone, Hope had a feeling she would've turned in his arms and jumped his bones right then and there. But they weren't, so she had to be content to turn her head and nuzzle against his cheek, scratchy with his ever-present barely-there beard.

"And that looks like our cue to go," Conor said with a laugh.

Hope blushed as everyone hooted and hollered at their public display of affection. Mackenzie helped pull her out of the beanbag, and Hope said goodbye to each and every one of the men and women who'd come over to see them.

When it came time to say goodbye to Blythe, Hope found herself getting extra emotional. This was the woman who'd almost gotten killed when she'd ventured back to the crappy part of town where the shelters were located, in the hopes of finding her and Billy.

"I'm glad you're all right," Blythe said. Her fiancé

155

stood next to her with his hand on the small of her back. The other woman looked happy and healthy, and Hope was so thankful for her friendship.

"You too. Thank you for having Calder look for me."

"As if I could have stopped him," Blythe said with a roll of her eyes. "Seriously, seeing you and Billy happy and relaxed is amazing."

"Thanks to you," Hope whispered. "Thank you for finding my son. For doing what you did." Hope's vision went blurry as her eyes filled with tears, but not before she saw Blythe's doing the same thing.

"Oh, jeez," Sawyer mock complained. "Here we go."

"Shut up," Blythe said and elbowed her fiancé.

Sawyer kissed Blythe's temple and said, "Come on. I'm sure Hope is tired after meeting everyone, and it's probably past Billy's bedtime."

It was. But Hope was loath to see Blythe go.

As if the other woman could read her mind, she said, "It's okay. I'll see you soon, I'm sure. Sophie wants to say hello, as do the other firefighter wives and girl-friends."

"There's more of you?" Hope joked.

"Lots more," Blythe warned with a smile.

Then the two women hugged again and Calder gave Sawyer a chin lift. Then it was just the two of them once more...well, three if she included Billy, who was currently taking a bath before bedtime.

Calder pulled Hope close and latched his fingers

together at the small of her back as he held her. "Okay?"

"Yeah. I'm great. Thank you."

"For what?"

"For inviting them all over."

"Hon, I didn't invite anyone. They just showed up."

Hope giggled. "Well then, thank you for not kicking them out."

Calder returned her smile. "You're welcome. I'd do anything to see you smile like that."

Her smile faded as she looked up at him. "I don't know how I would've gotten through this without you."

"With no trouble whatsoever, I'm sure," he retorted.

At her uncertain look, he went on. "Hope, you're the most resilient and incredible woman I've ever met. You get knocked down and simply keep getting back up. You don't know how rare that is. I know how hard it must have been to get back on your feet after being homeless."

"I wasn't exactly standing," Hope said dryly. "More like kneeling."

"But you were up," Calder protested. "And you would've gotten there eventually."

"I don't know," she mumbled, looking at the button near the base of Calder's throat.

"Look at me," he said softly.

Hope brought her eyes up to his.

"You. Are. Amazing." He kissed her between each word, hard, yet chaste kisses on the lips. "Don't ever doubt yourself. I'm fucking thrilled to be standing here with you."

"Thanks."

Calder smiled and stepped back.

Hope held on to his shirt and stopped his retreat. "I...I want you, Calder."

He smiled then, a look so sexy, Hope felt her knees go weak. "I want you too," he said. "But not tonight. I want to woo you. I want to pick you up at your apartment and take you on a date. I want to kiss you at your door and feel frustrated as hell when I have to leave you there and go home and jack off just to be able to fall asleep. I want to send you flowers and candies and take Billy to his little league games and sit in the stands with you and cheer him on. I want to help him with his homework and be there with you when he starts speaking again.

"I want it all, Hope. But more importantly, I want *you* to want it all. And I know as soon as we find the perfect apartment for you, you will. You need to be on your own. See how it feels to have made it. I've just started sleeping through the night again because I know you're safe. That you and Billy aren't behind a flimsy door at that motel. If I make love to you tonight, and you leave, I'll go back to sleeping like shit because I'll be missing you. Missing the way you feel tucked against me. The way you smell. I want you, Hope. More than I've ever wanted anything in my life...but I'm not ready yet."

Hope had never met a guy who turned down sex.

She understood what he was saying because she felt the same way. If she slept with him, she'd never want to leave. Sure, she'd gotten her and Billy off the streets, but having an apartment seemed like the final step to proving to herself that she'd "made it." Him wanting to wait to make love made Calder that much sexier in her eyes. "Okay, Calder."

"Okay." He kissed the tip of her nose. "How about you go up and check on Billy? Get him tucked in and I'll come up and say goodnight."

She nodded and headed for the stairs. At the top, Hope turned and looked down at Calder.

He was still standing by the front door. His head was bent and one hand was clenched around the back of his neck. Not liking that he was obviously struggling with his decision, she nevertheless trusted him even more as a result.

Smiling, ignoring the need coursing through her body, Hope went to find her son and get him settled for the night.

CHAPTER TEN

"*H*ope, get up."

Hope sat straight up in bed and looked over at the doorway. She could just make out Calder standing there. The hall light was on behind him.

"Did you hear me?" Calder asked urgently. "You need to get up. Billy too."

She was moving even before she'd thought about it. The urgency in Calder's tone making it impossible to do anything else. "What's wrong?"

"The diner's on fire."

Hope stopped at the end of the bed and stared at Calder in shock.

"Hurry, honey. I got a call from Squirrel, Blythe's fiancé. You met him last night, he's one of the fire-fighters at Station 7. He's off tonight, but he knows you work there, and he gave me a ring when he heard it come over the radio. I don't know what's going on, but I want to head down to check it out, check on Joseph.

I'm not going to leave you here alone though, just in case."

"Joseph!" Hope practically screeched. The older man had an apartment not too far from the diner, but she knew he often slept on the couch in the office in the back. Said since he didn't have anyone waiting for him at home, it was easier to just stay there.

She hurriedly tore off her sleep shorts, ignoring the fact that Calder was still standing there, and put on a pair of sweats. Calder handed her one of his sweatshirts and she pulled that over the T-shirt she was wearing, not bothering with putting on a bra.

"Do you want to wake him, or should I just pick him up and put him in the truck?" Calder asked, gesturing to Billy.

"Truck," Hope said immediately. Billy had been exhausted when he'd finally fallen asleep, and it was likely that he'd continue to sleep as long as they were careful.

Hope watched as Calder gently scooped Billy up, blankets and all, and carried him out of the room. She frantically put on a pair of sneakers, picked up a pair of shoes for Billy, and followed. By the time she caught up with them, Calder had already put her son in the back of his truck. He'd grabbed some pillows off the couch and made sure Billy was comfortable after he'd buckled him in.

Ever the gentleman, even in a situation like this, Calder helped her into the truck before running around and getting in on the other side. He drove quickly but not recklessly.

"What do you know?" Hope asked as they drove toward downtown.

"Not much. Just that several fire departments were called in. It's big, sweetheart."

"Was Joseph there? Do you know?"

"I don't. I'm sorry." Calder reached out and grabbed her hand and Hope held on tightly.

"I can't lose him," she whispered.

"Don't borrow trouble," Calder warned. "Until we know what happened, you can't assume the worst."

"It seems like with the good, always comes the bad," Hope said quietly.

"Hang on to me," Calder said.

"Okay."

"I'm here no matter what. All you have to do is hang on."

Hope nodded but didn't say anything. She closed her eyes and tightened her grip on Calder's hand, reassured when he squeezed her fingers back. "Please be okay," she mouthed silently as they raced toward the diner.

* * *

Calder clenched his teeth and prayed harder than he'd prayed in a long time. He didn't know Joseph all that well but knew he and Hope were extremely close. He hoped like hell the old man hadn't decided to spend the night at the diner tonight. Or if he had, that he'd been able to get out before the place went up in flames.

They had to park several blocks away from the diner and, after waiting for Hope to put shoes on a still-sleeping Billy, Calder gathered the little boy from the backseat and cradled him close. He felt Hope grab hold of his shirt and they walked as fast as possible together toward the diner.

The second they turned a corner, his heart sank.

The fire was mostly put out, but the smoke still hung thick in the air. All that was left of the diner was a burned-out hull of a building. Blackened wood creaked and the lights from the firetrucks spun crazily around them.

"Oh my God," Hope breathed.

Calder wanted to take her in his arms, but since they were currently filled with her son, he couldn't.

Billy stirred and rubbed his eyes tiredly. "I'm going to put you down, Billy," Calder warned him.

He leaned over until the boy's feet were on the ground, and then he shifted him until he was leaning against his mom.

"I'm going to go see if I can find someone I know and find out what happened," Calder told Hope.

She nodded but didn't take her eyes off where the diner used to stand.

"Hope," he said, but she didn't look at him.

Calder moved until he was standing between her and the remains of the diner and put his finger under

163

her chin. "I'll be right back. Don't move from here, okay?"

"Okay," she whispered.

"Promise me," Calder insisted. There were a ton of people milling around and the last thing he wanted was to lose her in the crowd.

"Promise," she said in that same whispered tone she'd used before.

Calder knew she was in shock, but hoped she understood what she was saying.

"Billy, stay with your mom. She needs you right now, okay?"

The little boy nodded. He was fully awake now and, while he still looked confused, he got a determined look on his face when he realized Calder was asking him to take care of Hope.

Calder kissed Hope quickly, assessing her with his gaze, before spinning and heading toward the diner. It took him five minutes or so, but he finally recognized Cade Turner.

"Sledge!" he yelled, getting the man's attention by using his nickname.

Cade turned and said something to the firefighter next to him before coming over to Calder's side.

"I'm surprised to see you here," Cade said in lieu of greeting. "The vic isn't dead yet. Don't you only get called for DBs?"

"Someone was in there?" Calder asked sharply.

Cade nodded. "Unfortunately, yes. The first fire-fighters on the scene entered the building and found him in the back. They had to break down the office door because there was a four-by-four piece of wood nailed across the outside. Old guy wouldn't've had a chance if he'd been in there five more minutes."

"Arson?" Calder asked quickly. He had to get back to Hope and get to the hospital.

"Definitely," Cade told him. "The whole place smelled like gas. Was overpowering from the second I got out of the truck."

Calder nodded. "Thanks. One last thing, where'd they take the vic? What hospital?"

Cade studied his friend. "You know him?"

"Yeah. Long story. I found Hope...the homeless woman Blythe befriended. She's been working here. The owner, Joseph, was probably the vic from tonight."

Cade whistled long and low. "She the waitress that won the million bucks from a tip someone left her at the diner?"

Calder nodded.

"Wow. I'm guessing he was taken to San Antonio Memorial. It's the closest level-one trauma center near here."

"Yeah, they have the best burn center," Calder agreed.

Cade put his hand on Calder's arm when he turned to rush away. "The vic wasn't burned."

"What?"

"The old man wasn't burned. He was beaten to within an inch of his life. He's got some smoke inhalation, but that's minor compared to what was done to him. The guys on scene told me he had a few broken ribs and a ton of bruises and contusions. But worse, both his legs had been broken. Probably by a baseball bat or crowbar or something. Even if that door wasn't barred, he wasn't exactly going to walk out of there."

"Fuck," Calder swore. "Thanks."

"You takin' Hope to see him?"

"Yeah. He doesn't have any family that I know of and he's as close to a father as she's got right now."

"Make sure you warn her. He was pretty messed up, Calder."

"I will." Calder shook Cade's hand. "Tell Beth I said hello."

Cade nodded. "If I was a betting man, I'd say you're going to have lots of company at the hospital once everyone hears."

Calder nodded absently. He had no doubt their friends would show up en masse the second they heard someone close to Hope was hurt. But at the moment, all he cared about was getting back to Hope and Billy. He started to head back to them but stopped and turned once more toward Cade. "They have anyone in custody?"

His friend pressed his lips together and shook his head. "No. But...the first firefighters on scene found a message spray-painted on the front of the building before that wall collapsed."

Calder braced himself.

"It said, 'Mine,'" Cade informed him.

Without a word, Calder spun and jogged back to where he'd left Hope.

He didn't know for a fact that the message was directed at her, but he had a pit in his stomach that wouldn't go away. Her story had been plastered all over local media in the last couple days, and who knew how far it had spread.

Someone could be pissed that she won the money, or Earle could've seen it and headed down to Texas to try to get Hope back. At the moment, he wasn't going to try to guess what the mysterious message meant, but he wasn't going to let Hope out of his sight until the cops figured it out. Unfortunately, since the diner had burned down, the message had been destroyed, but Calder hoped someone had taken a picture of the word on the wall beforehand.

He scanned the crowd, thicker now, for Hope and Billy, panicking when he didn't immediately see them where he'd left them. But then he sighed in relief when he saw they'd simply backed away from the middle of the sidewalk and were now huddled against the wall of a nearby business.

He went straight to them and wrapped an arm around Hope's waist. He hated to be the one to tell them about their friend, but it was better to just say it and get to the hospital than try to pretend nothing was wrong.

"Did you find out what happened? Where's Joseph?"

"He was hurt, sweetheart," Calder said gently. "He was taken to San Antonio Memorial."

Her eyes got big and he saw tears immediately forming.

"He was in the building, but the firefighters got him out."

"What happened?"

"I don't know." Calder decided to leave out the part about the threatening message on the front of the building for the time being. "It looks like it was arson though."

"Oh my God, seriously?"

"Yeah," he replied grimly. "Come on, we need to get to the hospital."

That seemed to get through. Hope nodded. "Yeah, he doesn't have anyone else, really."

Billy pulled on his shirt and Calder looked down at the little boy. "Yeah, Bud?"

The tears in his eyes spilled over and ran down his cheeks. His mouth opened, but no words came out.

Calder leaned down and picked him up, holding him against his chest. Billy buried his face in Calder's shoulder and wrapped his arms around his neck. Calder could feel his little body shaking with sobs.

Rubbing Billy's back soothingly, he said to Hope, "Come on, honey, there's nothing more we can do here."

Hope nodded but instead of heading for the truck, she stepped into Calder and put one arm around Billy's back, and the other she wrapped around Calder.

He closed his eyes in both tenderness and yearning. He hated that the two people who meant the most to him in the world were upset. Hated that they had to deal with this at all. But he couldn't deny that they felt right in his arms.

It took someone jostling them as they ran by to jolt Calder back to the present. If someone really was pissed at Hope, or if Earle was in town, he needed to get her off the streets and somewhere safe, where he could protect her better.

"Come on," he whispered. "Let's go see Joseph."

Hope nodded and shifted next to him, and with their arms around each other's waists, they headed for his truck and the hospital.

Three hours later, they were sitting in Joseph's room and the doctor was going over all of Joseph's injuries. The older man was going to go to surgery within the hour to fix his broken legs and had agreed to let Hope and Calder stay in the room while the doctor went over his options.

Calder had been appalled when he'd first seen Joseph. Cade hadn't lied, someone had beaten the shit out of him. His face was black and blue with one eye swollen shut. The blood from the cuts on his head had been cleaned up, and it was obvious the man was in a great deal of pain, but he was lucid enough to understand what was going on around him.

"Joseph, who did this to you?" Calder asked.

"Don't know," he mumbled.

169

"Was it anyone you know?" Hope asked.

Joseph's eye opened slightly and he turned his head on the pillow so he could look at Hope while he answered her question. "I can't remember. The last thing I remember is going into my office to do some paperwork. It's all a blank after that until I woke up in the ambulance."

"It's okay," Hope whispered. "You just concentrate on getting better. The police will get to the bottom of it."

Joseph coughed then asked, "The diner?"

Hope pressed her lips together and merely shook her head sadly.

The older man closed his eyes and frowned.

Several moments went by and Calder put his arm around Hope's shoulders, feeling his heart melt when she gave him her body weight.

"He'll be here at least a week," the doctor said quietly. "He'll be immobile for a couple months after that. He said he doesn't have any family, so after he's discharged from here, we'll arrange for him to go to a nursing home to be cared for."

Hope gasped. "What? No! He hates those places."

The doctor merely shrugged. "Can't say I blame him, but he's going to be bedridden and he'll need help with everything. Bathing, using the restroom... Once he's ready, they'll start physical therapy so his muscles don't atrophy. I understand he's got insurance, so that won't be an issue."

Calder didn't need to see the tears coursing down

Hope's face to speak up. "Does he have to be in the nursing home for his health, or is that just because he doesn't have any family?"

The doctor shrugged. "If he had someone who could look after him, home health care could be arranged. But since he doesn't—"

"He can come live with me," Calder said immediately. "I've got a large house and there's an office on the main floor that can be converted to a bedroom."

The doctor stared at him in surprise, and Calder could feel Hope's eyes on him too.

"This isn't something to be taken lightly," the doctor scolded gently. "He'll be laid up for at *least* two months, maybe longer depending on how his bones heal. He'll—"

Calder interrupted again. "I understand that. But what *you* don't get is that this man saved my woman's life. Out of the kindness of his heart, he gave her a job when no one else would take a chance on her. Not only that, but he had no problem allowing her son to stay at the diner while she worked. There's no way I'd leave him to rot in a nursing home. He'd hate it there. He can come and recuperate in my house."

"My legs are broken, I'm not deaf," Joseph mumbled from the bed. His voice was slurred and he sounded out of it, but he obviously was still aware of what was going on around him.

"Sorry, man," Calder said. "You understand what's going on?"

171

Joseph grunted. "Don't wanna go to no old folks' home. I'm not nearly old enough."

"So you'll come to my house?"

Joseph's good eye opened and he peered up at Calder. Then he looked at Hope. "On one condition," he said.

"Anything," Hope responded, squeezing his hand gently.

"You and Billy come too," Joseph said. "If I'm gonna be flat on my back, I'm gonna be bored. Gonna need someone to entertain me."

Calder blinked in surprise, then nodded. It was perfect. He honestly hadn't thought much beyond making sure Joseph was safe and had a place he could recuperate. But having Hope there was a great solution. She could make sure all was well with Joseph when Calder was working and the home-health nurse could take care of the older man's needs.

And, of course, that meant Hope and Billy would be living with him—something he wanted more than anything.

"Oh, uh…I don't know," Hope said, stumbling over her words.

"That would be acceptable," the doctor declared. "Now, if you folks would say your goodbyes, it's time to get Mr. Roberts prepped for surgery."

Hope looked from Calder, to the doctor, to Joseph in consternation.

"Come on, Hope," Calder said softly. "We need to get Billy home." They'd left the little boy sleeping in the nurses' station. One of the nurses had procured a cot from somewhere and gotten him a blanket. Within seconds of lying down, he was out. It had been a long, stressful night for him, and for Hope.

She kissed Joseph and said they'd see him after the surgery, and Calder led her out of the room. He stopped in the hallway and backed her up until they were chest to chest. He put his hands on her hips and held her still as he looked down at her.

"Move in with me, Hope," Calder said quietly. "Joseph needs someone to look after him. You can enroll Billy in the school nearby, the same one you'd have put him in if you'd rented one of those apartments. I've got plenty of space for all of you."

"You can't— This is moving so fast," she mumbled.

"I can't lie...I'm not thrilled about the reason," Calder said honestly. "I'm not happy about the diner burning down or Joseph being hurt. Though now you don't need to make the decision about whether or not to continue to work there. But...I actually dreaded you getting an apartment."

"But you said you wanted to date me. Wanted to pick me up at my apartment, kiss me at my door...you know...all that."

Calder could tell she was flustered, and tired, but he thought she was simply adorable. "Right. I *did* want that. I *do*. But the thought of waking up and seeing you sitting across from me as I eat breakfast is more alluring. Of helping Billy with his homework. Of watching movies with the two of you. Of being there when Billy finds his voice again. Of seeing you smile at me while we make dinner together. Of being able to touch and kiss you whenever the mood strikes...can't deny, sweetheart, that I want that more than I want the other stuff. But make no mistake, I'll still be wooing you. As much as I want you in my bed, under me, over me, in my shower...I'm willing to wait until we're both ready."

He watched Hope swallow and when she gazed up at him, her green eyes held so much emotion, it almost brought him to his knees. "How'd I get so lucky?" she whispered.

"Karma," Calder said immediately. "Although, I'm hoping after you're in my house for a while, you won't decide I'm too messy, or anal, or annoying, or anything else to want to stay. I sometimes get called out in the middle of the night for my job and I do work long hours. When I go into autopsy, I lose track of time, and I'll probably miss dinner a lot, and—"

Hope reached up and put a finger over his lips, silencing him. "I don't want to impose. It's a lot, Calder. Not only with Joseph, but with me and Billy too. You're going from being a bachelor living alone to having three other people in your space all the time. I know what it's like to feel like you have no privacy."

Calder reached up and grabbed her hand, kissing the palm before intertwining his fingers with hers. "Sweetheart. I'm forty years old. I've lived by myself for more than twenty years. I'm looking forward to having someone to talk to, even if that someone is a seven-year-old kid who, at the moment, doesn't talk back and a sixty-five-year-old man. I can't deny it'll take some getting used to on all our parts, but my house is big. There's more than enough room for any of us to find privacy when we need or want it. Say yes. Please. I'll beg if you want me to."

She chuckled, then quickly sobered. "I'm scared."

"I know. But, honey, this is a good thing. You've got plenty of money in the bank so you don't have to worry about finding a job right away. You can concentrate on Joseph and Billy. You can be waiting for him when he gets home from school, and if you need to meet with his teacher and administrators about his special needs, since he isn't speaking, you'll be able to do that without having to worry about taking time off work. I don't expect you to clean my house, do my laundry, or fix all my meals. I've been doing all that on my own for most of my life. I don't want a housecleaner or maid. I simply want *you*."

"It sounds too good to be true," she hedged.

"Say yes," Calder begged. "Please."

"Yes." It came out as more a breath of air than an actual word, but it was loud and clear for Calder.

He pulled her into his embrace, cradling her head with one of his hands as he held her to him. He wanted to reassure her. Wanted to tell her that everything would work out just fine. That he'd keep her and Billy safe. That whoever had burned down the diner wouldn't ever get his hands on her...but he couldn't say a word. His throat had closed up and it was taking all he had not to break down in tears right there in the hallway at the hospital.

It was weird the way things turned out. When he'd been awakened by the phone call saying the diner was on fire, he thought it was the worst thing that could happen. And while it wasn't exactly a good thing, by this time next week, he'd have the most important people in his life under his roof. He'd take that as a win.

CHAPTER ELEVEN

*H*ope looked around the living room and could hardly believe this was her life. It had been two months since the diner had burned to the ground and she, Joseph, and Billy had moved into Calder's house. She thought it would be weird, that she and Calder would tiptoe around each other as they tried to figure out how to live with other people. But that hadn't been what happened at all.

Maybe it was because at first, they were occupied with making sure Joseph was settled, or maybe it was because they were both busy, but whatever it was, it worked. *They* worked.

Billy had started school. He was placed in the second grade and even though he was slightly behind his peers, because of the work Joseph had done with him at the diner, he wasn't too far behind. He still wasn't speaking, but each day it seemed he was closer and closer to breaking whatever mental barrier had been put up after he'd been kidnapped and scared half to death.

He also had a lot of friends, which wasn't surprising, since Billy was fun to be around. He was generous and generally happy. She supposed even without speaking, the other kids had figured out those things about him and taken him under their wing.

Joseph was a tough patient. He was grumpy and impatient to get the casts off and to be mobile again, but Hope didn't care because he was alive...that was what mattered. In the evenings, they'd wheel his bed out of the office they'd temporarily made into a bedroom—thankfully the room had huge double doors —so he could join them in the living room and watch TV with them. He almost always fell asleep, but at least he wasn't shoved away in a corner and was with people who loved him.

Calder had finally told Hope about the message that had been spray-painted on the diner before it had burned down. She'd freaked out, but Calder had reassured her that all of his friends were doing everything they could to figure out who had written it and why. Of course, so far, they'd had no luck, but he was hopeful after the results came back from the evidence collected at the fire, they'd have more leads.

Things had been going so well between her and Calder that she'd put the thought of getting an apartment, once Joseph was back on his feet, out of her mind for the moment. She knew she should be worrying about that, but she couldn't muster up the desire. Living with Calder was like a dream come true, and she hated to even think about separating Billy from the man he so obviously loved and adored. Every day, her son still wore the medical examiner badge Calder had given him. It was clipped to his waistband and he proudly showed it off to anyone and everyone he met.

Everything felt perfect—except for two small things.

The first was the letters. They were sent through the postal system. Since she was home during the day, she was the one to get the mail. She wasn't going to open them, but from almost the first day she moved in, Calder had told her she would be doing him a huge favor if she answered the phone if it rang and dealt with his mail. He had a huge stack of it and Hope had been appalled when he finally sat down to open it and had discovered he was late in paying two bills. He'd told her if she found something important to let him know and he'd deal with it, and she could throw away any junk mail.

At first, Hope thought the unaddressed envelope was a solicitation for a donation or something but had been confused when she'd opened the first one. By the time the third one arrived, Hope could no longer ignore the fact that they were probably aimed at her.

The notes were short and to the point. The first had said, "Hope your happy," complete with bad grammar.

The second one read, "Don't get comfortable."

The last one she received simply said, "Mine." Just like the message at the diner.

That one *really* freaked her out—because it was confirmation that the person sending the letters was most likely the same person who'd set the diner on fire. If it *was* the same person, he obviously knew Calder's address...and if he decided to burn down this house, Hope would never forgive herself.

The more she thought about the notes, the more she was sure they were from Earle. He'd found her and was fucking with her before he swooped in and taught her the lesson she knew he was eager to give her.

Hope knew she'd have to leave. Not only Calder's house, but San Antonio and the state. She'd have to start over somewhere else, hopefully somewhere Earle couldn't find her. She had money now, though, so at least she and her son wouldn't be homeless, wherever they ended up.

But she didn't want to go. Billy was finally happy and living a normal life as a seven-year-old. Joseph still needed her. Then there was Calder...

If he knew about the letters, he'd never let her leave. She knew him well enough to know that for a fact. He'd want to protect her. To make sure she was safe from her ex. More than anything, she *wanted* to be safe, wanted her son to be safe, but she couldn't risk Calder's life. She knew more than anyone how unstable Earle was. He wouldn't hesitate to hurt Calder. Look at what he'd done to the diner.

No, she couldn't tell him. For his own protection.

She also knew Calder was waiting on an indication from her that she was ready for a more intimate relationship. At first, it had been *him* holding back, but shortly after they'd moved Joseph into his house, he'd told her one night that he was ready to move their relationship to the next level. Hope had been excited about it, and was trying to find the perfect time to let him know she was ready...but then the second letter came.

If she slept with Calder, she'd never want to leave, just as he wouldn't want her to go. And the last thing she wanted was for him to get hurt because of her.

So this time, she'd told him *she* wasn't ready. He didn't push, but he didn't shy away from letting her know he cared. Whenever he got close, he'd trail his fingers around her hip or touch her arm. And every night as they watched TV, he held her hand, intertwining his fingers with hers and rubbing his thumb along the back of her hand over and over.

It was torture. Billy had begun sleeping in his own room, and with her newfound privacy, Hope was becoming more aware of her sexuality. She'd even ordered a vibrator online, although so far, she'd been too chicken to use it, not wanting Calder or her son to hear.

But it seemed like she was horny all the time. Just watching Calder eat, she'd fantasize about his hands on her. Even when he wasn't doing anything overtly sexual, her mind always ended up in the gutter.

But those damn letters made it impossible for her to move forward. Calder would never agree to let her and

Billy leave if he found out about them, let alone after they'd slept together. He was bossy and protective, and if she agreed to sleep with him, he'd move heaven and earth to get to the bottom of the letters and make her safe.

That wasn't a bad thing...but she still couldn't make herself tell him. She was stuck. Wanting him more than she'd ever wanted anything, but not able to move forward with him because of the threats hanging over her head.

"What on earth are you thinking about so hard over there?" Mickie asked.

She and Hayden had come over and were visiting before it was time to pick Billy up at the bus stop. Hope was nervous about letting him continue to ride the bus to school, especially in light of the letters that had arrived, but she waited with him at the bus stop and saw him off to school every morning, and met the bus at the end of every day. It was the best she could do at the moment. The other options were telling Calder about the letters and putting him in danger, or leaving. Neither was appealing.

Joseph was napping in his room while the girls hung out in the dining room and chatted.

"Calder," Hope blurted.

Hayden rubbed her hands together and scooted to the edge of the chair she was sitting in. "Yeah?"

Hope sighed and ran a hand through her hair. "I just...I like living here, but it feels weird."

"Weird how?" Mickie asked.

"Just weird."

"Do you get the impression that he wants you to leave?" Hayden asked.

Hope shook her head. "No. Not at all. But…I have no idea where we stand."

"What do you mean?" Mickie asked.

"We're close. I mean, he tells me about his job, what he can, and I think I help him unwind from that. He seems to love having Billy here. He reads to him every night and helps him with his homework. He doesn't demand I do anything in return for living here. He does his own laundry, has no problem cooking when he gets home if I haven't started anything, and he treats Joseph as if he's his own father."

"What about you?" Hayden asked perceptively. "How does he treat you?"

"Like no one ever has before." Hope sighed.

"And that's good?" Mickie asked.

"Of course it is. It's just…" Hope paused.

"Is the sex not satisfying then?" Mickie whispered comically. It was as if she were afraid Calder was standing nearby and would somehow hear the question.

"No!" Hope exclaimed. "I mean…I don't know."

"You don't know?" Hayden asked, her eyes wide in disbelief.

"Wow. I seriously don't see a man like Calder being celibate," Mickie said.

Hope jumped to his defense. "Oh, he wants to…It's me holding back. He kisses me all the time. Little pecks on the cheek and my temple. And we sit in the beanbag together almost every night after Billy goes to sleep. We talk about our days and what we have coming up. When he drives us places, he always holds my hand."

"Then for goodness sake, why aren't you guys gettin' it on?" Hayden asked.

"Because I think my ex was the one who burned down the diner," Hope blurted. "If I sleep with Calder, it's going to be nearly impossible for me to leave him. And I know he won't *let* me leave."

"You can't leave!" Hayden blurted.

"Seriously!" Mickie echoed. "You love it here!"

"I know," Hope whined. "I'm so torn up inside. I want him, bad, but the last thing I want to do is lead him on...be a tease. I can't sleep with him then disappear."

"Then don't," Hayden said bluntly.

"I don't want to," Hope whispered. "I'm pretty sure I love him...but I don't want him to have to deal with my baggage."

Hayden studied her for a long moment, then took a deep breath before she began talking. "I'm going to tell you something that I probably shouldn't. In my defense, I thought you knew about this already, but I can see that it's likely he didn't tell you."

Hope's stomach fell. "What? He doesn't like me? He just wants to be friends?"

"Hush. No. Remember that business trip he took last month?"

Hope nodded. "Yeah, he was asked to give a speech

at a conference in California for medical examiners. He didn't want to go to the whole thing, but he agreed to go for a few days. He made TJ and Milena come and stay here. Said he wanted to make sure I didn't get overwhelmed taking care of Joseph and Billy."

Hayden nodded slowly. "Right. He didn't go to California. He went to Seattle. To talk to your ex."

Hope stared at Hayden in disbelief. Then she immediately began to shake. "What?"

Mickie put a hand over Hope's on the table and squeezed as Hayden continued.

"Cruz and I went with him. He was concerned that it was Earle who came here and set the diner on fire. That he'd written that word on the building and beat Joseph up."

Hope felt lightheaded and dizzy.

"He took Cruz because he's a Federal agent, and having the backup of the government when dealing with an asshole like Earle Thyne is a good thing. I went with them because many times, abusers can't handle a female cop getting in their face, and they'll say shit they might not have otherwise. We confronted him. Asked him point-blank if he'd been to San Antonio recently. He denied it, of course. So Cruz pushed, saying he could easily check into his financial records, and flight information, and that he'd talk to his supervisor if he had to. Fucker lost it. Said he'd looked for you for a while, but when you never used the credit card he'd given you, and you ditched the car he'd put the tracker on, he couldn't find you. When people at work started asking about you, he told them *he* broke up with *you*, rather than lose face by admitting you'd left."

Hope swallowed hard and stared at Hayden in disbelief. "But now he knows where I am."

Hayden nodded. "Yeah. But he's got a new girl-friend, and I think he got the message that you didn't want anything to do with him anymore when you fled."

"Is he hurting her too?" Hope whispered. She felt Mickie's hand tighten but didn't take her eyes from Hayden.

"We believe so. But, Hope, that's not the point here. I know you want to save the world, but we're talking about the fact that Calder went out of his way to threaten your ex. To make sure he hadn't come to Texas to get back at you for leaving him, and wasn't *planning* on coming here. Calder is *already* dealing with your 'baggage,' as you put it."

"Oh."

"That's all you have to say?" Mickie asked. "Oh?"

Hope struggled to find the words to explain her feelings. "No one has ever had my back before. I've always felt like it was me against the world. I'm not thrilled Calder lied to me, but I know he did it because he was looking out for me and Billy."

"Lies have a way of coming between people," Mickie observed. "They almost killed my relationship with Cruz."

"Did you know Cruz went to Washington?" Hope asked.

Mickie nodded. "Yeah. But I didn't know why.

There are a lot of things he can't tell me because of his job. I've gotten past the point where I need to know all the details."

Hope thought about that…and then bit her lip guiltily.

"What?" Hayden asked. "What aren't you saying, Hope?"

She picked at a stain on the tabletop absently.

"Hope?" Mickie asked.

"A few letters have arrived. I didn't think anything about them at first because I was busy getting Joseph settled and Billy enrolled in school. With everything else that was going on, I actually forgot about the first one."

"Shit, Hope," Hayden said, leaning forward.

"I know. The second one came, and I decided to ignore that one too. But then the last one arrived…and I have to admit that it made me nervous. I thought they were from Earle," she hurried to explain when both her friends looked at her with wide, disbelieving eyes. "I figured he'd started that fire, and I'd have to leave. But I knew Calder wouldn't let me if he found out about the letters."

"Hope, we went to see your ex a month ago. Since then, Beth has dug into his life a bit. He hasn't been outside of Seattle in months. Hasn't called anyone out of the ordinary. He's too focused on controlling his new girlfriend to worry about you."

"He could still be sending letters," Hope said lamely.

"Tell Calder," Hayden ordered.

"You really do need to," Mickie added. "Sending threatening letters via the mail is a federal offense. The FBI can get involved."

"They're not exactly threatening." Hope tried to defend her decision to stay quiet, though, given what Hayden had told her, she knew she'd made a mistake.

"What'd they say?" Hayden asked.

Hope told them, and Hayden shook her head in disbelief.

"Hope. Those are *absolutely* threatening. And the fact that the last one said the same thing that was painted on the front of the diner before it burnt down isn't good."

"I thought it was Earle! I thought he wanted me back and was pissed that I'd moved on and was living with Calder."

"Wouldn't that be the very reason to *tell* Calder?" Hayden shot back. "What if it *had* been Earle? What if he'd burned down this house next? What if he'd hurt Calder? Or Joseph? Or your son? Because Calder didn't know there was a threat?"

"I know!" Hope exclaimed in agitation. "And that's why I still need to leave. To keep Calder safe."

"No. Tell. Him," Hayden enunciated. "You both need to discuss what's been going on. Calder needs to tell you what he's been doing to try to keep you safe, and you need to tell *him* about the letters. You do *not* need to run off into the wild blue yonder. Beth has some crazy hacker skills. She can work with her retired military friend and see what they can dig up."

JUSTICE FOR HOPE

"Not only that, but you need to tell Calder that you want to be with him. I've seen the way the man looks at you. I guarantee there's no way he's not going to understand why you waited," Mickie said in a tone much gentler than Hayden's. "Leaving isn't the way to deal with this, Hope."

"I'll show him the letters when he gets home tonight," Hope said.

"Good," Hayden said.

"And you'll talk to him about your relationship?" Mickie pressed.

Hope nodded. Something was bothering her even more now, though. "So, if it wasn't Earle who hurt Joseph and burned down the diner, who was it?"

The other two women didn't have any immediate answers, they simply shrugged.

"I'm sure Calder and the others are doing their best to figure that out," Hayden said.

Hope thought about the notes. They'd made sense when she'd assumed Earle had sent them. She'd thought he was saying she was his. "Hope your happy" wasn't exactly threatening on the face of it, but the "Don't get comfortable" also made more sense when she'd thought Earle had written it.

But now, she was baffled. If they weren't from Earle, who *were* they from? And having an unknown enemy wasn't exactly comforting. "Could the letters have been meant for Calder or Joseph?" Hope asked, grasping at straws. "I mean, they weren't addressed to anyone, they just had this address on them."

"It's possible," Hayden said. "The news made a big deal out of Calder taking in Joseph, and they certainly reported on you and Billy enough after you won that money."

"Am I putting them in danger?" Hope asked.

"Stop panicking," Mickie ordered. "You can't think the worst. Besides, Calder's been on this. You know he's got your back. Hell, you and Billy are never alone, are you?"

Hope shook her head. Even now, she wasn't home alone. Hayden and Mickie were there. Thinking back, Hope realized that Calder always made sure someone was with her.

"I need to talk to him," she surmised.

Mickie rolled her eyes and Hayden merely chuckled.

Hope's cell phone rang in the kitchen. Calder had taken her to purchase one the day after the diner burnt down. Said that she needed to have a reliable way to get in touch with him. Since then, she'd put so many numbers in her contacts it was almost unbelievable. From each of Calder's friends, to their women, to the firefighters and *their* women, to the school and some of Billy's classmates' parents...it was almost overwhelming how she'd gone from having no friends, to having a phone full of them.

Mickie looked at her watch and smirked. "Looks like it's about time for Calder to check in, huh?"

Hope rolled her eyes at her friend. Calder had been calling at regular intervals to say hello, to make sure all was well with Joseph, and just to chat. It felt nice. Comfortable.

She pushed back from the table and went into the kitchen to grab her phone where she'd left it earlier when she'd gotten drinks for everyone.

It wasn't Calder though. She saw it was the school calling. Looking at her watch, Hope realized it was nearly time for Billy to be getting on the bus. She had roughly thirty minutes before she had to go meet him at the bus stop.

"Hello?"

"Ms. Drayden?"

"This is she."

"This is Mrs. Melton from Cougar Elementary. There's been an incident, and I needed to call to tell you about it."

"Oh my God, is Billy okay?" Hope asked.

Within seconds, she felt both Mickie and Hayden flanking her. Supporting her. She would've been emotional about that if she wasn't so scared that something had happened to her son.

"Billy's fine," the secretary said quickly. "A man came in and said he was Billy's father and was here to pick him up. Of course, when we checked his file, we didn't see that his father was on the approved list. We told the man to wait and that we'd call you to double check, but he got upset and stormed out of the building."

"Billy doesn't have a father," Hope said quietly. "I mean, he does, but he's not in the picture at all."

"That's what Billy told us. Well, he wrote it down, you know what I mean," Mrs. Melton said. "We're keeping him in the office with us until his bus arrives and we'll escort him to it personally."

"No!" Hope exclaimed. "I'll come and get him. Oh, wait, crap, I can't leave…" She looked at Mickie and Hayden in a panic.

"We can stay with Joseph until you get back," Mickie said. "Do what you have to do."

Hope nodded and took a deep breath. "Okay, I can come and get him. Will you keep him there in the office with you until I arrive?"

"Of course."

"Okay, thanks for calling. I'll be there as soon as I can."

"Drive safely."

Hope hung up and quickly explained what was going on to her friends.

Hayden immediately pulled out her phone.

"Who are you calling?" Hope asked.

"My supervisor. Then Beth. Schools all have video surveillance nowadays. I know they'll show you the footage, I mean, it was your son who the person was asking for, there's no way they wouldn't show it to you. But the faster we can get our hands on the video, the faster you can see if you recognize the person and we can find him and see what the fuck he's up to."

"And if I don't recognize him?" Hope asked.

"That's where Beth comes in. She can see what she

can do to use her facial recognition software and figure out who he is."

Hope nodded. She hadn't even thought about that.

"Call Calder," Mickie ordered, nodding at the phone still in Hope's hand.

"Oh, but—"

"No. Call him," she interrupted.

Hope took a deep breath. "Okay. You're right." She dialed Calder's number and waited impatiently for him to pick up. She couldn't remember if he had an autopsy scheduled that day or not. Or he could've gotten called out on a job. He might not be available to—

"Hey, sweetheart," Calder said in greeting.

"Someone tried to pick Billy up from school. The staff wouldn't let him take him, since the guy wasn't on the approved list, but I'm freaking out," she said in a rush.

"I'm on my way to the school now," Calder said.

She heard rustling in the background and she could imagine him immediately standing up and headed for the door. "Oh, but, I'm leaving in a couple minutes," Hope told him. "Mickie and Hayden are here and they'll stay with Joseph."

"Stay put," Calder ordered. "I'll go get him. Is he safe until I can get there?"

"Yes. The secretary said she'd keep him in the office with her."

"Good."

"Don't you have to work?"

"You and Billy are more important than work,"

Calder retorted. "It'll take me about fifteen minutes to get there."

"I could be there in five," Hope protested.

"Hon, I want you safe at our house with Hayden. Not gallivanting around by yourself when someone may or may not be on the lookout for you. This could've been a ploy to draw you out. Stay put."

Hope closed her eyes. There he went, protecting her again. "Okay. Calder?"

"Yeah?"

"We need to talk. This…there's some stuff I need to tell you."

"I need to tell you about my trip last month too," Calder admitted. "But in the meantime, I need you to be safe. Okay? Hang tight, stay with Hayden and Mickie, and I'll have your son back to you as soon as I can."

"Thank God I put you on the approved list," Hope mumbled.

"Try to relax," Calder told her. "I'll be home before you know it."

"Drive safe."

"Always. Later."

"Bye."

Hope clicked off the phone and thought about what Calder said. Home. He'd be home soon. She should be stressed that *she* wasn't going to pick up Billy. But this was Calder. He'd do everything possible to keep her son safe. She knew that down to the marrow of her bones. She had nothing to worry about with Calder on his way to the school. He'd figure out what was going on and whether it was something to worry about.

"He's on his way to get him?" Hayden asked.

Hope nodded. "Said I was safer here than driving around by myself."

"That's true."

"Come on. Let's go see if Joseph is awake and get him in his wheelchair. He's going to want to be up and ready when Billy gets home," Mickie said.

Hope knew she was trying to take her mind off what had happened, and she appreciated it.

Taking a deep breath and trying not to worry, Hope followed Mickie and Hayden to Joseph's room. Calder would have Billy home safe and sound as soon as he could. She knew that without a doubt.

CHAPTER TWELVE

The moment Calder walked into his house with Billy, Hope was there. He'd called Quint the second he'd gotten in his truck and informed him of what happened. The other man said he'd already gotten a call from Hayden's supervisor. He was going to head to the school as soon as he could and get the video. Whoever had dared try to take Billy would be caught red-handed.

Calder knew he needed to talk to Hope. He should've told her before now that her ex-boyfriend most likely wasn't behind the fire at the diner, but he'd wanted to keep her as worry-free as possible. And if it wasn't Earle, then who was it?

He had no idea what the deal was with the message spray painted on the building. What did the perpetrator think was theirs? And now with Billy being threatened, the mystery only deepened—and the stakes were much higher.

He was going to sit down with Hope tonight and tell her the real reason for his trip out west last month. Explain what he and his friends had discussed as far as possible motives and suspects in the arson, and tell her once and for all how he felt about her. The last two months had been both the best in his life, and the most frustrating.

Calder hated saying goodnight to Hope at the door to his guest room every evening. Hated not taking her in his arms and kissing her senseless in the mornings when he woke up. Every morning in the shower, he fantasized about her being in there with him. He'd never been so horny in his life, but it was more than that.

He wanted the right to call her his own. He liked being her friend, but he felt as if they were so much more than that. She got him. When he had a shitty day at work, she was the first person he wanted to talk to about it. He couldn't wait to get home to hear about *her* day. He loved watching Hope spar with Joseph and browbeat him into eating, or exercising, or doing his physical therapy. The relationship she had with her son was simply beautiful. She encouraged Billy to be who he was without stifling him.

All in all, he wanted Hope in every way. He'd be the first to admit he'd been reluctant to start a physical relationship because he knew as soon as he did, he'd want to keep her forever, and if she didn't want the same thing, it would crush him. But after Joseph had been hurt, could have easily been killed, Calder decided life was too short not to go for what he wanted...Hope in his bed.

But then *she'd* been the one who'd said she wasn't ready. So he'd been patient and backed off, not wanting to pressure her. But he could tell something was weighing heavily on her mind. He wasn't sure she had any suspicions about the fire at the diner, but whatever was worrying Hope, it was preventing her from taking the final step in their relationship.

Calder knew it didn't matter if they made love or not...he was already attached. She wanted him; he felt it. Hell, she'd *told* him. Not just with words either. He saw the way she watched him. Saw how she broke out in goosebumps when he kissed the back of her hand. Recognized the longing in her eyes because he felt the same thing. But she was holding back.

Tonight was the night they got everything out in the open. Because now that someone had threatened Billy, nothing was off the table. He'd do whatever it took to keep that little boy safe. He loved Billy as much as he loved his mom.

"Billy!" Hope cried as Billy ran ahead of Calder into the house. She went to a knee and hugged her son as he crashed into her.

Calder shut the door and was careful to lock it behind him. Nothing could've stopped him from crouching down behind Billy and taking both him and Hope into his arms. He heard Hayden and Mickie come into the foyer but didn't look up.

Having both Hope and Billy safe, here in his house,

went a long way toward making the panicky feeling he'd had in the pit of his stomach ever since Hope had called him go away.

He pulled back. "You okay?" he asked Hope softly.

She nodded. "Now that you're both here, yes."

Her answer made that pit in his belly disappear altogether.

Calder scooted around until he could see both Billy and Hope's faces. "I feel like I have to say something here. I don't want to…and it kills me that I have to at all. But we need to have this conversation. Billy, it sucks that you have to hear this, but you, of all people, will understand. Can you handle it?"

Billy nodded, but Hope just stared at him, distress easy to see in her eyes.

Calder palmed the side of her head and said softly, "Trust me."

Finally, she nodded.

"Billy, your mom and I have talked to you about safety in the past, but I want to make sure you didn't forget. If at *any* time someone comes up to you and tells you to get in a car, or grabs you and tries to forcefully *put* you in a car or van or whatever…under *no* circumstances should you allow that to happen. Even if they have a knife or something and are threatening you. Do whatever it takes to get away. Hit, wiggle, kick, bite, pinch…all of it. Even if it hurts. Got it?"

Billy nodded solemnly.

"Do you know why you shouldn't get in the car?"

Billy shook his head.

"Calder, I don't think—"

"No, he needs to hear this," Calder said gently then turned to face Billy head on. "Because the person can take you somewhere private, where there's no one to help, and hurt you more. Do you understand?"

Billy's eyes got wide and he made a little sound in his throat as he nodded.

"I'm not telling you this to scare you, but, Buddy, you remember how the bad guy tied you up and put you in that closet in the empty building, right?"

The little boy nodded again.

"He hid you so good it would've taken someone a really long time to find you. You don't want that to happen again. So if *anyone* tries to make you go somewhere with them, and you don't know them or don't want to go, you run away as fast as you can and find someplace safe to hide or someone you trust to help you. If they grab you to try to force you, again, kick, bite, hit, whatever it takes to get away, *then* run. Got it?"

Instead of Billy looking scared now, he lifted his chin and nodded once.

"Good boy," Calder praised. "Why don't you go now and show Joseph what you made in school today. I know your mom will want to see it later too."

Billy shrugged his backpack off and headed into the living room to find Joseph.

The second he was out of earshot, Hope stood and said, "I hate this."

"I know. I do too. But the last thing either of us wants is someone kidnapping him again."

Hope just stared at him solemnly. Then she asked gently, "You've seen what can happen, haven't you?"

"More times than I care to remember. Assholes who prey on women and kids are generally cowards. They rely on their victims being scared and doing whatever they're told to do. But I've heard of cases again and again where the victims fight back, and the perpetrators give up. They want someone weak. Someone they can force to do what they want. Promise me, Hope, that if for some reason I'm not with you and something happens, you won't go with anyone willingly, for any reason."

"I promise."

Calder breathed out a sigh of relief then leaned forward and kissed Hope gently.

When he pulled back, she said, "Billy doesn't look all that upset about what happened today, thank God. What did the people at the school say? Did they tell you what the guy looked like? Is Billy in danger? Maybe he shouldn't go to school anymore."

Calder put his hands on Hope's shoulders and looked her in the eyes. "I think Billy's okay. He didn't even see the man. By the time he got to the office, whoever it was had taken off. The office staff told me mostly what they told you. That a man came in, said he was Billy's dad and was there to pick him up. When they said they had to call you to approve the pick up, he left. That's it."

"What did he look like? Maybe it really was his father," Hope said doubtfully.

"Fairly tall. Skinny. Had black hair and was wearing a pair of jeans and a leather jacket."

Hope shook her head. "That doesn't really sound like Ben."

"That's his name?"

"Yeah. Ben Montrone. But the last time I saw him was about seven and a half years ago. He could've changed a lot since then."

"I'll get a still from the surveillance tape," Calder reassured her. "You can look at it and see if you recognize him. In the meantime, the staff at his school knows to be on the lookout. They aren't going to let anyone other than you and me pick him up without calling to check to see if it's okay."

"I don't want him taking the bus anymore," Hope said.

"Me either. I can drop him off on my way to work, and if I'm not out on a call or in autopsy, I'll pick him up in the afternoons too."

"I can't ask you to—"

"You didn't ask," Calder interrupted. "I volunteered. But, Hope, we need to talk. I'd prefer if you weren't driving around by yourself until we catch this guy."

"On that note," Hayden said, "we're going to get out of here."

Calder turned, but kept one hand around Hope's waist. "Thanks for staying with her," he said.

"Anytime," Hayden said firmly. "And I mean that. You've got over a dozen friends that will do whatever it takes to keep them safe."

Calder met Hayden's direct gaze and nodded. He heard what she was saying without her having to say it. She was one of the toughest cops he knew. Hands down. She'd move heaven and earth to protect those she considered friends.

"'Preciate it."

"I called Cruz," Mickie said softly. "Hope, he's going to need to talk to you."

Calder looked from Mickie to Hope and saw that she knew exactly what Mickie was talking about, even if he was in the dark.

"Hope?"

"Later," she told him.

Calder wanted to protest, but Mickie had come forward and was hugging Hope. Hayden also gave her a brief but heartfelt hug, and then they were alone in the foyer.

"Is Billy really okay?" Hope asked.

"Yeah. I told him that someone came to the school and wanted to pick him up, but that neither of us knew who it was."

"How'd he react?"

"He seemed more curious than anything."

"Really? I'm surprised. After Jonathan Jones kidnapped him, he panicked if anyone even looked at him for too long."

Calder ran a hand over her head. "It was a while ago. Kids are resilient. He won't ever forget, but he's got you, and me, and he feels safe now. Besides, since he never saw whoever it was, it's harder to really feel like you're in danger."

Hope closed her eyes and took a deep breath. Then she looked up at Calder. "What am I going to do?"

"You're going to trust me. I'll keep you both safe."

"From who, though? And why?"

"I don't know, but I'll figure it out. *We'll* figure it out. What was Mickie talking about?"

Hope opened her mouth, but was interrupted by Joseph yelling, "Billy's hungry! Kid can't do homework on an empty stomach!"

Hope seemed relieved by the change in subject.

"We'll talk tonight?" Calder asked.

Hope nodded. "Promise."

"Good."

And with that, Calder put his arm around Hope and led her into the other room to see about getting her son a snack.

* * *

Later that night, after Billy had been tucked into bed and Joseph was back in his room, and all the doors and windows in the house had been double checked, Calder settled into the beanbag with Hope.

Beth had gotten a copy of the surveillance tape from the school and had sent over a couple of stills from it. Hope hadn't recognized the man, and had gotten frustrated, but Beth had told her not to worry and that she was working on figuring out who he was.

Sitting in the beanbag together was a tight fit, but it had become their tradition. Besides, Calder loved the way they were smushed together as they sat in the unconventional chair. He wanted to be as close as he could when he told her he'd lied about his trip last month, and where he'd really been. He decided to just say it, not beat around the bush.

"Last month, when I told you I was going to California to talk at a conference…I wasn't being honest with you," he started.

"I know."

Calder blinked. "What?"

"I know. Hayden told me today."

He wasn't sure whether to be relieved or pissed. "It wasn't her place," he grumbled under his breath.

Hope squeezed his hand. "She shared for good reason. I…I haven't been honest with you either."

Calder's brows furrowed. "About what?"

"There have been a few letters that have been delivered to the house."

His stomach clenched. "What did they say?"

"The first said, 'Hope your happy.' Complete with the wrong spelling of 'you're.' The second one said, 'Don't get comfortable.' I didn't tell you about them because I thought they were from Earle. I felt horrible that I'd brought him to your doorstep. I didn't want you to get hurt."

"And the last?" Calder bit out.

"'Mine.'"

"Fuck!" Calder tried to jackknife up and out of the

SUSAN STOKER

seat, but couldn't do it elegantly or quickly.

Hope grabbed his shirt and held on. "Calder, listen!"

"No. Jesus, Hope. I can't believe you didn't tell me."

"I just...I didn't want to have to leave!" she blurted.

Her words stopped Calder in his tracks. "Explain," he ordered.

Hope took a deep breath. "I thought Earle sent them. That he was warning me he would be coming for me soon, and so I'd have to disappear again. I was trying to protect you," she finished, not able to look Calder in the eyes as she said it.

Calder tried to calm down. He had no right getting pissed when he'd kept secrets from her as well. But he wanted to rail at her for even *thinking* about leaving him. For keeping something so huge from him. If she really wanted to protect him, she should've told him about the letters so he could be on the lookout for her ex.

"Do you *really* think this isn't Earle?" she asked before he could say anything. "I mean, those letters could've come from him. He always claimed I was his and that I could never leave him."

"I'm sure," Calder told her. "Trust me. Between Beth and her friend, Tex, they investigated him thoroughly. It wasn't him."

"Then who? Who tried to take Billy today? And why? I don't understand."

Calder wrapped his arms around Hope and tucked her head under his chin and held on tight as she shook. "I don't know. Unfortunately, it could be almost anyone. Your name was all over the news, everyone knows you won a million dollars. Maybe someone's jealous. Or maybe it's one of the people you knew from the streets...some may not like that you've moved on and gotten so lucky. Maybe it's someone who's upset with *me* and is trying to hurt those I love to get to me. I've testified on some pretty horrific murder cases. Last year there was even a killing tied loosely to the mob. And we can't discount Joseph. The diner was burned down before you got any letters, so *he* could be the target."

He looked down and saw Hope was staring up at him with an unreadable expression. "What? What's wrong?" he asked.

"Trying to hurt those you love?"

Calder's mouth dried up and he felt as if he'd been sucking on lemons. He hadn't meant to blurt it out like that, but now that he'd said it, he wasn't going to take it back. "You have to know how important you are to me," he said.

Hope nodded.

"I love you, Hope. You and Billy have literally changed my life. I can't imagine a day going by when I don't get to see you or talk to you. I get excited to see what Billy's learned at school each day and I'm in total awe of him because even though he doesn't talk, he's got tons of friends and he's reading at a fourth-grade level. The thought of anything happening to either of you makes me insane, and I want to lock you both in this house and wrap you in bubble wrap so no one can hurt you or say anything mean to you for the rest of your lives. If you had left me…"

His voice cracked, and he cleared his throat before continuing. "If you had left me, I would've searched every inch of the country until I found you again. So, yeah…I love you."

"I've been lying about something else too," Hope whispered.

Calder's arms tightened around her. He was disappointed she was changing the subject, but he wasn't going to call her on it. "What's that?"

"Well, not lying, per se, but not being completely honest."

"Spit it out, hon. Whatever it is, we'll figure it out and move on from here."

"I don't want to sleep in your guest room anymore. Billy has his own room and is doing great, thanks to you and Joseph. I know you were the one at first who didn't want to jump into bed together, and you were more than clear when you let me know you were ready. But I knew if I slept with you, and had to leave to protect you, it would kill me. I know it was stupid, I should've been soaking up every bit of affection I could get before I left, but I was trying to protect *myself* too. But instead, I was kidding myself. Leaving without knowing how you feel inside me, and above me, would hurt more than not ever knowing."

They stared at each other for a moment before Calder groaned and swooped down to kiss her. He knew they should probably talk more about her ex.

About who might have tried to get to Billy. But he couldn't think about anything other than taking Hope to his bed and making slow, sweet love to her all night long.

They made out on the beanbag for what could've been minutes or an hour before Calder reluctantly pulled back. He licked his lips, tasting her lip gloss on them, which made him want to kiss her all over again. But he took a deep breath and tried to concentrate. "I didn't want to rush you."

"You're not rushing me. I want you, Calder."

He grinned and shook his head in exasperation. "So we could've been doing this way before now, huh?"

She returned his smile. "I guess so."

"I want you in my bed, sweetheart, but be sure. If you come upstairs with me right now, I won't let you go. I already don't want to let you go but the feeling will be even deeper after I have you. There will be no more sleeping in the guest room. Tomorrow, I'll move all your things into the master bedroom and we'll figure out something to tell Billy."

In response, Hope began to struggle to stand.

Disappointed, but vowing never to force Hope into anything she didn't want, Calder helped her stand by palming her ass and pushing, helping her escape the clutches of the beanbag.

She stood in front of him and held out her hand. "I don't want to sleep in the guest room anymore. I told you that. Billy won't think twice about me sleeping in your room as he loves you just as much as I do."

Hearing the words come from her lips made Calder inhale sharply. He wasn't going to let her take them back. He reached up and clasped her hand, letting her assist him up and out of the beanbag, which felt as if it was trying to suck him back in even as he was standing. He immediately picked her up with one arm under her knees and the other around her back.

She quietly squealed, ever aware of her sleeping son and Joseph, and wrapped her arms around his neck.

Calder strode quickly toward the stairs, shivering when her lips latched on to the side of his neck and she began to stroke him with her tongue. Tilting his head to give her more room, he said, "You keep that up and we might not even make it to our room."

"Our room," she murmured, running her fingers through the hair at the nape of his neck. "I like the sound of that."

Calder growled low in his throat. When she nuzzled the underside of his chin and said, "I've always wondered what your beard would feel like against my skin," he truly almost lost control. The images her words evoked were so carnal, Calder could hardly breathe.

"You're about to find out," he said gruffly.

"Thank God," was Hope's whispered reply.

CHAPTER THIRTEEN

Calder kicked the door shut and immediately strode to his bed. He put Hope down, then dropped over her, crawling with her as she scooted back into the middle of the mattress.

Hope could hardly believe she was here in his bed. She'd fantasized about it so often, she'd begun to think it would never happen. When she stopped, he lowered his hips until they were pressed to hers, his erection hot and hard against her.

"Last chance to back out," he said.

"Why would I want to do that?" she asked. "But to make it clear, I love you, Calder Stonewall. I've been wanting to be right here for quite a while."

Without a word, Calder's head dropped and he kissed her. He didn't start off slow though, his tongue immediately plunging inside her mouth, wrapping around her own sensuously.

Hope speared her fingers into his short hair and

held him to her as she returned his kiss with equal fervor. After a moment, he pulled back and began to nuzzle her neck. One hand shifted under her shirt and moved upward. He palmed her breast over her bra, which made Hope arch her back into his touch. She wanted more. Wanted to feel him against her bare breast.

But before things went too far, she had to ask him something.

"Calder?"

"Yeah?" he asked, even as he nipped at the tendon in the side of her neck.

"I haven't done this in a while. Not since my ex. I'm not on anything...I stopped taking my pills when I left Seattle and haven't been back to a doctor to get them started again."

Calder propped himself on his elbows above her. She could feel him from thighs to chest. She felt surrounded...and safe. She moved her hands down to hold on to the sides of his shirt as she waited for his response.

"I've got condoms," he said. "I bought them the day after you moved in. Not because I had any expectations of anything happening between us, but because I hoped something would someday. But I've wanted you practically since I met you. And to put your mind at ease, I haven't been with anyone in years myself."

Hope raised an eyebrow skeptically.

"Seriously. I dated quite a bit in my early thirties, but when relationship after relationship ended, I got more and more cynical about women in general. After a while, I stopped trying altogether and concentrated on work."

"Okay," Hope whispered, happy that he hadn't been with a woman recently. It wouldn't have made her change her mind, but it definitely made her feel less awkward that she wasn't the only one who hadn't done this in a while.

"How would you feel about going back on the pill?" he asked. "I mean, I'm happy to wear condoms, but I know the lubricant on them, not to mention the latex itself, can bother some women."

She chuckled. "And it has nothing to do with the fact that you don't really want to wear them?"

Calder wasn't amused. "This has nothing to do with me and everything to do with you, Hope. I don't mind wearing condoms because I don't know what I'm missing. I've never made love to a woman without one before. I want what's best for *you*. If they're irritating to you, then we'll figure something else out."

Hope stared up at Calder. He wasn't kidding. His concern for her safety and well-being never ceased to surprise her.

"Were you serious about wanting kids?" she asked.

He blinked in surprise but recovered quickly. "Yes."

"Then it's probably better if I don't go back on the pill. It can take a while for the hormones to leave a woman's body. We can use condoms for now."

Calder groaned and closed his eyes. He didn't move

otherwise, and Hope had an up-close and personal view of the many emotions flitting across his face.

"Calder?"

His eyes popped open and Hope felt almost burned by the emotions shining through his brown gaze. "I'm going to ask you to marry me. Not now. But probably sometime soon. I don't want to wait to start on a brother or sister for Billy. I'm not getting any younger and I don't want to be sixty and still having to change diapers."

Hope swallowed hard but managed to say, "That's twenty years from now. I don't want to still be having kids when I'm fifty-two."

"How'd I get so lucky?" Calder whispered.

"I think that's my line."

"No way. Hell, I'm lucky Driftwood or Taco didn't find you first."

"Who?"

"The last two single firefighters from Station 7."

"Um…no offense…but they aren't you. I'm not sure I would've wanted anything to do with them. And why are we talking about them and not getting naked?"

"Good question," Calder said with a grin. Then he reached down and took hold of the bottom of her shirt. "Arms up."

Hope immediately complied, and felt cool air flutter over her naked skin, making her nipples pucker under the cotton bra she'd put on that morning. If she'd known she'd be in Calder's bed, she would've worn something a little more feminine and alluring.

Before she could think, Calder's mouth was on the swell of her boob. He nuzzled her cleavage and used his hands to plump her mounds.

"Fucking perfect," he murmured.

"I want to see you too."

Calder immediately reached up to pull his shirt off over his head. Of course, he did it the badass alpha-man way, pulling at the back of his neck. He didn't lift his mouth from her chest until the last possible second, and the moment the shirt cleared his head, his lips were back at her boobs.

Hope chuckled, but it didn't distract her from her goal…feeling Calder's skin under her fingertips. His back felt like one big muscle and he was warm, so warm.

Calder abruptly sat up, giving Hope the chance to see his chest. He was covered with a light sprinkling of dark hair and she ran her fingers up his pectoral muscles, shivering in delight when his nipples puckered under her touch.

He reached up and grabbed her wrists, halting her movements.

Hope pouted. "I wasn't done."

"I need to see all of you," Calder said gruffly.

"Only if I get to see all of you in return."

Nodding, he swung his leg over the side of the bed and stood next to the mattress. His hands went to the belt around his waist, but his eyes didn't move from her body.

Hope immediately mimicked him, undoing the

button and zipper on her jeans. She lifted her hips and pushed the denim down and off. Then she reached behind her back and unclipped her bra. She slowly drew it down her arms, prolonging the moment. She reached for her panties, but Calder got there first.

He was nude, having shoved his underwear down with his jeans. His cock was hard, jutting out from his body as if it were a heat-seeking missile. Hope could see a bead of come on the tip and even though she'd always hated giving head, had the sudden urge to take him in her mouth.

"If you don't stop looking at me like that, this is going to be over sooner rather than later," Calder warned.

Hope licked her lips and met his gaze. "I'm okay with that if you are."

"Not our first time," he said immediately. "I want to memorize every inch of your beautiful body. I want to taste you. Feel you come undone on my mouth, then on my cock. I want to feel your body squeezing me as I do what I've been dreaming about for weeks. Namely, driving inside you while you orgasm."

"Calder," Hope whispered, words beyond her.

Calder reached over and opened a drawer next to the bed. He pulled out a brand-new box of condoms and ripped it open. He took out a condom and put it on the mattress next to the pillow. Then, protection ready to go for when he needed it, Calder straddled her once more. His hands went to her hips and he asked, "May I?"

Hope nodded and lifted her hips to help him get her underwear off. He pushed them past her knees, then let her kick them the rest of the way off. He put his hands on the mattress on either side of her body and stared down at her. He didn't move. Didn't try to touch her. Just stared.

Hope squirmed uncomfortably. The urge to cover herself was strong, but instead, she waited for Calder to do, or say, something.

Finally, he looked up at her, and she was surprised to see that his eyes were wet.

"Calder?"

"You are so fucking beautiful," he whispered. "I can hardly believe you're here. I'll never forget this moment and I'll never, ever take you for granted. I'll move heaven and earth to make you happy and to give you everything you want."

"I don't want anything but you," she told him honestly. "I don't need stuff. When I lived on the streets, I learned exactly how useless material things could be. They could be stolen, or lost, or broken. Billy was the most important thing to me. When he was taken from me, everything else seemed so petty and stupid. I just need *you*, Calder. I need you to love me."

"I do," he whispered. Then his hands moved and he was cupping her breasts, his thumbs moving over her nipples, which peaked once more at his touch. "Beautiful," he moaned before dropping his head.

Hope arched her back when he took her nipple into his mouth. His teeth bit down gently and his tongue played with the taut point. He used his hand to plump up the mound as he sucked. His cock brushed against her pussy lips and Hope spread her legs wider, wanting him inside her.

They'd just gotten started and she was soaked. She'd waited for this moment for so long, wanted him for so long, the second he touched her, she melted.

Calder's lips left her breast with a pop and he smiled down at her. "Delicious," he said. Hope rolled her eyes at him.

He leaned over once more and began to move down her body. He kissed the underside of her breast, then her stomach. Then he nuzzled her belly button, and she laughed when his beard tickled her as he moved.

Then Calder settled himself between her legs. He put his hands on the backs of her thighs and pressed upward until her feet were flat on the mattress. Then he pushed her legs apart. Hope felt the muscles stretch and knew she'd be sore, but the second his lips touched her pussy, she forgot about everything but the feel of him between her legs.

Moaning, Hope grabbed his short hair with her fingers and held on as Calder explored. She wasn't sure when he let go of her thighs but she groaned when she felt one of his fingers ease inside her body.

"Fuck, you're tight."

"Told you it's been a while," Hope replied.

"Gonna have to go slow when I get in here," Calder said, more to himself than her. Then he shut up as his lips surrounded her clit and sucked at the same time his tongue lashed at the small bundle of nerves.

Hope felt her body tightening. It had been a long time since anyone had cared enough to give her an orgasm this way. Her ex sure hadn't. He was more about making her pleasure *him*. He didn't care if she got off as long as he did.

Hope widened her legs as far as she could get them and pushed her hips toward Calder's magical mouth. She felt him smile just as her orgasm washed over her.

Shaking, she felt his finger pushing in and out of her body as she clenched her eyes shut and let the pleasure overtake her. It seemed to go on forever, but eventually, it receded and she opened her eyes and looked down at Calder.

He was still on his stomach between her splayed legs, but when he saw her looking at him, he removed his finger from her body slowly and stuck it between his lips. Hope knew she was blushing but didn't look away.

"Delicious," he said again, reverently.

Then he slowly sat up and got to his knees, forcing her to keep her legs open. Hope stared down at his erection. "Does that hurt?" she asked, then winced at the inane question.

"Not like you think," he responded easily. "Give me your hand."

Without hesitating, trusting him more than she'd trusted anyone in a long time, Hope lifted her hand and placed it in his. He kissed the palm, then wrapped it around his cock. Oh so slowly, he closed his hand over hers and squeezed.

Another bead of come dripped out of the tip and Calder moved their hands, catching it before it dropped onto her pussy. Without prompting, Hope moved her hand up and down his shaft, learning its texture and shape. Paying attention to what obviously felt good for him as she stroked.

Way before she was ready, Calder removed her hand.

"I wasn't done," Hope complained.

"*I* was about to be done if you kept that up much longer," he told her with a grin, then reached for the condom.

He deftly rolled it down his cock then asked, "You ready for me?"

"I've been ready for you my whole life," Hope blurted. She was embarrassed at her sappiness, but when she saw the emotion glittering in his eyes, she felt better.

Holding himself at the base of his cock, Calder scooted forward, pressing Hope's legs apart as he went. She lifted them and squeezed his torso as she felt the tip of him press against her sopping-wet folds.

She couldn't help but tense. The last time she'd done this hadn't been pleasant. Her ex had been rough with her. Upset that she wasn't as wet as he thought she should be. Instead of taking the time to make sure she was ready for him, he'd pushed inside her without a second thought.

"Easy, sweetheart," Calder murmured. "I'm not going to hurt you."

She knew that. Consciously relaxing her muscles, Hope put both arms over her head and arched her back, showing Calder without words that she trusted him.

"Damn, you slay me woman." And with that, he ever so slowly inched himself inside her. When she tightened involuntarily, he immediately stopped and brought his fingers to her nipples. They'd softened after her orgasm, but the second he began to lightly pinch them, they hardened into little rocks once more. "That's it," Calder praised as she relaxed around him.

He alternated playing with her nipples and rocking in and out of her, the combination eventually driving Hope crazy.

She was surprised when she felt his balls against her ass and looked down. She could see the root of his dick, but the rest of him was buried inside her.

"Okay?" Calder asked gruffly.

Hope nodded and slowly reached down and grabbed his arms. "I feel so full."

"That's because you are," he replied, then eased his hips back an inch before pressing in once again. He repeated his slow in-and-out movement until Hope was squirming under him.

"More," she said.

Without a word, Calder did as she asked, pulling out until just the tip of his cock was lodged between her folds, then pushing back inside just as slowly. He did this several times and Hope could see her juices glistening on the condom as he made love to her. It was carnal and sexy. She'd never seen that before.

"Harder, hon," she told him, pressing up with her hips when he moved inside her.

Cautiously, after he'd pulled back once more, Calder dropped his hips. Hope moaned and he froze. "Are you okay?" he asked anxiously.

"Yes!" she said in frustration. "I need more though. Harder. Faster. Fuck me, Calder. You feel good like this, but it's not enough."

"Fuckin' perfect," Calder whispered before thrusting inside her so hard, Hope could feel her boobs bounce up and down on her chest.

"Yes! Like that," she encouraged.

It was as if her words had removed whatever self-imposed barrier Calder had set for himself. He began fucking her like she wanted—and needed. His balls slapped against her ass over and over again. The wet sounds of sex filled the room. They both grunted and moaned as Calder continued to pound into her body.

Hope felt herself getting closer and closer to orgasm, but knew she'd never get there without touching her clit. Not thinking about anything other than getting off, she moved a hand between their bodies and frantically began to strum herself. Calder's stomach slapped into the back of her hand with every thrust, but she barely registered it.

Wanting him to enjoy this as much as she was, Hope adjusted her hand so her pinky lightly scraped against his dick as it exited her body, and again when he pushed back in. Her index and middle fingers were slippery against her bundle of nerves, and she was about to go over the edge when Calder pushed himself all the way inside her and held still.

"Fuck, yeah," he said. "That is so fucking hot."

Hope saw him looking down at their bodies and her eyes followed his gaze. She saw him buried to the root inside her, her hips jerking up and down against him as she fingered herself.

"I'm coming!" she breathed, seconds before her entire body tensed and she came.

"Oh my God, that feels so...you're so hot and tight around me...yesssssss."

Hope knew Calder was coming too because his own hips jerked a few times. She wished she could feel his come inside her body, but knew the condom was a good idea for a while.

Seconds after he stopped jerking, Calder's eyes popped open. Turning but keeping them connected, he looked up at her.

Hope blinked in surprise when she found herself lying on top of Calder. Her knees were drawn up and she was crouched over him.

"I love you," Calder said. "That was perfect."

"It was," Hope agreed. "Thank you."

He chuckled. "You don't ever have to thank me for making love to you, sweetheart. It was my pleasure, believe me."

"Mine too," Hope joked. She lay her head down on

his shoulder and slowly stretched her legs out. She felt his cock slip from her body and gave a little groan of complaint.

His chest vibrated under her with an accompanying moan.

"I need to take care of the condom."

"Mmm hmmm," Hope murmured, suddenly exhausted.

She felt Calder shifting her but didn't open her eyes. His lips touched her temple. "I'll be right back. You need a washcloth?"

She shook her head. "No. I'm good."

"Yes, you are," Calder agreed.

Hope smiled but didn't open her eyes. She felt as if she weighed eight hundred pounds and had melted into the mattress. Calder returned in what seemed like seconds and she let him arrange her so she was on her side, using him as a pillow this time. His arm was tight around her back and he felt nice and warm against her belly.

"I'll get you up in a bit and we can put on pajamas," Calder told her. "Don't want Billy coming to look for you and finding us naked."

He was so thoughtful. Hope sighed in contentment. "Okay."

"Hope?"

"Umm?"

"Are you awake?"

"Umm."

He chuckled. "Okay, I'll shut up. Sleep, babe."

"Calder?"

"Yeah?"

"Thank you for picking Billy up today. And for teaching him how to be safe."

"I'd do anything for him. And you."

"Love you," Hope whispered.

"Love you too. Now, sleep."

It usually took Hope half an hour or more to fall asleep. Nighttime was when she worried about everything. Billy. Money. Joseph. A job. But not tonight. Tonight, she was out within seconds.

CHAPTER FOURTEEN

a week later, Hope was standing in Calder's kitchen getting Billy's lunch ready. Calder was sitting at the bar eating a bagel and drinking a cup of coffee. Joseph was in the other room, entertaining Billy before it was time to go to school.

She froze when she heard what Joseph was saying.

"Grandparents' Day is in two weeks, huh? Are you sad that you won't have anyone to visit the school with you? Me? What *about* me?"

Hope put down the knife she was using to spread peanut butter on Billy's sandwich and turned to stare at Calder. She wasn't sure whether to be upset, happy, or to run into the other room and comfort her son. Before she could decide, Joseph spoke again.

"I'd be honored to come. I'm supposed to get these casts off today when I see the doctor. Maybe I can actually walk in there instead of being wheeled in."

There was silence for a moment, then Joseph said, "You know, this would be much easier if you just *asked* me what you wanted instead of writing it down."

Billy made a noise in his throat and before Hope knew it, Calder was standing at her back. He had his arms around her and had put his chin on her shoulder. Hope clasped his forearms where they rested around her upper chest and held on as they continued to listen to Joseph talk to Billy.

"You can call me whatever you want, son. I'm not that partial to 'Grandpa' though. Makes me sound like an old fart. What do you think of PopPop? That's what I called *my* grandpa. Yeah? You like that? Good. Me too."

Hope turned watery eyes up to look at Calder. "Did that just happen?" she whispered.

"Yup," Calder said with a smile. "Looks like Joseph is now Billy's unofficial grandfather. You okay with that?"

"Am I okay with that?" Hope echoed. She turned in his arms and wrapped them around his neck. "You have no idea how sad I've been that Billy wouldn't ever know his grandparents. There's no way I'd want him around them anyway, but it's been just me and him for so long, I knew he'd benefit from having someone else to talk to. Having Joseph in our lives is a miracle."

"You aren't alone anymore."

"I know. Although sometimes I still have to pinch myself to believe it."

"Not only does Billy now have his PopPop...he's got my folks too. We'll have to think of different nicknames for them though, so we all don't get confused. They're going to spoil him rotten."

Hope bit her lip and whispered, "Calder."

He leaned down and kissed her, lingering.

His touch brought back the night before, when they'd spent an hour caressing, licking, kissing...no part of their bodies was off limits. It had been extremely intimate and carnal at the same time. By the time he'd entered her, Hope had been on a hair trigger. He'd fucked her hard and fast, and nothing had felt better.

"I love you," she whispered when he pulled back.

"I love you back," he told her. "What's the plan today?"

"Joseph has his doctor's appointment at noon. He's supposed to get his casts off, as you heard, but at the very least they'll change them out if he still needs them. I'll take him with me to pick up Billy after school and, depending on how Billy's test goes today, I thought I'd take him out to celebrate."

"I wish I could come," Calder said.

"I know, but there will be other tests to celebrate," Hope told him.

"If I could reschedule the autopsy, I would."

"I *know*," Hope told him. "It's fine."

"You'll be careful?" Calder asked. "I'm not happy we haven't been able to figure out who the man was who came into the school, or who sent the notes."

Beth was still trying to figure out who the mystery man was. Hope had insisted on watching the video, even though she hadn't recognized the man from the still pictures Beth had sent over. It hadn't helped. Even seeing the man in action hadn't done anything to help her figure out who he was. She knew Calder was worried, not only about Billy, but her too.

"Of course. I'm not going to do anything to put any of us in danger," Hope reassured him. "I've had enough of living on the edge to last me a lifetime."

Calder kissed her again, then leaned over to grab the rest of his bagel. He put the plate in the sink even as he was shoving the bread into his mouth.

Hope rolled her eyes at him. Calder wasn't exactly the most couth man at times, but he'd been a bachelor for years, and she'd rather him eat what he wanted, how he wanted, than be stiff and uncomfortable around her. It was amazing how at ease they were with each other. She'd thought after living with her for a while, he'd miss his solitude, but he'd told her in no uncertain terms that he loved having everyone in his house…that it made it more like a home. Less lonely.

"I gotta get going," Calder said after he'd washed down his bagel with the last swig of coffee.

"I know." Hope kissed him one more time then called for Billy.

The little boy came running into the kitchen, all smiles.

"You ready to go?" Hope asked.

He nodded quickly.

"All right. Go say bye to Joseph, then grab your bag. Don't forget to make sure your homework is in there."

Billy held up a piece of paper that had the word "PopPop" on it and pointed.

"Right. Sorry. Go say bye to PopPop."

Billy beamed and spun on his heels. Hope smiled at her son's retreating back. For so long, Billy hadn't been allowed to be a normal little boy. He'd had to be quiet and fade into the woodwork, for their own safety. She loved seeing him blossom now. Loved seeing his natural energy not be suppressed.

"I'll call before I head into autopsy," Calder told her, before leaning down and kissing her once more.

"Okay. I'll probably be at the hospital."

"I'll text if you don't pick up."

"Sounds good. Have a good day. Good luck."

"Thanks."

Hope followed Billy and Calder to the garage door and waved after they were in the truck and backing out. She closed the garage behind them, then closed and locked the kitchen door. She wasn't taking any chances with her and Joseph's safety. Anytime they were in the house, the doors were secured. When they went out, the car doors were locked and she made sure to always park near other cars, just in case.

She didn't like not knowing who seemed to be upset with them. Thinking it was Earle had actually been easier because at least she knew him. Knew what he was capable of. A nameless enemy was much scarier.

Hope headed for the living room and Joseph. They had a few hours before they had to leave for the hospital. She was looking forward to sitting and chatting with the man her son now called PopPop.

* * *

Hours later, Hope sat in the waiting room at the hospital. She was frustrated that Joseph's appointment was taking so long. Calder had called earlier, as he'd said he would. They'd had a short conversation about their day and what to have for dinner before he'd had to hang up and get back to work.

She'd hoped they'd be done at the hospital in time for her to go pick up Billy, but it wasn't looking like that was going to happen. Sighing in frustration, Hope called Milena. She didn't pick up. So she then called Mickie, who also didn't answer.

Starting to worry she wouldn't be able to find someone to help her, Hope called Mackenzie.

"Hello?"

"Oh, thank God you're there."

"Hope? What's wrong?" Mackenzie asked.

"Well, nothing really, but I need help."

"Of course. What can I do?"

"I'm at the hospital with Joseph. He's supposed to be getting his casts removed today, but there was an emergency and we had to wait an extra hour before he could be seen. He's back with the doctor now, but it's

231

been a while and I haven't heard any news. If I left right now, I could get to the school in time to get Billy, but I can't leave Joseph here. Would you mind going to the school in about half an hour and picking him up for me?"

"Of course not. I have a short meeting to go to first though. Is that all right? I'll probably be about fifteen minutes late."

Hope sighed. It wasn't ideal, but since Mackenzie was doing her a favor, it would have to work. "Yeah. I'll call the school and let them know that you'll be picking him up and when you're getting there. Are you sure it's okay? I hate to impose."

"Hope, of course, it's okay. We're friends, it's what friends do."

"Thanks."

"You want me to bring him to the hospital?"

"No. I'm hoping we'll be done soon. We'll just meet you back at the house. Billy has a key in his backpack so you can get inside."

"Sounds good. I'm glad Joseph is doing so well. I remember when I was growing up, there was an old guy who fell on the stairs in front of his house. He was bedridden for months because he broke his hip. My mom brought him food all the time, but eventually, he died. I don't know of what, because I was little and no one would tell me, but I remember feeling sad because he was really nice."

Hope smiled a little. Leave it to Mackenzie to make

her feel better with her babbling. "Yeah, well, Joseph isn't going to die. He's too ornery and stubborn to die of broken legs."

"Of course he's not. He's had you and Calder to look after him. Not to mention Billy. I've heard that older people do much better in the long run when they're around kids. I think it was a study on grandparents, that if they babysat their grandkids they lived longer and had less issues with dementia...or something like that."

"I've heard that," Hope agreed, feeling happy that Joseph had taken to Billy as he had. "Anyway, thank you for helping me out today. I didn't want to have Billy take the bus, just to be safe."

"Yeah, the whole situation sucks. I'm happy to help. I know Daxton has been working with Cruz to find out what they can, but they don't have much yet...other than the fact that it's not your ex."

"Ms. Drayden?"

Hope looked up at the nurse standing in the doorway of the waiting room. "I need to go, Mack. The nurse is calling me back."

"No problem. I'll take care of Billy. See you later."

* * *

An hour later, Hope was pulling into the garage at Calder's house, a happy Joseph sitting beside her. He'd gotten both casts off and now had a walker to get around with. He was going to need some physical therapy to help build his muscles back up, but he was determined to walk on his own rather than use his wheelchair, claiming he'd been "sitting on his ass long enough."

Hope's phone vibrated with an incoming call just as she stopped inside the garage. She put the car in park and looked down to see it was Mackenzie.

"Hey," Hope said in way of greeting. "I just got home. I'll be inside in a second."

"Hope, I'm still at the school. They can't find Billy."

Those four words sent ice racing through Hope's veins.

She had a flashback to when Billy disappeared when they were on the streets. It had been the worst feeling in the world.

Taking a deep breath and telling herself it wasn't the same thing, she asked, "What?"

"I got here and went to the office to sign him out. The secretary checked the paperwork and saw that you'd called to approve me picking him up. They went to the playground to get him…and he wasn't there. None of the other kids had seen anything, and even the teacher on duty hadn't seen anything out of the ordinary. They're looking through the school now."

"Maybe he grabbed the bus," Hope said desperately, and made her way toward the door to the house, Joseph following behind her as fast as he could. He wasn't moving too quickly, but without the casts, he was at least upright and mobile now.

"Billy?" Hope called as she entered the house. She was met by nothing but silence. "Billy, I mean it. If you're playing a game, it isn't funny. Come out right now!"

But he didn't appear.

Hope leaned heavily against a wall and slid down it until her butt hit the floor. "He's not here," she whispered into the phone. "Mackenzie, he's not here. Where is he?"

"I'm calling Daxton," Mackenzie said. "They're still searching the school, but we can't wait any longer on this. Call Calder," she ordered.

"He's in autopsy. He won't pick up," Hope said.

"Then call his boss. Call *someone*. Make them go in and get him."

"I...he's busy," Hope said, feeling conflicted. "I mean, I know he'd want to help, but he's working, trying to figure out why and how someone *died*. It's not like he can just put that to the side and leave."

"Is Joseph there?" Mack barked.

"Yeah."

"Give him the phone."

Without thought, Hope held out her cell phone to Joseph.

The older man took it and put it to his ear. "This is Joseph," he said. He listened to whatever Mackenzie was saying for a long moment before replying, "Will do." He clicked off the phone then pressed on some other buttons before bringing it back up to his ear.

"TJ? This is Joseph Roberts. Billy's missin'. Calder's

in autopsy and needs to be notified. Hope is headed to the school, have him meet her there."

Hope heard him, but it was as if she was at the end of a very long tunnel. This couldn't be happening. Billy couldn't have been taken again.

Joseph clicked off the phone then said, "I'd help you up, but you'd probably pull me over."

When Hope didn't move, he nudged her with his foot. "Hope. Get it together. You need to get to the school."

Hope looked up at the man who was like a father to her. "I can't do this again," she whispered.

"Tough shit," Joseph said unsympathetically. "You don't have a choice."

Hope stifled a sob.

"Seriously, Hope. Get. Up. You can't fall apart right now. This sucks, and I want to rail against God and sit down on the couch and cry, but I can't. You know why? Because Billy's out there somewhere and we have to find him. There'll be time to break down later."

Hope took a deep breath and closed her eyes. Joseph was right, she knew he was, but pulling herself together was one of the hardest things she'd ever had to do. Even getting beaten by Earle was easier than this.

Her baby was missing. Someone had taken him. *Again.*

Then, as she sat huddled on the floor of Calder's house, something clicked inside her.

As if a switch had been flicked, she got mad. *Furious.*

Billy was *hers*. No one was allowed to mess with him. Steal him away. Hurt him.

She pushed herself to her feet and took Joseph by the arm. "How're your legs?"

"They hurt," Joseph said bluntly. "I can't go to the school with you. I'll stay here and call in the troops. If Billy comes home, I'll be here, and I'll call and let you know."

Hope nodded. That was a good idea. The last thing she wanted was for everyone to be running around and miss Billy if he showed up here. "Okay."

Joseph reached out and yanked Hope into his arms. "He's okay," he said quietly. "That boy has a core of iron inside him...just like his mom." Then he pushed Hope back and put his hands on her shoulders. "Go get him, Hope. Bring him home."

"I will." Hope took the phone Joseph was holding out and stuffed it into her pocket before turning around and heading for the garage once more. She drove like a bat out of hell to get to the elementary school, hardly remembering anything about the trip once she'd arrived.

She jogged up to the doors and went straight to the office. The principal met her there, and immediately started apologizing and telling her that they were reviewing the security tapes that overlooked the play area, to see if they could determine where Billy went.

Hope was trying not to break down, and feeling frustrated that there wasn't more they could do right now, when there was a ruckus at the doors.

Turning, she made a weird little noise in her throat that she knew was pretty pathetic, but she couldn't have stopped it if she tried. She'd been holding herself together pretty well up to this point, Joseph's little pep talk being immensely helpful, but the second she saw Calder, she felt her composure start to break.

Hope rushed to him. She barely noticed the other men with him. She only had eyes for the man she loved. Calder would know what to do. He'd find Billy.

Calder wrapped his arms around her and Hope buried her face in his chest, clenching his shirt with both hands. He was wearing what she called his "work uniform." A suit coat, nice shirt under and a pair of black pants. She knew he'd been in autopsy, and could smell the slight stench of chemicals. She also knew the mortuary didn't really smell bad, like one might expect with all the dead bodies. The building and autopsy room were well ventilated and washed incredibly frequently. But she still knew when Calder had been in autopsy because he simply smelled…off.

But at the moment, she didn't care what he smelled like or where he'd been, she only cared that he was here with her right now.

"Calder," she whispered.

"We're going to find him," Calder said without hesitation. "All the guys are on this. TJ and Hayden went to the house. Weston and Dax are organizing a search party, and all our firefighter friends are going to be assisting them. Quint and Cruz are with me to interview and question everyone who was here when he disappeared. "

"The principal said she was going to look over the surveillance tapes," Hope said, looking up.

"We'll take a look at them too. Hopefully one of us will recognize who it was, and then we can call Cruz, and Beth, if necessary."

Hope took a good look at Calder for the first time. He. Looked. Pissed. And the anger on his face somehow calmed her. She wasn't alone this time. When Billy had disappeared before, no one had seemed to care. The cops had come, but she could tell that because she was homeless, they didn't take her as seriously as they might someone else.

Having Calder at her side, organizing things, getting their friends involved, Hope had no doubt he'd not rest until Billy was home.

"Okay."

"Okay," Calder said firmly. "Come on, let's go talk to the principal." He turned her and, with his arm around her waist, they headed back into the office, where Quint and Cruz were already deep in conversation with the principal.

* * *

Two hours later, Calder and Hope returned home without Billy.

They'd looked at the surveillance tape at the school and, even though the footage was grainy, realized the man on the video was the same man who had come to the school previously and pick up Billy. But this time he hadn't bothered to try to be subtle about things—he'd simply snatched the little boy right out of the playground and run off with him in his arms.

Hope was sitting on the couch between Mackenzie and Mickie, holding her cell phone and staring at it, as if her gaze alone was enough to make it ring.

She knew Beth had been sent the surveillance footage from the school after Hope and Calder had watched it. Beth was still working on making an ID, as well as searching for other glimpses of the man from nearby traffic cams. Now they were all waiting to hear from her about what she might've found, or not found.

Calder was in the kitchen with Dax, Cruz, and Quint. It was getting dark, and any search efforts were on hold, since the assumption was that the mystery man had gotten him in a car and driven off with him... and that was absolutely terrifying

Joseph was sitting in a chair near the women, looking concerned and pissed off at the same time.

"The amber alert will be going out within the hour," Quint told Calder.

Calder nodded.

"And every law enforcement agency has been given pictures of Billy and the mystery man. They'll be on the lookout."

Calder nodded again, his eyes focused on Hope sitting in the other room.

"If there's a ransom call, we'll get it on tape," Dax added.

"Agents in Seattle went to Thyne's house to check out his alibi. It's not him," Cruz added. "He was at work all day and was in the process of berating his new girlfriend when they knocked on the door. They could hear him screaming at her as they walked up."

"He could've hired someone to snatch Billy," Calder said in a voice that held no emotion.

"The paperwork's been submitted to check his phone, his girlfriend's phone, as well as his phone at the police station. His computers will also be seized so they can look for emails and messages. If he's involved, they'll find out soon enough," Cruz told him.

Calder pulled his eyes from Hope to look at his friends. "Where is he?" he asked softly. "He's a little kid. A kid who doesn't talk. He can't scream for help. He can't call out. He's at the mercy of whoever took him."

"He's a *smart* kid," Dax said immediately. "He might not be able to talk, but that doesn't mean he can't fight back."

"Yeah, he's street smart," Quint added.

"But he's still a kid," Calder said. "He only recently got the confidence to sleep in his own room by himself. He was scared to sleep anywhere but near his mom. I'm not sure how much more he can handle." Calder turned to look back at Hope. "How much more *she* can handle."

"She's also stronger than you're giving her credit for," Quint said.

Calder turned to pierce his friend with a murderous look. "Don't give me platitudes," he growled. "When Corrie was missing, I didn't tell you that she was strong and you shouldn't worry. This is Hope's *child*. She's given up everything in her life for him. If something happens to him, if his mental health takes a hit because of this, she'll never forgive herself. She'll blame herself...hell, she's *already* blaming herself. I can sense it."

"I'm not telling you not to worry," Quint returned. "All I'm saying is that with you by her side, she—and Billy—will get through this."

"I didn't think Mack was going to be able to bounce back after that asshole buried her alive," Dax added. "I was afraid to let her out of my sight for the longest time after that. Hell, man, she was *dead*. When I pulled her out of that coffin, she was fucking dead. But by some miracle, I was able to bring her back. From everything I've heard about Hope and Billy, they really shouldn't be as healthy and happy as they are. From her douchebag ex, to living on the streets, to Billy's being snatched before. And now they have you. And Joseph. And all of us. There's no way in hell we'll stop before we find him. And no matter what, we'll be there for all three of you afterward."

Calder took a deep breath, dropped his head, and shut his eyes. He knew he had good friends. He'd been by their sides when shit had happened to their women. He'd never, not once, lost faith in their abilities to save them. But this was different. This was *his* family. Billy was his, just as his mom was. He hated seeing Hope upset and couldn't stomach thinking about what Billy was going through.

He'd seen all the ways humans could be vile to each other on his autopsy table. The thought that *Billy* might be the next body to lie there was unacceptable and loathsome. He was hoping like hell Beth would be able to find something when she widened her search for cameras around the school. It seemed like forever since they'd last heard from her.

He looked up at Cruz. "How much longer—"

Calder's words were interrupted by the ringing of Hope's cell phone. Calder was on the move before the first ring had finished echoing in the room. He leaned over her and saw the display said "unknown."

"It's not Beth," Calder said as he turned to look at Cruz. "It could be whoever took him."

"Take a deep breath," Cruz instructed Hope, who was staring at the phone anxiously. "We've been over this. Put it on speaker when you answer. Try to keep whoever is on the line as long as possible so Beth can track the call."

Calder knew Quint was already on the phone to the computer genius, telling her about the incoming call. He maneuvered his way between Mackenzie and Hope on the couch and wrapped an arm around Hope. "Answer it, sweetheart. We need to get our boy back."

Nodding, Hope reached for the display. Calder saw her hand shaking and wished he could turn back the clock and reschedule the autopsy he'd had that day.

Wished he'd had his assistant take over so he could've gone to pick up Billy. There were a hundred things he wished he'd done differently, but it was too late now.

"Hello?" Hope said shakily after she'd put the call on speaker.

The response was digitally altered, but it was obviously a female's voice. "We have your son."

CHAPTER FIFTEEN

*H*ope inhaled sharply at hearing the words she'd dreaded since Billy had disappeared. She wanted to fall apart, but Billy was depending on her to keep her shit together. She could feel Calder beside her. She could do this.

"Where is he?" Hope demanded.

"Somewhere that you won't find him. Not until you give us what we want."

"And what's that?" Hope asked.

"Five hundred thousand dollars in cash."

Hope gasped. "I don't have that kind of money," she told the kidnapper.

"Of course you do," was the response. "You just won a million bucks. I'm being nice and only asking for half."

"How is Billy? I want proof he's okay," Hope demanded, keeping in mind what Cruz had told her earlier. He'd gone over what she should and shouldn't say to the kidnapper if they called. He insisted that they needed to make sure Billy was okay, and that she tell the kidnappers no money would be delivered until they had proof of life.

Hope had shuddered, hearing him say it like that, but she knew he was right.

"You don't get to make the demands here," the disembodied voice said. "You'll do what I say if you ever want to see your son alive again."

Hope swallowed hard. She wanted to insist the person take a picture of Billy and text it to her, but she also didn't want to do anything that might make them hurt him. "I'm not sure I can come up with the cash very quickly."

"Bullshit," the woman on the other end of the line said. "You go to the bank. Tell them you want five hundred thousand in small bills and leave. Easy."

Cruz leaned down and held up a piece of paper with two words on it. Hope nodded and asked, "How am I supposed to get you the money? And where?"

"Bamberger Park. There's a nature trail there. Go down it about half a mile. There's a trash can. Put the money in it and leave. I'll be watching. If you involve the cops, I'll know. If you don't leave after dropping off the money, I'll know."

Hope looked back at Calder. She had no idea where the park the kidnapper had mentioned was. When he nodded at her, she swallowed hard. Okay, if Calder knew it, then she'd just go with it. "When?"

"Tomorrow. Eleven o'clock in the morning."

Hope wanted to agree right away. The sooner she paid the money, the sooner she'd get Billy back. "Fine. But how do I know you'll let Billy go if I give you the money?"

"You don't. You'll just have to take that chance," the kidnapper said. "Sucks to have to rely on someone else for something you want, doesn't it? Maybe you should've thought about that before you screwed people over. If you don't show tomorrow, or if you try to trick me, you'll never see your precious mute again."

"Wait, I—" But the person on the other end of the line had already hung up. Hope spun and looked at Calder with big eyes. "Was it long enough? I tried to get her to—"

"Shhh," Calder soothed. "It was long enough."

"Are you sure?"

"We're sure," Quint said. He still had his cell phone up to his ear. "Beth is tracking the number now. She says she's also working to strip out the layers of the digital alteration too. Says she'll have an unaltered file to us in about thirty minutes so we can see if we recognize the voice."

Hope blinked. "That fast?"

Quint grinned. "She apologizes that it'll take so long. Says since she's doing two things at once, triangulating the number and stripping the file, it'll take a little longer."

Calder turned to Quint. "Have her check the waitresses who worked at the diner. I can't think of anyone else who might think Hope screwed them over."

"Seriously?" Hope asked, her brows drawn down in a frown.

"I don't know for sure, but it makes sense," Calder told her. Ignoring the conversation Quint was having with Beth, passing his request on to her, Calder cradled Hope's face in his hands and rested his forehead against hers. "Hang on, Hope. Just hang on."

"I'm trying," she whispered, grabbing his wrists and squeezing. "Are you okay?"

He huffed out a breath. "No."

For some reason, his answer made her smile. "Me neither."

"I know."

The next thirty minutes were the longest of Hope's life. She held on to Calder's hand, digging her nails into his skin, needing him there to keep her from flying into a million pieces. She had no idea how she was going to get half a million dollars to the drop-off point by the next day. It wasn't the money, she didn't care about that. She'd give up everything she had and gladly live on the streets again, if it meant having Billy back safe and sound.

"How much does five hundred thousand dollars weigh, anyway?" Mickie asked. "I mean, the kidnapper said she wanted it in small bills. Will it even fit inside a trash can?"

"If it's a big trash can, possibly," Cruz said. "But the weight is the bigger issue. Five hundred thousand in one-hundred-dollar bills weighs about ten pounds. But in fifties, it doubles to twenty pounds. And in twenties, it's around fifty pounds. So that would mean a hell of a big duffle bag to put all those bills in. And the trash cans in Bamberger Park aren't exactly Dumpsters."

"Not to mention there's absolutely no place to hide out there. I mean, it's a nature reserve, yes, but someone emptying that trash can of all those bills won't exactly be inconspicuous. They have to know we'll be casing the place, waiting on them to pick up the cash," Quint said.

"Well, obviously the person isn't exactly the sharpest knife in the drawer," Joseph said dryly.

"They were smart enough to take Billy without anyone noticing," Hope said softly.

"Don't give up," Calder ordered, squeezing her hand. "When this person comes to pick up the money, we'll grab her and make her tell us where Billy is."

"What if she's already hurt him, and that's why she didn't want to do the proof-of-life thing?"

"You can't think that way," Mickie said. "You can't ever give up."

Hope saw Cruz put his hand on Mickie's shoulder and squeeze. She'd heard their story, and knew what Mickie said was true, but it was really hard to think positive.

Quint's phone rang, and Hope jumped about a foot.

"Easy, sweetheart," Calder murmured, but Hope could feel the tension in his muscles. He was just as worried and scared as she was, he was merely hiding it better.

"Hello?" Quint said. "I'm going to put you on speaker, Beth. Hang on. Okay, go ahead."

"Hi, can you guys hear me?" Everyone said they could and the computer genius continued. "Okay, so I stripped out the kidnapper's voice from the lame alteration she used. It was a shitty program that she downloaded from the Internet. It took me like two seconds to separate her real voice from the digital alteration. You ready to listen?"

"Ready, sweetheart?" Calder asked softly.

She wasn't, but Hope nodded anyway.

"Play it," Quint ordered.

There was a pause before the recording played, but the second Hope heard the woman speak, she knew who it was. "That's Donna."

"Who?" Cruz asked.

"Donna Swann. She was a waitress with me at the diner," Hope said.

Joseph had been sitting off to the side, listening to everything that had been going on. "That fucking bitch!" he exclaimed, struggling to get to his feet. "I can't believe it, after everything I did for her. She was a piss-poor waitress but I still didn't fire her. Nope, I knew she needed the money. I even paid her a month's severance after the diner burned down."

"Did she have a boyfriend?" Cruz asked. "An ex? A brother? Someone who might have helped her?"

"Hope?" Calder asked.

She shook her head. "I don't know. We weren't exactly close."

"A brother," Joseph confirmed. "Lincoln Swann. He worked for me too about a year ago, but it didn't work out. He was lazy as hell, and when I caught him dipping into the cash register, I fired him. Donna wasn't working that day. Since I didn't have any reason to can her too, I let her stay on. I kept my eye on her for a while but she never did anything suspicious."

"Beth?" Cruz asked.

"On it," came Beth's voice from Quint's phone. Everyone could hear keys clacking in the background as Beth began typing. "I had already traced the call to within a ten-mile radius, but since we know who was on the other end of the line now, and who her brother is, I'm guessing we don't need *that* anymore... Ah!" she exclaimed. "Bingo. Stupid bitch called from her brother's house. The phone seems to be a throwaway, but it's still on and pinging off a cell tower near his house."

"Was he the one who went to the school the other day and who took Billy?" Mackenzie asked.

"Hang on, hang on," Beth complained. "One thing at a time. Let me pull up that other surveillance...okay... comparing...oh, yeah...that's definitely him. And, as you know, the video from today was grainy, but the general characteristics, hair color, height, and build, match what's on Lincoln's driver's license. I'll let you know if I find out anything else."

"You're the best. Thanks, Beth."

"Shut up," she chided. "You don't thank me for taking care of family. Especially not when there's a kid involved." Then she abruptly hung up.

Hope looked around the room, wondering why Cruz and the other law enforcement guys weren't rushing out of the house to arrest Donna and Lincoln and to get Billy back. "Why aren't you going to get my son?" she asked.

Calder was the one who spoke up. He turned her face to his. "We can't just rush over to their house and knock the door down," he said softly.

"Why not? It's *her*. I know it's her! Even Joseph knows it's her!"

"They have to do everything by the book to make sure they don't get away with it," Calder said. "Search warrants, things like that. Besides, Beth doesn't work for law enforcement. Yes, she's a consultant, but she has to get the files to the FBI's data folks so they can officially analyze them."

"But, Calder, she's got Billy!" Hope said, tears filling her eyes. "What if they're hurting him? We can't sit here and do nothing while they hurt my baby!"

Calder pulled her into his embrace and Hope fought against him. She didn't want to be held. She wanted to *do* something. Go to Lincoln's house and force him to tell her what they'd done with Billy. To get him back.

Calder didn't even seem to notice her struggles, he simply buried his nose in her hair and held on tighter. Eventually, the fight drained out of Hope and she clung to Calder as tightly as he was holding her.

"I'm sending men over there right now," Cruz said. "They'll keep an eye on both Donna and Lincoln. If they go anywhere, they'll follow them and check things out."

"They're not going to hurt Billy," Joseph said.

Hope looked at him. "How do you know?"

"Because they just want the money. I heard her bitching with the other waitresses about you winning that money. Hannah demanded you give her and the other waitresses a cut of your winnings, and I know Donna agreed with her. I should've thought about them when the diner burned down. Even that graffiti that was painted on the side of the building makes sense now. 'Mine.' She thinks the money should be hers."

"Do you remember them coming in and beating you up?" Quint asked.

Joseph shook his head. "No. I still can't remember anything about that night. But if Lincoln was involved, it would've been fairly easy. He knew the layout of the restaurant. I'm guessing he thought the place would be empty, and when he broke in and realized I was still there, and saw him, he panicked. Beat on me, trapped me in my office, and set the place on fire. I'm lucky I didn't die...but he *also* lucked out because I don't remember anything that happened."

"I'm guessing maybe torching the place wasn't his original plan," Dax added. "I mean, he was probably just going to rob you, but when he went into your office where the safe was and found you, he probably freaked. Figured you'd rat him out."

"Here's what I propose," Cruz said. "But, Hope, the decision is yours."

Hope looked up from where she was huddled against Calder. "What?"

"We'll get a duffle and stuff it with both fake money and real bills on top. You'll make the drop tomorrow at the park. You'll be covered at all times by all of us. We'll make sure they don't hurt *you* in any way. At the same time, we'll raid Lincoln's house. If Billy's there, we'll get him to safety while Donna and Lincoln are otherwise occupied."

"What if only one of them goes to the park to get the money?" Calder asked.

"Then we'll arrest whoever stays back at the house," Cruz said. "And the second the money is grabbed, we'll arrest whoever is there to pick it up. If we haven't found Billy at that point, we'll interrogate both of them until they tell us where he is."

"I'm not sure I can wait until tomorrow," Hope said softly. "That means Billy'll have to spend the night somewhere without me. Probably scared out of his mind. What if they've hurt him? What if they've stashed him somewhere? What if they never say where he is?"

"Is there *anything* we can do tonight?" Calder asked his friends quietly.

Hope watched as Cruz pressed his lips together tightly before saying, "Unfortunately, no. Not legally. Beth's sending the information she has to the FBI and it'll take them some time to get what they need out of it. Then we'll need to get search warrants so we can enter Lincoln and Donna's residences legally."

"Then we'll wait until tomorrow," Calder said, a note of resignation in his tone. He turned to Hope. "I hate this just as much as you do, sweetheart. But we have to believe in Billy. He's smart. He's tough. He knows we're looking for him and he'll do whatever it takes to hang on until you can get to him."

Hope closed her eyes in despair...and nodded. She knew she didn't have a choice. Tomorrow seemed like forever away. All she could do was hope and pray that Lincoln and Donna hadn't done anything drastic to her little boy. As long as they hadn't killed him, they could work through everything else together when he was home.

She heard Mackenzie and Mickie saying their goodbyes and heard people moving around, but she didn't open her eyes and she didn't move from her spot in Calder's arms on the couch.

When it was quiet, Joseph asked, "Do either of you want something to eat?"

"No, thanks, Joseph," Calder answered.

"I'm so sorry this happened," the older man said. "I feel as if it's my fault."

Hope's eyes popped open at that. "This is *not* your fault," she said firmly. "It's *theirs*. Two greedy assholes who are pouting that they didn't get that money. Maybe if Donna was nicer, I would've shared it with her, but she wasn't and I didn't. That doesn't make it my fault. Or yours. Or Eli's or Billy's."

"Proud of you, Hope," Joseph said. Then he pushed himself to his feet and headed for his room.

When it was just the two of them in the living room, Calder turned until they were both lying on the couch. Hope's back was against the cushions of the sofa and her front was plastered to Calder. He held on to her just as tightly as she held him. She knew Calder was just as worried about Billy as she was.

"When we have Billy back, and things settle down, I'm going to ask you to marry me," Calder said quietly several minutes later. "I want to spend the rest of my life with you and Billy. I want to give you more children to fill this house of ours."

"Calder, I—"

He put a finger over her lips, stopping her words. "When I got the call that Billy was missing, I panicked. That kid has burrowed his way into my heart just as much as his mom has. Don't *ever* be afraid to call me, Hope," he chastised gently. "I don't care where I am or what I'm doing, if you need me, you call."

"Okay," she whispered.

"You're more important to me than my job, or anything else. I've never felt like this before. I love you, Hope. I want to wake up with you beside me every day for the rest of my life and I want to go to sleep with you at my side as well. I'm just giving you warning that my proposal's coming. Whatever kind of wedding you want, you'll have. Big, small, whatever. You've been through enough, and it's time you and Billy started experiencing the good that life has to offer rather than the shit. Got it?"

"Got it," she parroted quietly.

He didn't say anything else. They lay that way for hours. Neither sleeping, just soaking up as much love from each other as they could and watching the clock slowly tick away the seconds. Tomorrow couldn't come soon enough.

* * *

Billy tightened his arms around his drawn-up legs and buried his nose in his knees. He was scared and a little cold, but not as cold as he'd sometimes been when he and his mom had to sleep out in the open at night.

The wood planks under his butt hurt, but he barely noticed. The only sound he heard was the leaves rustling overhead and the occasional dog barking. Sleeping outside in the suburbs at night was very different from being in the city. It was a lot darker, for one. Billy could barely see his hand in front of his face. But it also felt safer. There weren't as many people around, and he would definitely hear if someone approached.

Billy didn't dare move from his hiding spot. Didn't try to go for help. The man could be out there. Waiting for him to show his face so he could try to grab him again. His mom had always told him that if he got lost, he needed to stay still. That she'd do whatever it took to find him.

And he knew without a doubt that his mom, and Calder, were looking for him. He'd heard sirens earlier and had hoped they'd come closer, but they never did. But he didn't lose hope. He was Billy Drayden, and he was one tough, strong little boy. Calder had said so.

One tear escaped before he took a deep breath and forced the rest back. He was seven, almost eight, too big to be crying.

Closing his eyes, Billy spoke for the first time in over a year. His voice felt rusty, and his words were only a whisper, but they were there.

"I'm here, Mom. Please come find me."

$\mathcal{C}$alder looked over Hope's shoulder as they watched the surveillance tape Beth had emailed over. She'd obviously been up all night, like they had, and had gathered more videos, the best of which was the one from a traffic camera at an intersection near the school. Any of the other law enforcement officers could've gotten the tapes and reviewed them, but having Beth obtain them was faster...even if it wasn't exactly legal. At the moment, however, no one cared about that. They were only concerned about finding Billy.

It was a little past eight the next morning and the entire team was gathered at Calder's house once more. Everyone was there, Joseph, Cruz, Quint, Wes, Hayden, Conor, and TJ.

"Keep your eye on the back corner of the playground," Cruz told everyone.

Calder felt Hope lean forward and knew she was

squinting at the screen. They'd seen this tape at the school the day before, but the others were viewing it for the first time. Seeing it again was just as horrifying as it was yesterday. Hope was shaking, the horror of watching her son being kidnapped obviously making her distraught.

Hope reached out and grabbed Calder's hand and squeezed as they watched what had happened the day before.

A man approached the far side of the fence—it was impossible to identify the person because of the distance and the quality of the video—and stood there for a second. Then, as a group of children ran by, the boy at the back of the group stopped to speak to the man.

Twenty seconds later, the man abruptly reached over the four-foot fence and grabbed the child, hauling him over the chain-link fence easily. The child struggled, but was carried off, out of the view of the cameras covering the school playground.

The entire abduction had taken only thirty seconds, if that.

"Why'd he stop?" Quint asked.

"I don't know," Hope said softly, her eyes still staring at the computer screen. The video had been stopped, but she didn't take her eyes off it, as if the footage would continue and show Billy coming back into the frame. "Maybe he thought he recognized him, even though he's never met him. But he probably said something that caught his attention. Whatever Lincoln said after that though, it obviously alarmed Billy." She looked up at Calder. "Did you see him take a step away right before Lincoln reached over the fence? He knew something was wrong."

"Here's the other clip," Cruz told them, and Calder focused his attention on the screen. This video they hadn't seen before. It was the one Beth had found from the traffic camera. He knew she'd been up all night reviewing all of the footage she could get her hands on. Cruz clicked on the second video and it began to play.

Calder held his breath as the view on the school changed from the playground to a street behind the school. The people in the clip were in the background and blurry, as the camera was focused on the cars going through the intersection, but they could see a man hauling a struggling child toward a car parked on the side of the street in the upper left-hand corner.

Before they reached Lincoln's car, he lost his grip on a wildly struggling Billy. The boy took off running across the street toward a field across from the school.

"He got away!" Hope breathed.

"Good for him," Joseph said under his breath.

The video ended with the man standing by the side of the road next to the field looking pissed, then turning around and running back to his car and driving away.

"Did you see that?" Hope asked, looking at Calder. "He got away!"

"I saw it, sweetheart," Calder told her. He turned her in the chair and kneeled down in front of her and grabbed hold of her hands. "We don't know for sure that he escaped Lincoln though. He might've cut him off on the other side of that field."

Hope shook her head. "No. Remember when you talked to him about never letting anyone get him in a car?"

Calder nodded.

"Me and Billy had a talk about that afterward. We both promised that we'd do whatever it took to get away. I asked if he remembered when he was little and we were still living in Washington and we were at the mall. I looked away from him for two seconds, and when I turned around he was gone. I searched the mall for an hour before I finally found him. Turns out we'd both been wandering in circles and missing each other. Billy remembered. I told him that if he was ever lost, that he should stay put. Let the people searching come to *him*. After we talked about your lecture, we discussed running away and hiding. That it would be safer for the police to come to us, rather than for us to wander around where the bad guy might find us again. I *know* he's hiding somewhere, Calder. I just know it!"

For the first time since Billy had disappeared, Calder began to feel a ray of hope.

He was a realist. He knew firsthand what could happen to people at the hands of others. There were some awful, sick people out there. He saw the results of that evilness on his autopsy table every week. But hearing that Hope had had a conversation with Billy gave him a glimmer of hope that he really *was* out there hiding, and not at the mercy of Lincoln and Donna.

He turned to Dax. "Call Sledge and the other fire-fighters. Tell them what happened and where to start searching. Explain that they should check every single nook and cranny where Billy might be hiding. He can't respond to people calling his name."

"I'll let him know," Dax reassured him. "I know all of the guys are standing by ready to help. If Billy's somewhere around the school hiding, they'll find him."

Calder turned back to Hope. "They *will* find him," he said without any doubt in his tone. "Are you up for doing the money drop today?"

Hope swallowed hard and nodded. "I can do it."

Calder wanted to be out looking for Billy, but he wasn't going to let Hope stroll through Bamberger Park by herself. Well, he knew she wouldn't be by herself, as all the men around them right now would be there watching over her, but he wasn't going to leave her side. No way in hell.

"I'm extremely proud of you," he told Hope quietly. "I know this isn't easy."

"That's the understatement of the century," she said. "I really feel the need to go to the school and look for Billy myself, but I can't let Donna and Lincoln get away with this. I almost wish I'd never won that stupid money in the first place."

Calder didn't know what to say that would reassure her. He didn't give a rat's ass about the million bucks because he wanted her and her son just the way they were. But he knew the money would give her the confidence to get herself back on her feet and not feel beholden to anyone, even him.

TJ came over to them then. He put his hand on Hope's shoulder. "I used to question fate all the time. I thought I was being punished when I got hurt when I was in the Army. I didn't feel as if I deserved Milena. And when I found out she'd had my son, and had raised him by herself for two years, that feeling got even stronger. But you know what? I finally pulled my head out of my ass long enough to realize that if I hadn't gone through what I did in the Army, I wouldn't be able to appreciate what I have now."

Calder watched as Hope's eyes filled with tears and she nodded.

"It sucks that you were homeless. Even more so that you were homeless with a child. But I truly believe that your experiences are helping Billy today," TJ said.

"Thank you," Hope whispered.

"Are you ready to go?" Hayden asked.

Hope took a deep breath and nodded. Calder stood and pulled her up next to him, keeping his arm around her waist.

"Okay," Hayden said. "Conor's talked to his game warden friends and they're already stationed around the park, undercover. They're posing as civilians hiking and enjoying the nature reserve. Cruz and Wes are going to head out before us and get in place to apprehend whoever goes after the money you leave. Quint and I will be in the parking lot, making sure neither escapes if they manage to evade Cruz and Wes."

"Where are you going to be?" Hope asked Calder.

"At the park with you," he told her.

"But…they said no cops."

"I'm not a cop," Calder said immediately. He lifted his hands and framed her face, forcing her to look at him. "I won't walk right next to you, just in case they're watching you, but I'll be nearby just in case you need me. There's no way I'll let you go in there by yourself. Don't ask it of me, Hope. Please."

She licked her lips but nodded.

"They aren't going to do anything to mess up the money drop," he reassured her. "I'm not dressed like a cop and I won't be wearing my badge."

"Donna knows who you are from when you ate at the diner though," Hope said.

"Those two are obviously desperate for money," Quint said. "The FBI did a background check and found that Lincoln has been dabbling with gambling and owes ten thousand to a local loan shark. They aren't going to risk the deal going bad if Calder's with you."

"Especially if they don't have Billy in the first place," Hayden added. "They're going to want to get their hands on the money as soon as possible and get the hell out of town. I have a feeling it's why they contacted you so quickly after the attempted abduction. They wanted to get the money before Billy was found and they lost any leverage they had."

Hope took a deep breath. "Okay. I trust you guys."

Calder dropped his hands from her face and wrapped an arm around her waist once more.

"But, right after we do this, can we go and join the search around the school?" she asked.

"Absolutely," Calder reassured her.

Hope moved away from him but when she reached for his hand, Calder relaxed. She intertwined her fingers with his and took a deep breath. "I'm ready."

"Let's do this," Hayden said.

Everyone headed for the door except Hope and Calder, and Joseph disappeared into the room he'd been using to give the couple some privacy. Since he'd be a liability rather than a help, with the shape his legs were in, he'd offered to stay at the house and once more monitor the phone, and to be there in case Billy came home.

Calder waited until everyone had exited before he turned to Hope. "I love you."

She licked her lips but didn't hesitate to return the words. "I love you too."

"Let's get this done so we can find Billy and get on with that wonderful life, yeah?"

"Yeah."

Calder felt Hope squeeze his hand as they headed for the garage.

* * *

At precisely eleven o'clock, Hope walked as fast as she

could down the nature trail toward the trash can she was supposed to put the money in. She usually loved being in the outdoors, but not this morning. Every chirp of a bird made her flinch; every time the wind blew, she whipped her head around, thinking Lincoln would be standing there.

She was sweating, and she knew her heart was racing. Her shoulder hurt from the weight of the bag she was carrying and she was nauseous from nerves. But she didn't let any of that stop her. Putting one foot in front of the other, she kept going.

Billy and Calder were the two things keeping her moving forward. Billy, because she knew whatever happened in the next couple minutes could determine his fate. And Calder, because she knew he was watching over her. He wasn't right by her side, but she knew he was behind her somewhere. As were the other law enforcement officers.

They'd arrived at Bamberger Park thirty minutes before she had and fanned out, forming a protective circle around the path, the drop point, and her. She didn't see Lincoln's car parked anywhere, but she hadn't bothered taking the time to inspect every car in the lot either. Her only job was to get the money to the trash can and leave.

The sticks crunched under her feet and she could feel her heart beating way too fast in her chest. She had no idea if Lincoln would decide to just pop out from behind a tree and kill her and steal the money, or if he really would wait for her to leave the cash in the trash can she was headed toward. She was terrified, but nothing was going to make her turn back now. No way.

As she walked around a bend in the path, Hope came to a stop in the middle of the trail. Right in front of her was a bench—and next to it, a large metal trash can. It looked sturdy enough to withstand a hungry animal trying to get a meal.

Looking around, Hope didn't see or hear anything out of the ordinary. The birds were still chirping, and that was the only thing she could hear, other than her own too-fast breaths.

She slowly made her way toward the trash can and reached for the lid. She panicked when she couldn't figure out how to get it off. It was a bear-proof trash can, and for a second, she envisioned Lincoln killing Billy when she couldn't leave the money because she was too flustered to figure out how to open the damn thing.

After a few seconds, she realized how the mechanism worked and the top popped open. Without hesitation, Hope dropped the bag on the ground and started removing the money, both the real and fake. She was glad the fake money looked almost exactly like the real stuff...she almost couldn't tell which was which. The bag wouldn't fit inside the small opening and she wanted to get rid of the money as fast as she could. She dropped a couple bundles of cash in her haste to make the drop, but she didn't even glance at them. Her only concern was doing what Donna had told her to do so she could get Billy back.

When she was done stuffing the money into the trash can, she folded the bag and pushed that in too. Then…she stood there. Not sure what she was supposed to do next. It seemed anticlimactic to just turn around and leave, but after a moment, she realized that was exactly what she was supposed to do.

Calder had said that Conor's game warden colleagues were ready and waiting to pounce on Lincoln and Donna when they showed up to grab the cash, and TJ and Conor himself were there somewhere as well. But she had the intense urge to stand by the trash can and yell at Lincoln to come out and give her son back.

Instead, she took a deep breath and turned her back on the trash can and the money, and made her way back to the parking lot. It was one of the hardest things she'd ever had to do in her life, but she knew Calder and his friends would do whatever it took to take down Lincoln and Donna and find Billy.

It was the thought of Calder watching over her, of knowing he'd join her back at the parking lot, that gave Hope the strength to walk away.

* * *

Two hours later, Hope and Calder stood in the parking lot of the nature area at Bamberger Park and watched as both Donna and Lincoln were put in separate cop cars. They were handcuffed and had been yelling at the officers even as they were placed in the backseats.

TJ and Conor walked toward them.

"How are you two holding up?" TJ asked.

"We're okay," Calder said. "Can you tell us what happened?"

"After Hope put the money in the trash can and left, Lincoln appeared out of the bushes where he'd been hiding," Conor said. "My game warden colleagues got everything that happened next on film. He had trouble getting the trash can open, since it's designed to keep animals out. Donna came out of hiding to help and they had to tip the receptacle over and shake the money out, since they couldn't figure out the release mechanism on the front panel. They quickly realized some of the money was fake, but were greedy enough to waste time trying to fish every bill they could out of the trash can. It's a good thing we had the park locked down because it took them so damn long to get the cash, someone would've certainly come upon them. The second they headed back down the path, they were apprehended."

"What'd they say about Billy?" Calder asked.

"That they didn't know where he was. Said they never had him," TJ said with a shake of his head.

"They could be lying," Calder said.

"I don't think they are. The second they heard about the kidnapping charges, they fell all over themselves trying to explain what happened at the school, and how they never found him after he ran off. We even had to tell them to shut up so we could read them their Miranda rights to make everything legal. Right after that, they repeated what they'd said, that they never had Billy, and had only used his disappearance to their advantage so they could get their hands on the money. And Cruz called. Both houses have been searched and they didn't find any sign of Billy at either, or that he was ever there."

Hope didn't care what happened to Donna or Lincoln. They'd get what was coming to them. They might not have kidnapped Billy, but they'd tried. And they would've if Billy hadn't outsmarted them. All she cared about was finding her son. "Can we go?" Hope asked Calder.

He turned and kissed the top of her head. "Yeah, sweetheart. We can go." He looked at their friends. "We'll be with the search party around the school. You'll call if anything happens with those two that we need to know about? If they have any information at all about where Billy might be?"

"Of course," TJ said. "Go. Find Billy and bring him home. Tell him he won't have to worry about these assholes again."

"Will do, thanks," Calder said, shaking both TJ's and Conor's hands.

When they were finally on their way to the school, Calder asked, "Are you okay, Hope?"

"Yes. But I'll be better when we find Billy." She turned to him. "We *are* going to find him, aren't we?"

"Absolutely," Calder answered without hesitation.

Hope swallowed the lump in her throat. She couldn't fall apart now. She glanced at her watch. It was after lunch. Billy had been out there somewhere on his own for almost a full day. He was probably hungry and scared.

"He's fine," Calder said softly.

"How'd you know what I was thinking?" Hope asked.

"Because I'm thinking the same thing."

Hope studied Calder. He had dark circles under his eyes, much as she did. He wasn't taking this any easier than she was...though he was hiding it better. Even though Billy hadn't been a part of his life for that long, he loved him. He'd told her that, but a part of her hadn't really processed it. She'd lived with Earle for years, and he'd never shown even a third of the emotion toward her son as Calder was right this moment.

The man sitting next to her had been emotionally supporting her since Billy had gone missing, and she'd selfishly not returned that support. Billy might not be related to Calder by blood, but it was more than obvious to her, now that she was looking for it, that it didn't matter.

Reaching out, Hope put her hand on Calder's thigh. He glanced at her quickly before his eyes returned to the road in front of them. He reached down and covered her hand with his own.

"Yes," Hope said softly.

"Yes, what?" Calder asked.

"After we find Billy and things settle down, my answer will be yes," she told him.

She saw the second her words penetrated because his entire body seemed to sag in understanding. He didn't answer her in words, simply picked up her hand and kissed her palm reverently, before placing it back on his thigh. The rest of the drive to the elementary school was done in silence.

CHAPTER SEVENTEEN

*C*alder told Hope he wanted to start their search for Billy at the exact location on the street where he'd escaped Lincoln. Cade Turner, one of the firefighters from Station 7, had met them at the school and had updated them on the search, indicating what neighborhoods had already been combed through and what clues had been found...which had been nothing.

There was a group about to start a new search about three miles from the school, but something inside Calder told him that would be a waste of time. He stood at the edge of the street and stared across the field where they'd seen Billy running on the surveillance video.

"What are you thinking?" Hope asked.

Calder shook his head. He wasn't sure *what* he was thinking. He looked beyond the field on the other side of the road at the neighborhood on the other side. The houses weren't big, but they weren't small either. It was a typical middle-class neighborhood, normal for this part of town. He tried to imagine, if he was Billy, what he'd do...where he'd go. He suddenly regretted that he hadn't taken Billy camping. Or taught him more about the outdoors. There simply hadn't been time. In some ways, it felt as if Hope and Billy had been living with him forever, but in reality, it hadn't been that long. But he regretted not spending more time with Billy. Vowing to change that, Calder looked down at Hope.

She was staring at him, concern easy to read in her expression. She was worried about her son, that was obvious, but he could see that at the moment, she was also very concerned about him. "I'm okay," he told her. "I'm just trying to think about where Billy'd go. What he was thinking as he ran across this field. How comfortable was he with nature?" he asked.

Hope blinked in surprise at his question but answered without hesitation. "I'd have to say not very. I mean, when we stayed outside while we were homeless, he always complained about the bugs and stuff. He always preferred we find a place to stay that wasn't out in the open in the parks."

Calder nodded and reached for her hand. They were both wearing bright orange vests supplied by the search organizer. He started walking with Hope's hand in his, his eyes constantly scanning their route as they walked in the direction Billy had fled. "I'm sorry that I haven't spent more time with him outside. Little boys should love the great outdoors. Getting dirty, lying in the grass. When we find him, I intend to change that. Maybe we can all go camping or something."

When Hope choked back a laugh, he looked at her. "What?"

"Seriously? Camping?"

"What's wrong with camping?"

"Calder, we spent a year basically camping when we were homeless. I can't say it was all that pleasurable."

Calder hated to think about what she and Billy had been through, but he pushed the bad thoughts back. "I'm guessing you guys didn't exactly get to sit around a campfire and listen to the crickets chirping." He waited until she shook her head before continuing. "And that you didn't make s'mores around that campfire. Or fish in the nearby lake just for fun."

When she shook her head again, he stopped and put his hands on either side of her face, tilting it up so she was looking him in the eyes. "I can't promise that nothing will remind you of what you've been through in the past, but I *can* promise to do my best to give you and Billy new memories. Good ones."

"I'd like that," she whispered.

Calder kissed her swiftly, then took her hand in his and started walking again.

"What does camping have to do with finding Billy?" Hope asked.

He wasn't surprised she wasn't following his train of thought because all her mental effort was concentrated on finding her son. "Billy doesn't like being outside, at least out in the open. So if he was running from Lincoln, he'd want to hide someplace sheltered. He'd want to find someplace that made him feel safe. I'm going to need you to keep your eyes peeled for anywhere that might remind you of the city and where you guys holed up. He'll pick something familiar to him."

"He's good at climbing," Hope said. They'd reached the end of the field and had to decide which way to turn. To the right toward a neighborhood or left toward a small shopping area. "He had no problem scaling fences when we were homeless. He had to help me over more than one."

Calder looked toward the buildings to their left. Then he turned and looked at the neighborhood. Most of the houses had fences around their manicured lawns. At first glance, it seemed as if there were many more places to hide at the shopping complex, but when he thought about it, he had a feeling Billy wouldn't have gone that way.

"If he was trying to get as far away from Lincoln as possible, he would've tried to go somewhere that a car couldn't get to," Hope concluded.

"That's what I was thinking," Calder said, turning right and heading for the neighborhood.

"The cops said they went door to door here already," Hope protested. "No one said they saw him."

"Billy's smart, but he's also shy and mute. He wouldn't have gone up to a door and knocked to ask for help. He'd hide, making himself feel safe in the process. You said it yourself, he's a good climber. He could get over these fences without a problem...especially if he had adrenaline on his side."

"So what do we do?" Hope asked as they stood on the side of the street looking at the rows of houses on either side of them. "How do we find him if he's hiding? He didn't come out when the searchers came through here yelling for him."

"He was probably still scared. But I truly think if he hears *you*, he'll come out."

Hope put her free hand on Calder's arm. "You too."

"Me too, what?"

"If he hears you, he'll come running. I know it."

Calder wasn't as sure as she was on that. He wasn't Billy's mom. The little boy and his mom had been through a hell of a lot together. If he was in this neighborhood somewhere, he'd probably stay hidden until his mom came for him...just as she'd instructed him to do.

"Come on," Calder said. "You walk on that side of the street and yell his name. Reassure him that it's really you and that he can come out, that Lincoln has been caught. I'll do the same on this side."

Calder loosened his fingers from Hope's but was surprised when she held on.

"Thank you."

He could barely hear the words because they were said so softly. "You don't thank me for this, Hope," he scolded. "Billy might not be my blood, but that doesn't mean I don't think of him as my son." He saw she was struggling to keep from crying. "Now, come on, let's go find Billy and get him home. I'm sure he's hungry and scared."

"Right," she choked out. "I love you."

"And I love you," Calder returned.

Hope stood up on her tiptoes and kissed him quickly, then took a deep breath and squeezed his hand before letting go and wandering over to the other side of the street.

Calder stared at her for a long moment, wondering how in the hell he'd gotten so lucky, before mentally shaking his head and following his own advice about finding Billy and getting him home.

* * *

Billy sat huddled in his hiding spot, wondering for the hundredth time if he should get up and go looking for his mom himself. But then he'd remember her lecture about staying put when lost. He *wasn't* lost. He knew exactly where he was, but the last thing he wanted was for the scary man to find him instead of his mom.

He'd heard people yelling his name the night before, but he'd refused to budge. It could've been the man who tried to kidnap him or his buddies playing a trick on him. No, he was better off staying right where he was.

His stomach rumbled and Billy did his best to ignore it. He'd been a lot hungrier when he and his mom had been homeless. He'd be fine for at least another day. He'd lucked out when he'd found his hiding spot had a few bottles of water tucked away.

When he'd fled the school, he'd had no idea where he was going, but then he remembered Jaylen talking about his treehouse. He'd said that his dad had made it for him, and how cool it was. He'd described the rope ladder that, when pulled up, meant no one could get up there. How the roof was a *real* roof, made from the same shingles that were on their house, and how he even slept in it when it was warmer out.

Billy knew where Jaylen lived because he'd seen where he got off the bus...when Billy was still *riding* the bus. With no other plan in mind other than to hide from the man who'd tried to snatch him, he'd run as fast as he could to his friend Jaylen's house. The fence around the yard had been no problem for Billy, and he scampered up and over it as if he were part squirrel.

He'd pulled up the rope ladder as soon as he was inside the treehouse and hadn't done anything that would bring attention to the fact he was there.

Billy had no idea why the man had tried to grab him. He'd seen him at the fence around the playground at school and had stopped when the man said he'd lost his dog nearby and asked if Billy had seen him. But almost immediately he realized the man was lying, because the man wasn't telling him the name of the dog. Anyone who was really looking for a lost pet would know what they'd named it. Billy had tried to back away, to go to the teachers for help, but the man had reached out and grabbed him.

Remembering what Calder had said about not getting in a car with someone, he'd fought like crazy and the man had dropped him. His knees still hurt from landing on the ground, but at the time Billy hadn't felt it. He'd just run as fast as he could across the field and into the trees by the school to get away.

But even with the water that Jaylen had stashed in his treehouse, Billy was hungry and wanted to go home. He wanted his mom. Wanted Calder. They'd keep him safe from the man, he had no doubt.

Sighing, he put his head back down on his up-drawn knees and did his best not to cry.

He had no idea how long he'd been sitting there, when he thought he heard something. Lifting and cocking his head, Billy strained to hear something other than the dang birds chirping.

"Biiiiiiiilly!"

His heart started beating fast and Billy quickly climbed to his feet. He tiptoed over to the window in the treehouse—yes, Jaylen's dad had even put a small glass window in the amazingly awesome treehouse—and peered out.

He could only see a part of the street because the leaves on the tree and Jaylen's house blocked most of it, but Billy stared through the glass at the section of road he could see and tried to determine if he was hearing things—or if he really had just heard his mom's voice.

"Billy! Can you hear me?"

That was Calder's voice!

Billy's heart was really thumping now. His mom and Calder were there! They'd found him!

He opened his mouth to yell back—but nothing came out.

Frustrated, Billy scrambled over to the opening in the floor and lowered the rope ladder. He could still hear his mom and Calder calling his name, but their voices were getting farther and farther away.

Panicking, Billy shrugged his backpack over his shoulders and hurried down the ladder. He missed a rung on the way down and fell. Luckily, he was almost at the bottom and the only thing hurt was his pride. He sprang up and ran for the fence. He could barely hear his mom's voice now. She'd passed the house and was leaving him behind.

"Mom!" Billy croaked as he leaped at the fence to climb it. He miscalculated and didn't quite reach the top, slamming his body against the wood.

Terrified he was going to miss his chance to be found, Billy stepped back away from the fence in order to make another run at it—and yelled at the top of his lungs, "Calderrrrrrr!"

He didn't hear anything now. Not his mom's voice yelling for him, or Calder's. He ran at the fence and this time managed to grab the top of it when he jumped. Using all his strength, he pulled himself up far enough so he could throw a leg over the top. He peered over the fence at the road where he'd heard his mom...and stared in disbelief and joy at the sight in front of him.

* * *

Calder hadn't ever heard Billy's voice before, but the second he heard his name being yelled in a desperate, scared-out-of-his-mind way, he knew it was Billy.

He spun at the same time Hope did and began running back the way they'd come. It was hard to figure out where the voice had come from, but he was close, that much Calder knew.

He scanned the fences and yards as they ran, and when he saw Billy's head pop up over the top of a six-foot wooden fence to his left, he almost cried. Without waiting for Hope, his only goal to get to Billy, Calder sprinted toward the little boy.

Their eyes met as Billy pulled himself high enough up the fence to get his leg thrown over. Billy froze as he stared at both his mom and Calder running as fast as they could toward him.

Calder didn't even slow down. The second he was within reach, his arms went up and he plucked Billy off the fence as if he were a toddler, instead of a quickly growing boy. He wrapped his arms around him and held on tight, his relief so profound, so overbearing, he fell to his knees right there in the yard.

Seconds after he hit the ground, Calder felt Hope's arms come around both him and her son. She was sobbing and almost incoherent, but all Calder could do was clasp Billy to him and thank God he was all right.

Hope pulled back and took Billy's head in her hands and said, "Are you okay?"

Expecting Billy to nod, Calder was shocked when instead he said, "Yeah. I'm good. I knew you'd come for me."

It wasn't until that moment that Calder fully comprehended what had happened. Billy had yelled his name. Out loud. The sound had made both him and Hope come running, but he still hadn't truly processed the fact that Billy was no longer mute.

"I'll always come for you," Hope told her son, tears once again falling down her cheeks.

"And that goes double for me, Bud," Calder added, his own tears squeezing out of his eyes.

When Billy buried his face against his neck once more, Calder looked up at the woman he loved more than life itself. Hope was smiling and crying at the same time.

He mouthed, "I love you." When she mouthed it back, Calder felt his throat close up once more. He'd never been happier in his life than right that moment, with the two most important people in his life, safe and happy in his arms.

CHAPTER EIGHTEEN

"*A*fter the basketball game, me and Jaylen are going to get to spend the night in his treehouse. His dad said it was okay, and we're gonna eat popcorn and cake at the game and then go out for burgers."

"Jaylen and I," Hope corrected and smiled at her son.

It had been a month since he'd almost been kidnapped, and he was back to being a normal seven-year-old. He didn't continue talking immediately after he'd been rescued, but with patience and a few visits with the school psychologist, he'd slowly come out of his shell. His friends at school were excited to hear him talk, and Jaylen was his new best friend. His parents felt horrible that they hadn't noticed the rope ladder was up inside the treehouse instead of hanging down, as it usually was. Hope was just happy that her son hadn't been wandering the streets while he'd been missing.

Joseph had decided it was time he moved into his own place once more, using the money he'd received from the insurance payout for his diner to purchase a small condo nearby. He'd said that as Billy's "PopPop," he needed to stay close.

Hope was thrilled he'd decided to move out to the suburbs and was also relieved he'd decided not to reopen the restaurant. It was a lot of work, and Joseph wasn't exactly getting any younger.

Tonight was the first time Billy was spending the night at someone else's house, and Hope thought the entire experience was harder on her than her son. He'd talked about nothing else but the game and the treehouse and how much he was going to eat. She'd tried to talk to him about what to do if he got homesick, but Calder had pulled her aside and told her to chill out.

"What time should we come and pick you up, Bud?" Calder asked Billy, putting his arm around Hope's waist as he pulled her into his side.

Billy shrugged.

Calder chuckled. "Right. I'll walk you to the door when I drop you off and have a word with Jaylen's parents, how about that?"

"Okay. Did I tell you that Jaylen got a hockey goal for his birthday? His dad is gonna set it up in the driveway so we can play!"

"He's going to be there to watch you though, right?" Hope asked, imagining the two little boys playing without being supervised and someone pulling up and luring them away.

She felt Calder squeeze her waist reassuringly even as Billy rolled his eyes and said, "Of course, Mom. He's going to be goalie!"

Hope tuned out her son's rambling when she felt Calder's lips brush against her temple. "Stop worrying," he said quietly. "The Jacksons aren't going to leave him unsupervised. They know what happened and will make sure he's safe."

Hope nodded and smiled at her son as he continued to bounce around babbling about his upcoming overnight.

"Hope," Calder said, turning her face so she had no choice but to look up at him.

"Yeah?"

"Nothing I say will make you worry less, will it?"

She knew she was overreacting, but this was the first time she'd intentionally spent the night away from her son. Billy might be excited about it, but she was not. She shook her head.

"I know you've been thinking about Billy, but you know what this means?"

Hope focused on Calder. "No, what?"

"We'll have the house to ourselves. No more worrying about how much noise you make when I'm deep inside you. We can sleep naked next to each other. We won't have to worry about him bursting into our room in the middle of the night."

Hope knew she was blushing but couldn't help it.

She and Calder had a healthy sex life, but they were always careful because the last thing she wanted was Billy walking in on them. The thought of being able to completely relax and not worry if she was being too loud or if Billy might wake up and need her was exciting.

Calder chuckled. "I see you like that idea."

"Yeah, I like it," Hope told him with a shy smile.

Calder kissed her temple once more, and she felt his fingers ease under her shirt and trace the sensitive skin of her lower back. Shivering, she shot him a warning look before pulling away to head into the living room to make sure Billy's bag had everything he'd need for the night.

Two hours later, they were back home after dropping Billy off. Hope paced, feeling restless and jittery. She really didn't like not having her son by her side.

"Hope. Come here," Calder said.

"This was a bad idea," Hope said, ignoring Calder. "What if he wakes up in the middle of the night, freaked out? What if he remembers he had to spend the night in that treehouse while he was hiding from being kidnapped?" She gasped as something just occurred to her. She turned to face Calder. "Did you hear from the detective? Are Donna and Lincoln still behind bars? What if they got out and they want revenge? We need to go and pick Billy back up. He's not safe. It's—"

Hope's words were cut off with a shriek as Calder easily picked her up. She threw her arms around

Calder and said, "What are you doing?" as he headed for the stairs.

"Taking you to bed. You're way too wound up. Billy's fine. Donna and Lincoln are still in jail, awaiting their trial. The Jacksons said they'd call if anything happened or if Billy got homesick. He's fine."

Hope knew she was acting crazy, but she couldn't help it. "But—"

"No buts," Calder said firmly. "We have this whole house to ourselves. I'm not on call. It's Saturday, and you don't have to be at Billy's school to work until Monday. We have a day and a half to ourselves—and I'm taking every minute of it."

Hope forced herself to relax. She knew Calder was right. She just didn't think being away from her son would be this hard. She loved her new job as an aide in a special-needs classroom at Billy's school, but between that and Calder's odd work hours, they hadn't had a lot of time to spend together one-on-one.

"You think you can take my mind off the fact that this is the first time since he was born that I've purposely been away from Billy?" Hope asked, running her fingers through the hair at the nape of Calder's neck. She felt him shiver, but he didn't slow down and never faltered as he headed up the stairs with her in his arms.

"I don't think it, I know it," Calder answered a bit cockily.

"Wanna make a bet?" Hope teased.

Calder pushed open their bedroom door with his

foot and strode inside, not bothering to close it behind him. There was no need. They were alone in the house. "Yes."

Hope smiled up at him as he stood over his bed and dropped her. She laughed as she bounced on the mattress. She propped herself up on her elbows and smiled coyly at him. "What are the stakes?"

Calder began to unbutton his shirt, not taking his eyes from Hope as he disrobed. "If you can still think when I'm done with you, I'll buy tickets to the game tonight and we can go and spy on Billy and make sure he's having a good time."

Hope's eyes lit up. "That's a great idea!" she enthused, sitting up. "I'll go get my computer and—"

Calder put a hand in the middle of her chest and gently pushed her back down, crawling up the bed until he was straddling her. His chest was bare and Hope was momentarily distracted.

"We'll do that, *only* if you can't stop thinking about Billy."

"And if I do?"

Calder shifted until his knees were inside hers and he pushed outward until her legs were splayed open around him. She was still fully dressed, but she shivered at the carnality of the action.

"Then you'll agree to marry me."

Hope stared up at Calder. She knew her mouth was open, but she couldn't help it. "What?"

He smirked. "If I make you lose your mind, where you can't think of anything other than me and what we're doing here in our bed, you'll agree to marry me. The sooner the better. I want to make Billy mine in all ways, but before I adopt him, I want you to marry me. Then I want to create some siblings for him."

"I thought I already did," she said with a small smile.

He returned her grin. "Then you'll actually start planning our ceremony then."

Hope's brain was reeling. She knew Calder loved her, and she loved him in return, and they'd even discussed getting married at some point, but even though she'd said yes, he hadn't brought it up again... until now. Then there was the fact that he'd said he wanted to adopt Billy. Then that bit about siblings. She couldn't stop smiling at him.

"See? I'm already winning. You can't think about anything other than me," Calder said with a chuckle. Then he dropped his head and took her lips, plunging inside her mouth and kissing her as if he needed her to breathe.

* * *

Hours later, Calder had no idea how much time had passed, just that it was now dark outside, he held Hope in his arms, and was stroking her hair lazily with his fingers. She was lying boneless against his side, naked as the day she was born. They'd gone downstairs at some point to get some snacks, her wearing his blue dress shirt and nothing else. He'd ended up eating her out on the kitchen counter before hauling her over his shoulder and bringing her back upstairs.

"You win," Hope whispered. "Although you don't fight fair," she complained. "How in the world I ever thought I could think of anything other than you and what you were doing to me when you refused to let me come, I don't know."

Calder smiled in the dark room. A light was on in the bathroom, giving just enough light to see by. He turned until Hope was on her back. He propped himself over her with his elbows. His cock wasn't hard; he was exhausted and there was no way he was getting it up anytime in the next hour or so. But he fitted his hips against hers, loving how hot and wet she still was after their last bout of lovemaking.

He stared down into her eyes and asked, "Hope Drayden, will you marry me? Will you let me into your and Billy's lives permanently? I promise to never raise my hand in anger against you or your son, and I won't do anything to hurt either of you emotionally. When I look into your eyes, I see our future, which hopefully will include many children to love and nurture. I'll live anywhere you want and I'll bust my ass to make you happy. My job has consumed me for as long as I can remember, but for the first time in my life, when I go to sleep at night, I don't think about tissue damage, blood spatter, or doing chemical analyses... The second I walk out of the autopsy room, my only thoughts are of you. Marry me, Hope. Please. I—"

He stopped talking when Hope brought a finger up

between them and placed it over his lips. She stared at him for the longest time, making Calder's heart race and anxiety settle in his belly.

"Of course I'll marry you. I love you, Calder."

He breathed out a sigh of relief. "Thank God."

She giggled. "Did you seriously think I would say no?"

"I was confident hours ago, but the second the words left my mouth, I thought about all the ways I could fuck this up," Calder admitted.

Hope lifted her head and kissed him before falling back again. "I think I want two more."

"Two more what?"

"Kids."

Calder knew he was smiling like a goof but couldn't help it. "Six."

Her eyes got big. "Six? No way! Three, but that's it."

"Five," he returned.

Now she narrowed her eyes at him in mock rebuke. "You'd better be kidding."

"There's nothing I want more than to look into the eyes of our sons or daughters and see their mom in them. But I know no matter how many we have, even if we have to adopt, they'll have the most awesome mother in the world. Protective, loving, and you'll teach them to be resilient and to stand up for others."

Hope sighed. "Four. And that's my absolute max."

"Done. Four it is."

Hope smiled, then asked, "You totally played me, didn't you?"

SUSAN STOKER

"Who, me?" Calder asked.

"So…when are we going to get started on these four kids? I'm not getting any younger, you know."

Calder stilled over her. They'd been using condoms because they were still settling in after everything that had happened. But at the thought of taking her bare, of starting their family, he felt his previously exhausted dick swell with need.

Hope obviously felt his reaction and spread her legs, lifting her hips a bit so she pushed up against him.

"Are you sore?" Calder asked, trying to hold himself back.

"No." One of her hands brushed down his side and latched onto his butt cheek.

"Fuck," he swore and reached down to make sure she was ready to take him. She was. So Calder took hold of his cock and fit it to her opening.

They both sighed as he eased inside her without any barrier between them for the first time. "I don't care what kind of wedding you want," Calder said as he slowly pumped in and out of her body. "Big, small, fancy, laid-back. But you need to start planning it as soon as possible."

Hope moaned as she wrapped her legs around his hips.

"I'm sure Milena, Mack, and the others would be glad to help. But I plan on fucking you as often as humanly possible, so if you don't want to be hugely pregnant when we say 'I do,' you'd better get on that sooner rather than later."

"I'll call Mack tomorrow," Hope promised. "How does two months from now sound?"

At her words, Calder closed his eyes and huffed out an emotional breath of air. He pressed inside her as far as he could go, then opened his eyes. "Perfect," he told her.

"I'm paying for it with my winnings," she informed him.

Calder's mellow mood fled. "No, you're not. That's your money. For you and Billy."

"It's my money, so I'll spend it how I want," Hope insisted.

"Absolutely not," Calder said firmly.

"We'll see."

"Hope," he warned.

"Are you going to fuck me, make me scream in satisfaction, then impregnate me, or do you want to have this conversation instead?"

"We aren't done talking about this," Calder told her.

Hope smiled at him. "I didn't think that for a second."

"I have a ring for you."

She arched a brow. "You do?"

"Yeah. I got it weeks ago."

"Okay."

"I love you, Hope," Calder said as he thrust in and out of her lazily.

"Love you too. Now...can you please fuck me like you mean it?"

Calder smiled and said, "Yes, ma'am."

* * *

An hour later, Hope sighed in contentment. Calder was sound asleep next to her. She was exhausted but couldn't sleep. She was mentally planning their wedding, and making lists in her head of things she needed to do, when Calder's phone vibrated. Reaching over his chest, she grabbed it off the bedside table, thinking it might be an emergency at work that he'd need to take. She knew he wasn't on call and technically didn't have to work until Monday, but she'd learned over the last month that things happened.

She stared at the text for a second, then smiled. It was from Billy. She'd said she wasn't going to get a phone for him until he was older, but after the almost-kidnapping, she'd caved. If he'd had a way of getting in touch with her, a lot of stress and worry could've been avoided.

Apparently, Billy was returning a message Calder had sent earlier, the little sneak. He'd told her to leave the kid alone, that he was having a good time and if he needed her, he'd get in touch. But then he went and texted him.

But Hope couldn't be upset. Not when it meant he was as worried about Billy as she was. Her son's text said,

Billy: Im fine. Game was awesome. I miss you too. Tell mom hi and not to worry.

.   .   .

She put the phone back down without replying and snuggled into Calder. Her movements must've woken him because his arm tightened around her. "You okay?" he mumbled sleepily.

"Great. Go back to sleep."

"'Kay. Love you."

"I love you too."

Within seconds, he was asleep once more.

Hope couldn't help but wonder how in the world she'd gotten so lucky. Most people would say that being abused, then homeless, wasn't lucky at all, but she knew better. Everything that had happened in her life had led her to Calder.

"*B*uttery nipples for everyone!" Sophie shouted to be heard in the crowded bar.

It was a small group, as a lot of the others were busy. Hope was on her honeymoon, Blythe was pregnant and feeling bloated so she'd cried off, and Beth hardly ever came out because of her agoraphobia. So, besides Sophie, Adeline was there (she'd left Coco, her service dog, at home this time), as well as Quinn, Penelope, and Mackenzie.

They were supposed to be celebrating Hope's pregnancy and recent nuptials, but it was simply an excuse. Sophie was worried about Quinn, and had shared her concerns with the others, and they'd all decided an intervention was in order.

Many people had told Quinn that she was beautiful, but because of the port-wine birthmark on her face, and the abuse and teasing she'd grown up with, she couldn't see it.

Defending Allye
Defending Chloe
Defending Morgan
Defending Harlow
Defending Everly
Defending Zara
Defending Raven (June 2020)

Silverstone Series

Trusting Skylar (Dec 2020)
Trusting Taylor (TBA)
Trusting Molly (TBA)
Trusting Cassidy (TBA)

SEAL of Protection Series

Protecting Caroline
Protecting Alabama
Protecting Fiona
Marrying Caroline (novella)
Protecting Summer
Protecting Cheyenne
Protecting Jessyka
Protecting Julie (novella)
Protecting Melody
Protecting the Future
Protecting Kiera (novella)
Protecting Alabama's Kids (novella)
Protecting Dakota

Stand Alone

The Guardian Mist
Nature's Rift
A Princess for Cale
A Moment in Time- A Collection of Short Stories
Lambert's Lady

Special Operations Fan Fiction
http://www.AcesPress.com

Beyond Reality Series
Outback Hearts
Flaming Hearts
Frozen Hearts

Writing as Annie George:
Stepbrother Virgin (erotic novella)

John "Driftwood" Trettle was head over heels in love with Quinn, but she refused to do more than text him. Refused to give him a chance.

Penelope had finally overheard Driftwood saying that he'd done his best, but if Quinn truly didn't like him, he needed to move on. She'd called Sophie, who'd talked to the other women, and here they were. It was time to set Quinn straight.

"Drink up, Quinn!" Sophie ordered.

"I'm already plastered," Quinn protested. "And I still don't see how getting drunk to celebrate Hope getting knocked up makes sense when she isn't even here to partcipatate."

"Participate," Penelope corrected.

"That's what I said!" Quinn said with an eye roll.

The others all laughed and they clinked glasses before throwing back the sweet shots.

Mackenzie raised an eyebrow at Sophie.

She nodded and leaned forward over the small table. "Here's the deal, Quinn. While we're here to celebrate our friends getting m-married and being pregnant, that's not why we're *really* here."

"It's not?" Quinn asked.

"Nope. We're here because you're an idiot."

Quinn blinked. "Well, shit, Soph. Don't hold back, tell me what you really think."

Everyone giggled.

"John likes you. I m-mean, *really* likes you. I've s-seen the texts he's s-sent you. Why are you not giving him a chance?"

SUSAN STOKER

"You know why," Quinn fired back.

"If you're talking about your birthmark, I can guar-antee Driftwood doesn't even notice it," Penelope said.

"Riiiight," Quinn drawled sarcastically. "Because it's so easy to miss."

Penelope smacked her hand down on the table, the loud sound making everyone jump. "I get it. I do. You've gotten teased your entire life and you had that bad experience with a man. But Driftwood is nothing like those boys you used to know. I saw him literally jump Squirrel when he made a totally innocuous comment about your birthmark. Tried to beat his ass *right there* in the fire station."

"He did?" Quinn asked, much more subdued now.

"Yes. He said you're beautiful, and anyone who said something about your birthmark, to your face or behind your back, would regret it," Penelope informed her.

"Remember when you told m-me that you'd do anything to have a m-man who was protective and bossy? Well...there's one who's practically begging to be that for you, and you won't let him," Sophie added.

Mack reached over and took Quinn's hand in hers. "What's *really* bothering you about John?"

Quinn's eyes filled with tears. "You guys wouldn't understand."

"Try us," Adeline said.

Quinn took a deep breath. "Once, when I was little, we read the story of *Beauty and the Beast* at school. At recess, a group of girls surrounded me and told me that

I was the Beast. That kids would be crazy to play with me. One of the boys I liked overheard and for the rest of the school year, he wouldn't have anything to do with me."

"They were kids," Mack said gently.

"Right. I was also passed over for adoption time and time again because of the way I looked. Parents would grab hold of their children's hands and pull them away, as if their kids could catch something if they were too near me. Don't even get me started on my own mother and how *she* treated me. Those were all *adults*, Mackenzie."

"Assholes," Sophie muttered.

Quinn wanted to smile but couldn't. "I liked this one guy in college, and we talked all the time. He seemed to really like me back. I got up the nerve to ask if he wanted to get something to eat sometime...and he looked at me like I was insane. Told me we were just friends, and that his fraternity brothers would make fun of him forever if he went out with 'the chick with the thing on her face.' It was so embarrassing, thinking I'd found someone who was into me, only to find out he just wanted to be friends."

"This isn't like that," Penelope protested.

"I wasn't done," Quinn said, holding up a hand. "I finally decided I'd never lose my virginity if I continued to be picky enough to want a man who could overlook my birthmark. So I started going to bars. And it worked. A guy finally took me home. But in the morning, when he woke up and wasn't drunk, he looked like he was going to puke when he got a look at my face. I'm lonely, I'll admit it, but watching movies by myself and cooking for one is a hell of a lot better than having to figure out a man's motives."

"Quinn—" Sophie started, but she was interrupted.

"When I find a man who makes me forget that half my face is covered by this birthmark, maybe I'll take a chance on him. But so far, that hasn't happened. If it's not the people around us staring, it's the way the guy's eyes continually go to my face and neck. As if he's hoping it'll somehow disappear."

"Driftwood can be that man for you, *if* you give him a chance," Penelope said, not letting it go. "I won't deny people are often assholes. But not all of them."

"I have to admit s-something," Sophie said.

Her voice was so contrite, Quinn immediately got suspicious. "What?"

"The guys are coming in about," she paused to look at her watch, "fifteen m-minutes."

"Seriously?" Quinn griped. "I thought this was a girls' night out."

Sophie shrugged. "You know how they are. There's no way they would let us get a cab home."

Quinn plunked her head down on the table, not even caring about germs and stuff. "Kill me now," she mumbled.

The others all giggled at her theatrics.

"Come on, Quinn. Give John a chance. He likes you. *Seriously* likes you," Mackenzie said. "I know I don't hang out with you guys as much as I'd like to, but it's obvious even to me, and that's saying something. Put the poor man out of his misery and tell him you'll go out with him."

Quinn picked up her head and looked at her friends. She envied them. Their men were amazing. Even though Penelope wasn't officially with Moose, it was obvious that she was everything to him.

"Whoops!" Sophie said. "Looks like I was wrong. They won't be here in fifteen m-minutes after all."

"They won't?" Quinn asked, feeling relieved.

"Nope. They're here now. Guess they couldn't wait any longer."

Quinn turned to see Dean, Moose, Roman, John, and Dax headed their way. She put her forehead back down on the table and closed her eyes. "Seriously, kill me now. Please. It'd be more humane."

She heard her friends giggling again—but didn't lift her head until she felt a hand on her lower back and John whispering in her ear.

"You okay?"

Quinn sat up quickly, not noticing that she'd almost beaned John in the face with her actions. "I'm good. Great. I think I'll get another shot before I head home though."

She went to stand up and would've fallen if John hadn't been there to catch her. "Easy, Emmy."

Quinn almost groaned. He'd started calling her "Emmy" after deciding her eyes were the color of emeralds. She'd protested, saying it was ridiculous, but...every time he called her Emmy in his deep, rumbly voice, she got goosebumps. All her life she'd been given nicknames, but none were nice ones.

"I'm good. Fine. Great," she told him as she struggled to stand without keeling over. She always felt out of place around John because he was tall, blond, blue-eyed, and absolutely gorgeous. She was already self-conscious because of her looks, but being around him made it that much worse. She was almost jealous of him. How handsome he was. He had people staring at him all the time...but it was because people *admired* his looks, rather than being shocked or disgusted by them.

"Come on. Let's get you home," John said.

"Sophie said she'd take me," Quinn blurted.

"S-Sorry, Quinn. Roman and I have plans," her friend said, throwing her under the proverbial bus.

"Same here," Adeline chimed in.

"Us too," Mack said, barely keeping a chuckle from escaping.

Quinn turned to Penelope and Moose.

Penelope held up a hand and refused to say a word.

Sighing, Quinn said a little ungratefully, "Fine. Whatever. I'm ready." She turned to grab her purse from the back of the chair when she heard raucous laughter coming from a table nearby.

Turning toward the sound automatically, Quinn stiffened when she saw three men staring at her. She ducked her chin and turned away, but it wasn't quick enough.

"Damn, you're right, Jim. It's hideous."

"Right? I bet her boyfriend has to fuck her with a bag over her head."

When the laughter continued, Quinn tried to do what she always did…ignore them. But at the sound of a low growl from next to her, she couldn't. She turned to look at John—and froze at the fury on his face.

"I'll be right back. Don't move," he told her.

Quinn tried to grab his arm, to tell him not to worry about it. That she heard much worse all the time, but she was drunk, and uncoordinated, and her hand caught nothing but air when she reached for him.

"Oh, shit," Daxton said. "Mack, wait here."

Quinn stared at John's back as he stomped over to the other table and leaned on it. He was obviously exchanging words with the group of men, but she couldn't hear what they were saying.

"This is exciting," Sophie said with a grin.

Quinn turned to her and snapped, "It is not! Shut up."

"Yes, it is," Sophie returned without an ounce of worry on her face.

"I told you," Penelope said.

"Told me what?" Quinn asked.

"That Driftwood almost beat the shit out of *Squirrel* for saying something that wasn't even derogatory. That he wouldn't put up with anyone saying anything about your face." She gestured to the men. "Case in point."

Quinn turned back to look at John. His face was red and his stance was definitely hostile, and the men

SUSAN STOKER

seemed to get the message loud and clear. They looked worried and were nodding their heads rapidly.

John said one last thing to the group before turning and heading back in her direction, with Dax at his heels.

He didn't look at anyone but Quinn as he returned to her, and she couldn't take her eyes from his. When he got within touching distance, he reached out and put his arm around her waist and pulled her into him.

Quinn stumbled, but she knew John wouldn't let her fall.

"Enough is enough," John said gruffly. "I'm done with this shit. From this second on, we're dating. Anyone who *dares* say anything insulting about your beautiful face will have to deal with me directly."

"Um…" Quinn ventured tentatively, not wanting to upset him further. "We're dating?"

"Yes," John replied succinctly. Then he turned so they were hip to hip and started walking them toward the door of the bar without another word.

Quinn wrapped her arm around his waist to make it easier to walk and looked back over her shoulder at her friends.

All four were standing by their table, smiling hugely. Sophie even lifted a hand and gave her a thumbs-up as John dragged her off.

Quinn wanted to blame her immediate acquiescence on the amount of alcohol she'd consumed that night, but she couldn't. She'd had the biggest crush on

John ever since she'd met him, she'd just been scared to do anything about it.

She wasn't sure how she felt about him declaring they were dating, but she couldn't deny the little thrill inside of her at his protectiveness. Not once in her entire life had a guy stood up for her like he just had. Not. Once.

Sure, Sophie and the others were quick to come to her defense when someone said something insensitive, but somehow that was different than when John did it.

They exited the bar and headed for his truck. He got her settled inside and stalked around the front to get in on the driver's side. He took off without saying a word, but Quinn noticed they weren't going toward her apartment.

"Um…where are we going?" she asked.

"My place," John told her.

"I don't think that's a good idea."

"Tough. You're drunk. I'm not leaving you alone in your apartment. What if you puke in your sleep? You could die. Not gonna happen on my watch."

The thought of her throwing up in front of John made her panic. "I can't puke in front of *you!*" she exclaimed.

For the first time since she'd overheard the men talking about her, John's face relaxed. He didn't quite smile, but it was close. "Too bad."

Quinn groaned and rested her head on the seat behind her. "Next time Sophie wants me to go drinking with her, remind me of this moment, and lock me inside my apartment, okay?"

She didn't see him, as she'd squeezed her eyes shut, but she felt him pick up her hand and rest it on his thigh, covering it with his own large, warm palm. "You got it, Emmy."

"I think we should talk about this dating thing," Quinn ventured.

"Shhh," John said. "Later. Just rest. I'll take care of you."

And that was what Quinn was worried about. That she'd get addicted to him taking care of her. That she'd love him with everything that was in her, and he'd eventually get sick of defending her, of looking at her flawed face, of everything...and leave. Just like everyone she'd ever gotten close to.

"Don't leave me."

"I'm yours as long as you'll have me," John said.

Quinn was horrified she'd said the words out loud. She hadn't meant to. She wanted to believe him, but it wasn't that easy. Was it?

The last thing she remembered was John picking up her hand, kissing the back of it, and placing it back down on his thigh, before she finally passed out.

Look for the next book in the series...*Shelter for Quinn. As you can see by the end of this book, Driftwood is done*

messing around. See if he can convince Quinn that she's beautiful.

JOIN my Newsletter and find out about sales, free books, contests and new releases before anyone else!!
Click HERE

Want to know when my books go on sale? Follow me on Bookbub HERE!

Also by Susan Stoker

Badge of Honor: Texas Heroes Series

Justice for Mackenzie

Justice for Mickie

Justice for Corrie

Justice for Laine (novella)

Shelter for Elizabeth

Justice for Boone

Shelter for Adeline

Shelter for Sophie

Justice for Erin

Justice for Milena

Shelter for Blythe

Justice for Hope

Shelter for Quinn

Shelter for Koren

Shelter for Penelope

Delta Force Heroes Series

Rescuing Rayne

Rescuing Aimee (novella)

Rescuing Emily

Rescuing Harley

Marrying Emily (novella)

Rescuing Kassie

Rescuing Bryn

Rescuing Casey

Rescuing Sadie (novella)

311

Rescuing Wendy
Rescuing Mary
Rescuing Macie (novella)

Delta Team Two Series
Shielding Gillian
Shielding Kinley (Aug 2020)
Shielding Aspen (Oct 2020)
Shielding Riley (Jan 2021)
Shielding Devyn (TBA)
Shielding Ember (TBA)
Shielding Sierra (TBA)

SEAL of Protection: Legacy Series
Securing Caite
Securing Brenae (novella)
Securing Sidney
Securing Piper
Securing Zoey
Securing Avery (May 2020)
Securing Kalee (Sept 2020)

Ace Security Series
Claiming Grace
Claiming Alexis
Claiming Bailey
Claiming Felicity
Claiming Sarah

Mountain Mercenaries Series

ABOUT THE AUTHOR

New York Times, *USA Today* and *Wall Street Journal* Best-selling Author Susan Stoker has a heart as big as the state of Tennessee where she lives, but this all American girl has also spent the last twenty years living in Missouri, California, Colorado, Indiana, and Texas. She's married to a retired Army man who now gets to follow *her* around the country.

She debuted her first series in 2014 and quickly followed that up with the SEAL of Protection Series, which solidified her love of writing and creating stories readers can get lost in.

If you enjoyed this book, or any book, please consider leaving a review. It's appreciated by authors more than you'll know.

www.stokeraces.com
susan@stokeraces.com

facebook.com/authorsusanstoker

twitter.com/Susan_Stoker

instagram.com/authorsusanstoker

goodreads.com/SusanStoker

bookbub.com/authors/susan-stoker

amazon.com/author/susanstoker